P9-CEJ-003

Praise for *I'm Not Her*

"...rtler's writing unfurls with the exquisite grace of a flower. Readers ...heer Tess's triumphant awakening as she blooms in the shade of ...ity, family tragedy, and ...bling riva... ...o discover a strength and ...all her own."

...Ockler, bestselling author of ...*elilah* and *Twenty Boy Summer*

"...... A gripping read, Gurtler allows real life to prevail, avoiding ...t... easy, 'after-school special' ending many writers might have ... Major characters are well-developed, and even adults are portrayed in a realistic, although not always positive, light."

—*VOYA*

"Just right for fans of Sarah Dessen and Jodi Picoult, this is a strong debut that attempts to answer the question, What does it really mean to live?"

—*Booklist*

"Gurtler balances humor and tragedy beautifully and the plot moves along quickly, yet smoothly. Cute and quirky, with sentimentality reminiscent of Judy Blume, this is a book for the keeper shelf—one that readers will devour again and again!"

—*RT Book Reviews*, 4.5 stars

"Subtle, believable, and satisfying."

—*School Library Journal*

"Completely honest and realistic. The writing is crisp and the dialogue is authentic. The relationships are heartbreakingly truthful. This is a must read for teens and those of us who want to understand them."

—*Sacramento Book Review*

Praise for *If I Tell*

"Gurtler handles complex issues of race, identity, friendship and fidelity with laugh-out-loud humor and engaging frankness…once you're in you won't regret it."

—*RT Book Reviews*

"Gurtler unabashedly tackles several sensitive topics without sacrificing the story line and constructs a beautiful paradox."

—*Booklist*

"A touch of conflict stirred into a simmering romance."

—*Kirkus*

"The characters are believable, as is the small town setting. Recommended."

—*Library Media Connection*

"This character driven teen drama is a terrific tale…"

—*Midwest Book Review*

Praise for *Who I Kissed*

"A powerful look at the place where guilt and innocence collide into one confusing, heartbreaking, and life-changing moment that will leave you thinking about intent, assumptions, love, and the importance of hanging on…as well as letting go."

—Jennifer Brown, author of *Hate List* and *Bitter End*

"Without excess heavy-handedness, Gurtler weaves a tale of collective responsibility as several teens reflect on their actions that one fateful night. A well-crafted story about a student's fight to feel normal again when a community of peers turns on her."

—*Booklist*

"Gurtler demonstrates sensitivity toward her characters and insight into their emotional responses…the characters breathe with life."

—*Kirkus*

Praise for *How I Lost You*

"Gurtler gracefully negotiates the powerful emotions that accompany a changing friendship. Readers…will understand the difficulty of moving on from a toxic relationship that once felt like it would last forever."

—*Publishers Weekly*

"The novel explores female friendships in a thought-provoking way… There's no hurt quite like best friend hurt, and that's something Gurtler captures well."

—*Booklist*

"This is a relatable story about nurturing a friendship. The lesson that Grace learns is a good one, and the strong female characters are a plus."

—*School Library Journal*

"The all-too-relatable tale of two inseparable best friends, Grace and Kya, as they struggle when their relationship begins to fall apart. Perfect for any girl who's faced tough times with her own BFF."

—*Entertainment Weekly*

#16thingsithoughtweretrue

Janet Gurtler

sourcebooks
fire

Copyright © 2014 by Janet Gurtler
Cover and internal design © 2014 by Sourcebooks, Inc.
Cover image © plainpicture/Franke + Mans

Sourcebooks and the colophon are registered trademarks of Sourcebooks, Inc.

All rights reserved. No part of this book may be reproduced in any form or by any elec-
tronic or mechanical means including information storage and retrieval systems—except
in the case of brief quotations embodied in critical articles or reviews—without permission in writing from its publisher, Sourcebooks, Inc.

The characters and events portrayed in this book are fictitious or are used fictitiously.
Any similarity to real persons, living or dead, is purely coincidental and not intended
by the author.

Published by Sourcebooks Fire, an imprint of Sourcebooks, Inc.
P.O. Box 4410, Naperville, Illinois 60567-4410
(630) 961-3900
Fax: (630) 961-2168
www.sourcebooks.com

Library of Congress Cataloging-in-Publication Data is on file with the publisher.

Printed and bound in the United States of America.
VP 10 9 8 7 6 5 4 3 2 1

For Jean Vallestros

Because I told you I would. So I did.

chapter one

1. Working in an amusement park should be amusing.
#thingsithoughtweretrue

After pausing for a deep breath, I force myself to walk into the room with my head held high and my shoulders pulled back. *I can totally do this, show people who I really am—not the girl they saw dancing on the video.*

I'm focusing so hard on keeping my cool that I trip over a chair and it clatters to the ground. Everyone in the staff break room stops talking and stares. They're all wearing the same Tinkerpark T-shirts but in different colors. Red, blue, yellow, or green, we're all dressed as brightly as a package of Skittles.

"Awwwk-ward," someone mumbles. I see a girl waving and, relieved, I wave back but realize she's not even waving at me, but at a guy standing behind me. An idiot blush heats my cheeks, even though a blink later the tension evaporates and people go back to whatever they were doing.

I hold my tray high and hurry past a table lined with girls from the dance show that runs several times a day. They have big hair, lots of stage makeup, and sequins everywhere. I quickly claim an empty spot at a nearby table and turn my phone on to check for messages. This is my life now, and deep down I wonder if maybe, just maybe, they're right. Maybe I really am an attention whore who deserves to serve time in social purgatory for appearing in my underwear online.

At any rate, it serves me right for taking my brother's bet and hoping that today could be different, that today people would see past the rumors that float over me like rainclouds. At least Jake owes me ten bucks.

I stop chewing a French fry midbite when I get a feeling that people are staring and notice that one of the boys at my table is singing "Sexy and I Know It." Slowly I look up. People are giggling. Whispering. And pointing. At me. I drop my gaze back to my phone, but my eyes sting. Crying in public is not an option, so I need to get out fast. I push away from the table, abandon my fries and soda, and ignore a wiggle of guilt for leaving stuff on the table for someone else to clean up.

"You're a jerk," someone from the show-girl table calls to the boys as I zip by. That surprises me a little, but I don't look back.

Screw this. Why did I think I needed them anyway? I already have friends and I know where to find them, in a place where no one will bother me—an old restroom forgotten after renovations to the park.

I hurry to the bathroom, slip into a stall, and plop onto a toilet seat. Hunching down over my phone, my body finally relaxes. I'm finally free to check my Twitter feed without interruption. I breathe out relief and smile when I see my friends. And when I check my followers, see I'm up to 4,041.

OMG, almost at 5,000 followers. Help me reach 5,000. Please
RT for new followers!

A whoosh of air swirls at my feet as the main door opens right when
I send my tweet. The stall beside me is suddenly occupied, and
quiet sniffles invade my space. I try to focus back on my phone, but
the sniffling turns into gulping. I study the purple Converse sneakers under the stall door beside mine. They're clean; they look new.
The gulps from their owner are tears that don't want to be held in.
I know that kind. Whoever is in that stall is messed up.

I reach into my pocket for a tube of cherry ChapStick. "Um? You
okay?" My voice bounces around the tiny space and comes back at
me in a slight echo. I swipe some ChapStick across my lips.

The girl starts crying even harder, but helpful posts in 140 characters or less don't appear. Life should be more like Twitter.

"Are you all right?" I call.

There's no response, but then there's a clank and the stall door
opens and huge glistening brown eyes stare out at me. I recognize
the girl from the snack shop that's next to the gift shop where I work.

"You're Morgan McLean," she says. It's a statement, but her voice
goes up at the end, as if it's a question. She's short and skinny with
surprisingly chubby cheeks. She looks fourteen but she's wearing a
blue Tinkerpark shirt like mine, blue for concessions. There's rank
and prestige attached to different jobs as well as different colors.
Red is for the games people, yellow for rides. Blue shirts are the
lowest on the employee totem pole, and she swims in hers.

"Um. Yes," I answer.

She walks over and stands beside me at the sink, and then turns a knob to run water over her hands. "Ouch," she squeaks. "Hot," she says, turning the water off and shaking off her hands. "I'm sorry. I ruined your break."

I glance at us in the old mirror above the sink. It's dark and scratched, and our reflections are barely visible, but I see misery in the tightness of her lips and the droop in her eyes.

"No. No you didn't. What's wrong?" I ask her.

"It's Adam," she says and sighs. She reaches for the white, pulley, continual towel to dry her hands. I cringe at the germ count that must be on it.

"What did he do?" I ask.

She leans against the sink and sighs deeply. "He…yelled at me."

I lift my eyebrows. "Welcome to the club. He's the boss. It's pretty much his job to yell. Maybe you shouldn't take it so personally."

Adam is a senior next year, like me, but we never hung out with the same people even when I had people to hang out with. I've avoided him at work since he yelled at me on my second day when I forgot my name tag. He seems like he's trying too hard—probably that's why he's in management.

"But…I mean, I want him to like me," she says.

"Why?" Even as I ask the question, the answer is written all over her face. "Oh. You have a crush on him?"

She lifts her shoulder and chews her lip, sneaking a look at me. "Kind of?"

I can see how he's cute in a smart-nerd way, with black plastic-framed glasses and wavy hair. Not my type though. That makes me wonder for a fraction of a second if I have a type. "Why'd he yell at you?"

She tugs on the bottom of her T-shirt. "He saw me eating popcorn from a bag before I served it to a customer."

I imagine her dipping her fingers into someone else's food and then serving it to them. Ew. "Well, you know that's kind of against the rules, right?"

She bats her eyes and lowers her gaze to her purple shoes and shuffles her feet around. "It was a mistake." She sniffles and fresh tears brew in her eyes.

Mistake? How do you accidentally stick your hand in someone's food? "Still. Kind of gross," I tell her.

In the silence that follows, I realize I sound like a pompous jerk who's never done anything wrong. Ha. I am the queen of wrong. "But yeah. I get mistakes."

"Yeah. I know you do," she says and stares at me. Blinking.

My cheeks heat up.

"I was hungry," she says. "I never ate breakfast and I forgot to bring my lunch."

"Maybe you could have, you know, bought something to eat?" I glance at my phone. I haven't got much longer left on my break. My foot taps up and down and I glance at my Twitter feed. "You work in the snack shop, right?" I smile down at a tweet from one of my favorite Twitter friends, @debindallas. Her icon is of her in a flared black dress with red cowboy boots.

Dads are like noses, her tweet says. They're always in your face.

Dads aren't like noses, I tweet back. You're not allowed to pick them.

5

"Yeah. But. Um. I don't have money," she says.

I look up. "You get paid to work here. Right?" I return my attention to my screen, wishing she'd go away.

"I, uh, have to give my paycheck to my parents," she says quickly.

I frown and glance up to study her.

"We, uh, need the money. For groceries and rent and stuff." Her cheeks redden and she looks away.

"Really?" Great. Once again, I feel like a jerk. I turn my phone off and tuck it in my pocket. "You have to give them your paycheck for that stuff?"

She nods. She looks like an underfed dog with jutting ribs, like she needs a steak or something meaty and juicy to bite into. I dig into my front pocket and pull out a wrinkly five. "Here." I put it in her hand. "Go get yourself a hot dog. Don't eat from customer's stuff anymore."

She stares at the money and then slowly makes a fist around it. "Uh. Thanks." She pauses. "Do you think Adam will forgive me?"

"Why don't you explain it to him? Tell him the truth."

"I can't do that."

"Then maybe just avoid him."

"But I don't want to avoid him," she says quietly.

"The crush?" I guess, and she sniffles again and her eyes get brighter.

"At least he noticed me. No one ever notices me. My dad says it's probably because I'm so little." She stops to catch her breath. I ignore the roll of jealousy in my belly at the casual way she mentions her dad.

She sniffles again. "I'll pay you back."

"Don't worry about it," I say. It's only five bucks, and she obviously needs it more than I do even though almost every cent I make is going to my college fund.

"I could talk to him, Adam," I say without thinking. What am I doing? I don't want to get involved. But she bats those teary eyes. I'm a sucker. But what if he puts her on probation? She needs the money. Her family is poor.

"Really? You'd do that? For me?" She blinks fast, her eyes bright and sparkly with moisture. She sounds so grateful that I ignore the nausea building in my belly at the thought of confronting him.

"Sure." Great. I have to do it now.

She grins and it improves her looks about seven hundred percent. "That's super nice. You know everyone says you're stuck up." She stops and her eyes open even wider. "I mean, you're not. I'm sorry. Things just come out of my mouth sometimes."

"I'm getting that."

"I saw your video on YouTube." She clamps her hand over her mouth, and her wrist is covered in colorful string bracelets.

For the second time that day, I laugh out loud. It's kind of refreshing to have things said to my face instead of behind my back. My laughter bounces around the walls of the bathroom, and she half grins, as if she's a little confused but also encouraged. "Sorry. My dad says I don't have a filter on my brain."

Him again. "He may be right. But that's okay. What's your name, anyway?" I ask, noticing she's not wearing her name tag.

She crosses her arms. "You don't know my name?" She frowns.

"I work beside the gift shop. I say hi to you every time I walk by." She sighs dramatically. "My name is Amy."

"Nice to meet you. I mean officially." I walk toward the main door. "Okay. I should go. My break's almost over."

"I'll walk back with you."

"Sure." I hold the door open. "So, how'd you find this place?" I ask her as she slips by. "I thought I was the only one who knew about it."

She smiles. "Honestly?"

I squint at the glare of bright sun and then step outside.

"I saw you going this way last week and I checked it out. I didn't know you'd be in here today. I was upset and wanted to be alone. I didn't mean to butt in." She looks off the opposite way.

"It's okay," I say. Funnily enough, I even mean it.

As we walk side by side down the old cracked pavement that used to be the park entrance, strange noises fill the air—the buzz of the crowd. We reach a shaded tree area and a grass pathway back to our workstations.

"I'm taking my dad to Big Beautiful Burgers for dinner tonight. His favorite restaurant. He's an inventor." She takes a breath and glances at me. "When I get nervous, I talk too much."

"No kidding," I say but smile to soften it.

"What's your dad's favorite?" she asks.

I skip a breath. "My dad?" We walk past a janitor's cart, abandoned behind a huge tree on the pathway.

She stares. "Yeah. Where does he like to eat?"

I reach for my phone, pull it out of my pocket, and stroke the cover. "I have no idea."

"Why?"

"Because." I blow out long and hard, so the stale air from the bottom of my lungs leaves them. I glance at my phone. "I have no idea who he is." I glance up, and she's staring at me.

"What do you mean?"

"He took off before I was born. I don't even know his name." That's more than I've said about him out loud in a long time. It suddenly feels like I've just stripped down to my underwear. And there's a hole in the crotch.

"You don't know his name?" she repeats.

"My mom won't tell me. It's not even on my birth certificate."

"That's kind of weird."

"You're right," I agree. "But you should meet my mom." I start walking faster.

She matches my pace. "You want me to meet your mom?" Her eyes sparkle and her lips turn up into a smile.

I don't have the heart to tell her I don't mean it literally.

"You could come to my house, meet my dad," she says, trying to keep up with me on her short legs. "He's awesome. We're really close. My mom's okay too, but I'm closer to him."

"No thanks." Her comment makes me miss my best friend, Lexi. Well, ex-best friend. Her dad left her when she was in second grade to start a new family with a younger wife. She rarely saw him. We shared daddy issues. We got that about each other. But she left me too.

"Why not? Because you don't have a dad?" Amy hurries to catch up to me on the pathway. "That's sad."

We reach the end of the treed path that leads back into the crowds. Now I notice all the dads wandering around with their kids. Dads come in all shapes and sizes.

"My break is up. I have to go," I say.

She glances over to the snack shop to our right. Adam is visible at the till inside, serving ice cream to an elderly lady. To the left is the gift shop where I work.

"But you're going to talk to Adam for me right? Try to smooth things over?"

Her puppy dog eyes kill me. "Sure. Wait here."

She grins, and I sigh as I head toward the snack shop. I wish I had his number, so I could text him instead of having to talk to him. When I reach the snack shop door, I take a deep breath. It smells like hot dogs. Adam is at the counter with his head down. There are no other customers in sight. He glances up and squints at me when I come in.

"What are you doing here? Where's Amy?" he snaps.

"Uh. She's coming." I take a few steps forward, so I'm in front of a counter filled with oversized, overpriced chocolate bars and gummy snacks in the shape of dinosaurs.

"You got a second?"

"Not really." He sighs. "Too much to do, not enough time. What's up, Morgan?"

I blink, surprised he actually remembers my name. But he is the supervisor. I guess it's his job. And then I remember I'm wearing a name tag this time, and my cheeks warm.

"Um. It's about Amy. She feels really bad."

He frowns. "You mean for sticking her hand in people's food? Or for getting caught?"

"Um." I glance around. "It's gross, yes, but she was really hungry." I lower my voice. "I don't think her family has a lot of money,"

He makes a noise in his throat. It's not a nice noise.

"Seriously," I say, standing taller. "She gives her parents her paycheck for rent and stuff."

He stares at me over the counter. Not blinking.

"So, I promised her I would talk to you. She's upset. Maybe you could let her know you're not going to suspend her or anything."

"How do you know what I'm going to do?" Adam glares at me, making no attempt to hide that he's not happy with me running interference for Amy. I can almost see the pole he has shoved up his butt.

As he rants about customers and health regulations, my phone chirps, letting me know I have a new text. I pretend to listen to him, but my phone is burning a hole in my pocket. Technically I'm still on a break, so I pull the phone out and check my text while Adam talks on.

> Mom's in the hospital. It's serious. Get here as soon as you can.

CALHOUN COUNTY LIBRARY
P.O. BOX 918
GRANTSVILLE, WV 26147

chapter two

D id you hear what I said?" Adam asks. His eyebrows are arched way up. "Your break is over. Can you please turn off your phone and go back to the gift shop?"

"I have to go," I say. My heart thumps hard. *My mom's in the hospital?* I spin around and run for the door, clicking Jake's contact number.

"Did you talk to him?" Amy whisper-yells as I pass her outside the snack shop.

"Later," I holler and keep going, pressing my phone to my ear.

I race back to the gift shop and grab my backpack from the counter. "Family emergency," I tell Theresa, who's been watching the shop during my break. "I have to go."

I throw my backpack over my arm and keep running.

Adam is coming toward me. "I can fire you if you take off in the middle of your shift," he says.

"Congratulations," I call out and dart around families grouped together in clusters. A little girl is crying, and I pat her head as I run by and mumble sympathetic noises but don't stop. I jump out of the way to avoid an escaped toddler running for his life and bump into the back of a dad holding a screaming girl by her armpits. I press Jake's contact number again. It goes straight to voice mail. Great.

As I'm jogging through the parking lot, Adam yells my name, but I keep moving. The only thing on my mind is getting to the car.

I try my other brother's phone, but Josh doesn't pick up either. Something is very wrong.

"What the hell?" Adam yells, and I turn to see he's chased me all this way, even though I made it pretty clear I don't care if he fires me. His legs are frigging long, and clearly I'm no athlete. I reach Josh's car and jumble around in my backpack for the keys.

"Is this is about Amy? You can't just leave, you know."

My chest is tight, my breathing fast. "This has nothing to do with Amy." I'm about to tell him my mom is in the hospital when he interrupts.

"This is yours?" Adam stares at the restored '70s muscle car. Cutlass 442. A classic. I only know this because Josh drilled it into my head.

I unlock the door, ignoring Adam as I slide into the front seat. Adam moves quickly, standing in between the door and the car, so I can't close it. "Why're you taking off?" he demands.

"It's my mom," I say, and the tears I've been holding in pop out of my eye corners. "She's in the hospital okay? I have to go. Like NOW."

"Oh." He uncrosses his arms. "Which hospital?" he asks without stepping away.

"Shoot." I realize I don't even know. "I'm an idiot," I moan and grab my phone to madly text Josh and Jake at the same time. I stare down at the phone, willing one of them to answer right away. "My stupid brothers aren't answering my texts."

"If I drive, you can call hospitals and find her faster. It'll save time." He pulls out his phone and types a quick message. "Done. Theresa will cover me and the gift shop. I told her you have an emergency."

I want to refuse, but frankly I need the help. I swallow, tempted to tell him no, but this is too serious to worry about my silly pride.

"Fine," I say, even though he's already pulling me out and pushing me around the front of the car to the passenger door. He opens it and shoves me inside.

"Drive carefully," I tell him as I do up my seat belt. "This is my brother's car and he's very protective of it—and very muscular."

Adam's lip turns up for half a second as he gets behind the wheel and pushes the seat back to accommodate his long legs. Fuzzy dice hanging from the rearview mirror give off a slight scent of pine. I've never asked Josh whether they're ironic, but I hope so.

"Cool car. I promise to be careful. I'm not big on being beat up." Adam taps the fuzzy dice so they swing back and forth, and then pulls on the seat belt. "Why don't you start with the University of Washington Medical Center? Call the emergency line and find out if she's been admitted there."

He sprays gravel as he backs out of the parking lot. I call 411. They connect me to the hospital, but we're on the highway by the time I press enough buttons to reach a real person on the phone. A few minutes later, I find out my mom isn't there and hang up.

"Try the Virginia Mason," Adam says as he drives past an old farm with cows grazing on grass.

I wonder how he even knows this stuff but don't have time to ask. When I reach a person at the Virginia, I find out she's not there either. As soon as I hang up, Adam gives me the name of another hospital.

"The Marcede Grace Hospital. It's small, but closest to Tadita."

I get the number as we're reaching the outskirts of the city. Stretches of grass and farmland change to pavement and will lead to large buildings.

When I get the hospital on the line, they confirm my mom's admission but refuse to tell me what's wrong with her over the phone. I hang up frustrated and close to tears. I have no idea why Mom is in the hospital or how serious her condition is.

Adam reaches over and pats my leg and then presses his foot to the gas pedal and flies around the turnoff from the freeway. "Hang on," he says. "Ten minutes tops."

I picture my mom when I left for work. She had a package of cigarettes tucked in her bra, like she thought she was a glamorous movie star in an old movie. I squeeze both hands tighter around my phone.

"Don't worry," Adam says. "It's probably not as bad as you're imagining."

My ears heat up and I look out the window. There's a sign on the side of the road with a blue *H* and an arrow. "I hope not," I say, and my voice sounds funny.

"We're almost there," he says, and he reaches over to pat my knee.

I stare at his profile as he checks the rearview mirror. A motorcycle roars up from behind us, passing too fast and too close. "Idiot," he mumbles.

After a moment of silence, he asks, "Did your parents split up?"

He flicks on the turn signal and steers onto another off ramp, and I see the long brown building. It conjures up images of sick people in hospital gowns and doctors running to surgery.

The question about my parents hangs in the air, but I can't find words to answer.

"I assumed because you haven't said a word about your dad. Or is he dead?" His eyes open wider, and he sneaks a look at me. "God. Sorry. Stupid. I totally suck at bedside manners."

I blink at his profile. "Bedside manners?"

"Yeah. Um. I'm going to be a doctor someday." His chin lifts slightly, and he grips the steering wheel tighter but keeps his eyes on the road. "I've been applying to schools. Premed."

"It's summer," I remind him and turn my attention to the hospital as we get closer. My knee is bouncing up and down.

"It's only summer for a little while," Adam is saying. "Then senior year." He sighs. "A big year."

"Yeah," I agree and then, because he's being nice, add, "I have no idea if my dad is dead."

Usually I go for months without discussing my dad, but today he keeps coming up. "I think he was basically a sperm donor. I mean, my mom never went to a sperm bank, and as far as I know, I was conceived the old-fashioned way, but I never met him or anything. He took off before I was born. No interest in me."

I sneak a look, and there's pity in his eyes and I kind of hate it. "It doesn't matter," I say louder than necessary, as if adding volume will make the statement more true.

Adam speeds up to a set of lights, but they turn yellow and he slams his foot on the brake. The hospital is only a few blocks away now. "Yeah. It does," he says softly. "It matters. That sucks." I keep my eyes on the hospital, and we sit at the red light, staring ahead, but an invisible tentacle stretches over and wraps around my heart, bonding me to him just a little. "No one deserves to feel abandoned or unloved." The words reach inside and touch me, and he turns for a second to look at me, and something shifts between us.

"I'm sure your mom is going to be all right," he says quietly.

I nod and then stare out the window, afraid to admit to myself how much this connection means to me. He's like a full glass of cold water after a hot, muggy walk. I didn't know boys could be so nice.

"Do you have brothers and sisters?" he asks.

"Twin brothers. Twenty-one. They live at home. My mom still does their laundry and buys their underwear." I force myself to sound lively.

"Do you get along with them?"

I shrug and reach for my backpack. "Better now than when I was little. You're driving Josh's car, remember?"

"Yeah," he says.

"What about you?" I ask and search inside my backpack until I find my ChapStick and pull it out.

"One brother. Younger. He's cool. But if it's any consolation, my dad is kind of a jerk. For real. Sometimes I've wished my parents would split up. It would be easier for me in a lot of ways." He clears his throat as if he's embarrassed. The confession touches me. I glance over and his cheeks are red, and he keeps his attention on the lights.

I apply ChapStick and check my phone. A new follower. Normally that would make me more excited. The lights change and Adam speeds ahead, pulling into the hospital entrance.

"I'll drop you off at the emergency entrance and go and park this thing," Adam tells me.

I nod, glad he came along. "Thanks," I manage, but it's barely above a whisper. I wonder if he knows how much I want to cling to him.

He smiles at me, as if he understands the things I'm not saying. "When you walk inside, go straight past triage and take a right. Go down that hallway to the end and you'll find the information desk. They can tell you where your mom is."

How does he know this?

"I've volunteered here," he says. He pulls up to the emergency entrance and stops the car. "What's your mom's name? I'll park and come find you."

I grab the door handle, almost reluctant to get out now that we're here. "Maggie. Maggie MacLean." I give him a last longing look, wishing he could come with me and keep telling me what to do. My heart races as I hurry into the emergency entrance. I glance around the packed room and automatically pull out my phone to text my brother, but a nurse yells at me to turn it off, pointing to a sign with a picture of a cell phone crossed out.

I hurry down the hall, find the information booth, and explain to the elderly woman perched on the seat that my mom's been brought in. She looks her up, tells me she's on the third floor, and then points me to the elevator.

When I finally get to my mom's room, I find my brothers with their heads pressed close together. For the first time in a long time, I see how similar their faces are even though they're fraternal twins. They look over, and their blue eyes open wider. Their worried expression is identical.

"What happened?" I ask.

"Jake brought her in," Josh says, and their differences become apparent again. Josh is wearing a coat from some trendy store. Sunglasses are perched on top of his fluffy head of hair. Last November, he grew a mustache for Movember to raise money for cancer, and the fur on his lip seemed to awaken some latent hippy gene. He bought the muscle car in the new year and kept the mustache. He claims the girls love it, and he never seems to be without one on his arm. But that's been true since he was fifteen.

Jake is wearing old jeans and a plain T-shirt he probably picked up off the floor that morning. His shoes are plain white Vans but he colored them with Sharpies. He has mad drawing skills and tends to fall deeply in love with one girl at a time. I totally see him married with children running around his feet in a few years.

"I had to call an ambulance," Jake says, "since you had Josh's car."

I grab his arm. "What happened?" I repeat.

"It's her heart." Jake scratches his closely shaved head. It's less a fashion statement and more because he hates hair product. The twins have thick, wavy hair, less curly than mine and much darker. "I got home from lunch with my dad. Josh had a date. Mom was still home." He glances around at the walls of the hospital. "She was having pains in her chest. She was scared." He glances at me. "So I called 911."

"She was supposed to be at work," I say and it sounds stupid even as it leaves my mouth.

"She called in sick."

I frown. She never calls in sick. "Will she be okay?" The words tumble out in a rush.

"I don't know." Josh, who is never afraid of anything, who is never at a loss for words, sounds like a scared little boy. "They're running a bunch of tests. She's been complaining of being dizzy and short of breath for the past couple of weeks."

"She has?" I look around, wondering why she never said anything to me. Aren't moms supposed to tell their daughters that stuff?

There are footsteps in the hallway behind us, and I turn and see Adam. He pushes his glasses up his nose, but his shoulders are pushed back. He walks with confidence. For a moment, I can imagine him in the future—in a white doctor's coat with a stethoscope around his neck, walking the halls, in charge. I blink and he's a teenager again.

"He's obviously with you," Josh says, following my gaze.

I frown until I realize Adam's wearing a Tinkerpark employee shirt. "My boss," I mumble.

"How's your mom?" Adam says as he reaches us, and he stands beside me so we're in a semicircle in the narrow hospital hallway.

"It's her heart," I say and shake my head. "She's been dizzy and out of breath." I'm still trying to make sense of it.

Adam nods. "Have they done an angiogram?" he asks. I have no idea what he's talking about.

"To check for blockage," he adds.

"Not yet," Jake answers. "They did a CT scan but didn't find anything. They're setting up an angio as soon as they can get her in." I stare at Jake, a little surprised. He seems to be taking charge, and it's not the usual role for him. He scratches his chin and looks Adam in the eye. They're the same height. "Her blood pressure is through the roof," Jake tells Adam. "So they're going to keep her here." He sticks out his hand. "I'm Jake."

I feel like my brother has become someone I don't even know anymore. Jake isn't a guy who talks so freely to people he doesn't know—and he doesn't give out personal information.

Adam shakes his hand. "Adam Ranard." He turns to Josh and shakes his hand too, but Josh doesn't introduce himself. I wonder if my brothers switched bodies.

"If they find a blockage, she'll need a stent. They'll do it during the angiogram," Adam says.

We all stare at him.

He lifts his shoulder. "I want to be a doctor. This stuff interests me." He hands me the car keys and a ticket stub. "I parked in the east lot. Level four. Near the exit."

Josh reaches over and removes the keys from my hand. "You let this dude drive my car?"

"He drove so I could try and figure out which hospital Mom was in. Jake didn't leave that info, and I couldn't reach either of you." I glare at both brothers.

"Sorry, Chaps. I was kind of distracted," Jake says. He calls me Chaps because of my addiction to cherry ChapStick. I have spare tubes tucked away everywhere.

Adam clears his throat and stands taller. "I drove your car carefully and parked it on an angle so no one can park close on either side."

Josh looks him in the eye for a moment and then nods. "Okay. Thanks. Sorry. I'm a little freaked out here. Thanks for bringing Morgan."

Adam nods. "That car is sweet," he adds, and in spite of what's happening, I find it kind of funny that he cares about Josh's opinion so soon after meeting him. Even with his loopy '70s vibe, Josh has that effect on people.

"You want me to stay?" Adam asks me.

I shake my head, ignoring the way Jake looks, as if he wants him to. Adam walks to the nurse station down the hall to ask a nurse in pink scrubs sitting in a chair behind the desk some questions. When he returns to where we're silently huddled, he smiles. He tells us a few reassuring facts about heart disease and women, but we're all too freaked out to answer.

"Give me your phone," he says to me. I look at my brothers, but they step away from us, mumbling, and walk down the hallway so they're out of hearing range.

Adam holds out his hand. I dig into my pocket and hand the phone over. He punches his number into my contacts and hands it back.

He glances at his watch. "My dad said he'd pick me up on the way home from work and he'll be here soon," he says. "Call if you need anything. Or if you need to talk."

"Thanks," I tell him. "But I'm okay now."

He looks as me as if he knows I'm lying. He takes my shoulders and pulls me into his space. The hug is completely unexpected. I smush against him, and his fingers press on the small of my back. I hold my hands awkwardly up, unsure where to put them.

After a split second, I'm able to relax. I rest my head on his shoulder. We stand there and it feels so good until, all of a sudden, he steps back. I stare into his eyes and he stares back, holding my arm. I notice his long black eyelashes. He should wear contacts. Almost as if Adam can sense me thinking about how pretty his eyes are, he clears his throat and looks away. My cheeks burn.

"There's, uh, this girlfriend," Adam says as he glances around the hallway, and his voice cracks at the end of the sentence.

"Oh?" It's all I can think of. God, I'm such an idiot—my mom could be dying and I was getting all pervy over my boss.

"She wants to be a doctor too," he says, still looking around the pale-painted hallways, avoiding my eyes.

"Yeah, well. They say compatibility is important." I wonder if she's a douchebag too. But he left work early to drive me here. He's been helpful and kind and thoughtful. Not a douchebag at all. It's not his fault I reacted inappropriately to his hug. My anger isn't at him. It's at me for taking his kindness the wrong way.

"My girlfriend…" he starts to say.

"No. It's okay." Last thing I want is an explanation. I tap my fingers against my phone. "Thanks again. For driving me here. And, well, for everything." I'm finally able to look at him again and attempt a smile, but my lips quiver and quit halfway up. "Sorry if I was being a bitch earlier. At work."

He adjusts his glasses up on his nose. "You were just standing up for Amy." He meets my gaze. "You know I kind of have to be a jerk at work, right? Or no one will listen to me."

"At least you do it well." I grin as I say it. He doesn't laugh, but he does smile back. Something passes between us. Friends, I think. We really could be friends.

"See ya, Morgan," he says softly. "Keep me posted."

I have an urge to grab his arm and ask him to stay. I have a feeling he would, but he's walking, and he waves at my brothers and keeps going toward the elevator.

Almost immediately, Josh and Jake walk back to my side. "Was that your boyfriend?" Josh asks.

"No!" I glance at the back of Adam's head, hoping he didn't hear as he disappears around the corner.

"A good guy won't care about that video, Chaps," Jake says. "He was looking at you like a boyfriend," he says. "Do you owe me ten bucks?"

My cheeks burn. "Check your texts. Lunch was a disaster. You owe me ten bucks. He's my boss, and he already has a girlfriend."

There's a *rat-tat-tat* of clicking heels behind us, and we all turn. A woman in a white doctor's coat, carrying a clipboard and tapping a pen against the side of it, walks toward us.

She stops when she reaches us. "You're Maggie McLean's kids?" she asks.

We all nod in unison.

"Good. I'm Dr. Sally. Libby Sally."

I study her face. She has high cheekbones and dark lashes, and far as I can tell, she's not even wearing makeup. She's naturally beautiful. Not only that but she can slice into human skin and deal with copious amounts of human blood and save lives. It seems rather unfair.

"We need to talk about your mom."

I hold my breath.

The tone in her voice doesn't sound good.

"She's definitely got a heart condition. I suspect she'll be needing angioplasty surgery, but we don't know for certain until we go in."

chapter three

2. Heart disease happens to other people.
#thingsithoughtweretrue

Y ou can go in and see her. I'll be with you in a minute," Dr.
Sally says after delivering her news. She described how high
risk Mom is for a heart attack, with her smoking and high blood
pressure, and talked about other symptoms and probable causes.
Heart disease. My mom. It's hard to digest.

I step into the hospital room. Four beds. In the bed closest to
the door, a pale old man hooked up to a bunch of tubes lies on his
back, covered by a blanket. His papery white feet stick out of the
bottom of the blanket, his toes pointing straight to the ceiling. He
snorts and grumbles with his eyes closed.

Across from him, in an identical bed, there's another sleeping
man with tubes everywhere. He's old, with thin skin and white
hair. The bed beside him is empty, but across from it is my mom.
A half-closed privacy curtain separates her from the old man
beside her.

I walk closer and see she's tucked into a narrow bed. The steel
sides of the bed are pulled up, almost as if she's in a crib for adults.

Her eyes are closed, and plastic tubes stick out of her. She's attached to a pole with IV bags hanging from it and more tubes that run to another machine. It looks scary and obscene, as if she's a giant voodoo doll. I worry I'll trip on a tube and unplug her and try not to imagine what will happen if I do.

She looks tiny and vulnerable under the thin covers. Her hospital gown falls opens at the neck, and her skin is translucent. I study her pale face, and it occurs to me that she doesn't have her lipstick on. She always does her makeup so early in the morning, it's rare to see her without it.

She's incredibly still, no indication of her chest rising and falling even. Worried she's not breathing, I move closer and hold my hand above her mouth. She swats away my hand and rubs her nose. Then she sputters and opens her eyes and glares at me. I pull my hand back.

"Geez, Mom. You scared me," I say and drop my backpack on the ground beside her bed.

"Did you think I was dead?"

I frown at her, and she giggles, but it's frail and fades off. Jake steps behind me and reaches over and pats Mom's hand.

"Chaps, quit bugging Mom." He bumps my hip with his, and I shut my mouth even though I didn't mean to bug her. She actually freaked me out.

"Hi, boys," she says and smiles, but it's weak and fades quickly too.

Josh hangs back, behind Jake and me.

"I'm really tired," Mom says, looking at Josh.

He shuffles his feet but doesn't respond.

"You'll be fine, Mom. You're a tough old broad." Jake glances back at Josh and frowns and then turns back to Mom and pats her hand.

There's a cough behind us and we all turn. Dr. Sally grabs the privacy curtain and expertly swings it all around, so we have a false sense of isolation from the other patients in the room. "We have you scheduled for an angiogram in two days," she says to Mom. She turns to Jake and me. "We're keeping her admitted to keep an eye on her. Because her blood pressure is high, and she's been short of breath, we want to monitor her. She's high risk for a heart attack."

I picture a doctor on TV rubbing together a defibrillator and trying to shock someone's heart to start up. Mom closes her eyes.

"What exactly is an angiogram?" Jake asks.

"Basically an X-ray of her arteries, so we can see what's going on around her heart. We'll check for blockages. We can do the angioplasty if need be."

Dr. Sally goes on, describing what they're going to do in the angiogram, inject a dye into her and poke around her insides and what they'll see if she needs angioplasty. My stomach swoops, and my head sways with a dizzy queasy sensation. I shut my eyes. This is not supposed to be happening to my mom. She's not a sixty-year-old man with a bad heart. I open my eyes when the doctor stops talking, and she's glancing at her watch.

"Any other questions?" she asks briskly.

"How old are you?" Josh asks.

She blinks at him, presses her lips together, and raises her eyebrows. "I'm thirty-five. And if you're concerned, my credentials are impeccable. I've performed this procedure dozens of times."

Josh doesn't take his gaze off her. "You look young is all," he says.

I honestly can't tell if he's worried about her qualifications or if he's trying to flirt and figure out if she likes twenty-somethings with mustaches. It's hard to say which is worse.

"Thank you," she says without a trace of thankfulness. She looks down at her watch again and then up at us. "Right. Don't tire her out. I have another patient to see." She turns and leaves.

Mom feebly attempts to boss us around to give the impression she's in charge, but she tires quickly. "If I were to base my chances on the looks on your faces, I'd be a goner," she says.

Jake pushes down the side railing of her bed and sits, making sure he doesn't sit on any tubes. Josh doesn't move from where he's standing, his shoulders hunched over.

"You're going to be fine," Jake says. "If there's a blockage around your heart or anything, they'll take care of it right away. We'll have this done and get you rested and back on your feet," he says as if he knows it all now. He stands and walks to the window and stares out of it.

"I guess things happen for a reason," she says, looking at Josh.

That's her favorite saying. Things happen for a reason. Well, that and "pass the wine, would you please, sweetie." She loves her wine, that's a fact. I hope at least one of those will change.

Josh attempts a smile but looks lost. The whole scene feels like an awkward segment of a reality show. It would be nice to tell someone to turn off the camera. Mom fades back into her blankets. "I'm dying for a cigarette," she says.

"If you're not careful, you'll mean that literally," I tell her.

She sighs. "You're right."

I move closer to her side. "I'm going to get you Nicorette gum. You have to quit smoking, like, yesterday. No heart attacks allowed."

She nods, and I know she's definitely scared. The boys and I have been asking her to quit smoking for years. Even Jake's late-developing asthma didn't stop her.

"Boys," she says. "I want to talk to Morgan. Go get something to eat. You must be starving." She's probably right, because they're always hungry, but I remember I haven't had anything to eat besides one or two French fries on my embarrassing break, hours ago now. Josh and Jake mumble, and I watch them disappear from the room with a little dread and a little resentment.

When they're gone, she reaches out her hand. I move beside her and stare at the steel thing on her finger that looks like a splint. It's connected to a tube that runs to a machine.

"I think I knew this was coming," she says. Beeps and other noises from the machines hum in the background. "I've been having dreams."

I don't ask what kind. She's always believed she has psychic abilities through her dreams. She loves to describe them and analyze the meaning. In excruciating detail.

"You've always been the strong one in this family," she says to me.

I watch a monitor as it beeps out her heart's rhythm. "Me? I'm not strong."

"Yes, you are, Morgan. You're stronger than the boys. You've had to be." She sighs, and for a moment, her silence is deafening. This is not the usual script. She doesn't let go of my hand, and I barely resist an urge to pull away from her. She squeezes it. "I always hated it when my parents pried into my life when I was a teenager," she says, "but you know you can always come to me."

I gently pull my hand away, pretending to have a scratchy arm.

"I did silly things too, Morgan. Everybody does. If there'd been camera phones around when I was younger." She whistles, and I glance away and her gaze follows mine, and we both stare outside the tiny window at mist creeping up a red brick wall. "Honestly, I expected Lexi to be a better friend," she says. My jaw clenches tight, and I close my eyes to keep out the images of me in underwear. Dancing.

"Me too," I whisper and close my eyes, wishing I didn't have to feel so incredibly guilty about what happened with that video.

It's quiet except for the whirs and beeps in the room, and then she sniffles. "I'm scared, Morgan," she whispers. I reach for her hand this time and squeeze, trying to forget my own pettier problems.

"You're going to be all right," I say, but it's hard to make my voice sound convincing when I don't know. She's been a smoker as long as I've been alive. And she loves wine and hates exercise. "You have to make changes. You will make changes," I say.

"Listen to you, acting like the mother." She tries to giggle but it turns into a sniffle. I reach over to the table beside her bed and take a Kleenex from the box and hand it to her. She takes it and loudly blows her nose. "I wish you had more friends to talk to," she says with another little sigh. "In case something happens to me."

"You're going to be fine," I answer automatically. "And I have friends." She narrows her eyes. "I mean real ones."

Now this, this is the familiar script. I sit up straighter and hold in my comebacks. My online friends are real. No matter what she thinks.

"You're going to be okay, Morgan," she says.

I swallow and swallow again and breathe deeply, suppressing my urge to make this about me, to ask if I came with a money-back guarantee—or if a dream told her that. But this isn't the time or the place for old arguments.

"I'm not going to make it," she whispers.

"Mom. You'll be home before you know it." I wiggle myself a little closer to her on the bed, so my knee touches her hip. It's bony. She's always kept herself so thin. "You're going to be fine."

"No." A single tear plops out of her eye and runs down her cheek.

My heart beats faster, and for a moment, I have an urge to throw up. She's not going to die. She's scared. She's going to have an operation and she's being melodramatic. I close my eyes and fight an instinct to flee the room, run to my phone.

"Yes," I say softly.

I stare down at her hand and notice age spots. I close my eyes and say a silent prayer to God. We're not always on great terms, but I hope He's listening.

"I owe you some explanations," she says.

I open my eyes, and she's staring at me so intently, I frown.

"Mom? You don't owe me anything," I say quietly. "And even if you did, you'll be home soon and can tell me then."

Frrrrrrrrrrapppppppppppp.

There's a loud sound from the bed across the room. I turn my head, startled, and realize the old man across from her farted. It's drawn out and loud and travels through the privacy curtain to us. Mom and I stare at each other for a second and then we both start to laugh. The old guy snorts.

"Sorry 'bout that," he calls out. "Damn medication."

Mom and I laugh softly, but it dwindles quickly, and the room is quiet again, except for the whirring.

"I'm sorry for so many things," she says. "For not telling you…" she continues, in a quieter voice.

My entire body goes stiff, on full alert. I don't move. I can't move.

"I should have told you I love you more." She wipes away a tear, and my own eyes fill up. I'm not used to this person; it's much easier dealing with the less helpless version of my mom.

I rub my eyes and wipe my nose with the back of my hand. "I know you love me," I say softly. The words taste foreign in my mouth.

In the back of my mind, I'm composing a tweet to make this funny somehow. Hashtag #awkwardparentmoments. It would probably trend on Twitter. I want to laugh at this to make the whole situation less real.

"Do you?" She stares intently at me, not blinking. "I've never been, you know, good at expressing things. And with you, you've always been so self-sufficient. You were an old soul, even when you were a baby. I swear you did everything on your own. I guess with the twins and the energy and attention they consumed, well, maybe I took your independence for granted." She stops talking and stares off past me, at the curtain separating us from the rest of the room. I remember being younger and trying desperately to earn her attention. The things I did never seemed to matter as much as the boys' things.

This hospital version doesn't look the same or talk the same way as the mom I know. She doesn't even smell the same. "You're a lot like your father, you know, and sometimes I guess I resented you for that."

Everything in my body goes on high alert. I don't move. Something fills my stomach, but it's impossible to tell if it's excitement or anxiety. My dad?

I don't even blink, yet somehow a tear rolls down my cheek and slides into the corner of my mouth. I ignore the salty taste and hold my breath, waiting for her to continue. I've never been this terrified, terrified she'll say more about him—terrified she'll stop and leave me with nothing but this one small mention. I'm like him?

Layers of silence pile on top of each other. Finally she sighs. "He had a dry sense of humor, your dad." She says it quietly and then laughs, staring off out the window, seeing something I can't. A memory of him? My dad. I want to see it. I want to peer inside her head and see it.

"You're smart like him. He could do math in his head in seconds. And he could turn on the charm." Her eyes focus, and she turns to me. "You'll be able to do that someday—when you grow into your skin."

Her specialty—the backhanded compliment. Still, I lean forward and will her to continue. My heart beats so fast and loud I feel it in my throat, but if she doesn't say more about my father, it will stop and I will die. My math comes from him? What else?

"Your awkward phase won't last forever."

I close my eyes and breathe deeply. No. This isn't what I want. I don't want to hear about my faults. I open my eyes. She's about to have surgery. I shouldn't upset her. But she brought him up. My insides are close to exploding, wanting to demand more. But I breathe and wait, reminded of the silent treatments I used to get if I dared ask questions about my dad when I was little. She never told me anything about him. Not if I cried, not if I had a tantrum, not even if I refused to eat. She knew eventually I'd stop and get hungry enough to leave her alone. And I did. I heard that being ignored has the same effect on the brain as being physically hit. My bruises were invisible.

She reaches up and moves my hair from my eyes. "Your blond hair is his too."

She smiles but it's low voltage and never reaches her eyes. "I loved him. It was different than with the twins' father. Than with any other man." She shakes her head and stares off again, caught up in her own memories. Ones I've never been privy to. She loved him? My dad?

"I was so young when I had the boys."

I don't want to hear about Josh or Jake but don't dare interrupt.

"He swept me off my feet." She reaches up and traces her fingers over her lips.

Footsteps traipse by outside the hall, and I glance over and see a nurse hurry past.

"He asked me out at work. Before he knew I was a mom. I mean, he found out eventually, of course, and he met the twins. He liked them enough, but the boys were two and kind of a handful. When we spent time together, the twins usually stayed with their dad, with George."

I hold my breath.

"He didn't want to be a father."

I strain to keep my emotions off my face, to hide the wound, the puncture she pounded into my chest. "When I realized I was pregnant…" She sniffles. "Well, he didn't want to be a father," she repeats and closes her eyes and folds her hands over her chest.

I wonder if the old men are listening through the curtain, hearing the truth about me—if they feel sorry for me that my dad didn't want me, or if they wonder if I got what I deserved.

"Do you ever talk to him?" I ask softly. "About me?"

"He's never asked," she says without opening her eyes.

Boom. Right through my heart again—an even bigger puncture. I lift my chin. "Is he dead now?"

"Dead?" She opens her eyes, frowning. "Of course he's not dead. Why would you think that?"

As if I haven't imagined ways he's died hundreds of times. As if I never wondered about him just because she didn't want me to. "You never told me anything," I whisper. "I didn't know what to think."

"He's not dead," she repeats.

The pain in my chest expands. I hope I'm not close to having a heart attack too. I have a father. It wasn't immaculate conception.

Mom presses her lips tighter and then turns away from me, staring out the window. "I'm the one who's dying."

"No, you're not." I fight to keep bitterness from my voice—and the fear. If she leaves me, I'll be all alone. The twins aren't exactly responsible-adult material. I reach for ChapStick in my pocket, pull it out, yank off the lid, and jab my lips. "You're having surgery. You're going to quit smoking, and you're going to be fine." I shove my ChapStick back in my pocket and stand.

She turns back to me then, her face panicky, and shakes her head. "No. I'm dying. My dream…"

"Mom," I say, placing my hand on her hip. "You're not going to die," I say firmly.

"But…" She stops and glances around the room and then whispers, "The insurance won't cover all of this. Not all the tests they're doing. The surgery."

For a second, I think about grabbing her hard, physically jolting her and shaking sense into her. We'll have bills whether she dies or not. "It doesn't mean you're going to die. We'll figure it out." For a brief second, I imagine the worst-case scenario. If she dies, Jake and Josh have their dad. Is it possible I could have mine too?

"The boys need you," she says, as if a death warrant with her name on it has already been scribed.

But who's going to be there for me? An image of the father I don't know tries to form in my head, but I can't see a face.

"Mom," I repeat. "You're going to be okay. And don't worry about the money." I have money in my savings account. I've been saving for years. There's a nice chunk. It's supposed to be for college. But if she needs it, I know I'll hand it over.

Silence in the room thickens. I try to say something…*I love you...I'll help you.* But I don't. Her eyes water, and I can see the fear swimming among her tears.

There are footsteps around us, and then the boys walk into the curtained area and the air returns to normal. Mom glances at me, puts a finger to her lips, and sits up a little higher. She pastes a brave face on for her boys. While Jake settles on the side of the bed, Josh takes the chair by her feet and I back away.

"I'm going to get a coffee," I say. Jake is telling her about a nurse Josh hit on in the cafeteria, and I wander out, unnoticed. I head down the hallway to the elevator and find my way to the coffee shop on the main floor. I absently watch visitors, patients, and hospital staff all hurrying around in different directions as I order the hospital's version of an overpriced vanilla latte and sit at a table for four all alone. When I take a greedy sip of coffee, my lip burns.

I try to imagine life without my mom in it, but it's impossible. Instead, I imagine the faceless man. The man who didn't want kids. The man who never wanted me. I sip at the coffee and try to swallow back my emotions.

"Daddy!" a little girl screams. She runs past me, her face streaming with tears and terror. No one pays attention, so I stand and run and catch up. I place my hand on her arm, and she stops and I kneel down in front of her.

"You okay, honey?"

Her lip quivers, and she shakes her head. "I can't find my daddy."

"It's okay. I'll help you find him." I put out my hand, and she fits her teeny one inside mine. I smile. I've always loved little kids. I've been researching degrees that lead to careers working with kids. We walk to the information desk, and there's a man standing beside it. The little girl drops my hand and runs to him, hugging his legs. He bends over and scoops her into the air, swinging her around and planting a kiss on her cheek.

"Where did you go, my little monkey?" he says. "I was so worried." I turn and walk back to the coffee shop. "Thank you, miss," the man is calling, but I ignore him and go back to my table and pick up my full coffee. I walk to the garbage can and pitch it in the trash. Five bucks down the drain but what does it matter? I probably won't be going to college now anyhow.

When I get back to my mom's hospital room, the nurse is inside checking Mom's vitals. Josh and Jake are standing by the window. The nurse pointedly looks at each of us and tells us Mom needs to rest. The boys kiss Mom on her cheek and I pat her arm, and we leave.

"She's going to be fine," Jake says as we wait for the elevator in the hallway.

"We need to get her a truckload of Nicorette gum. Hopefully, she'll go through most of the withdrawal while she's here," I say. "She has to quit smoking."

Jake agrees, and then the elevator door opens and we all pile inside. Josh presses the parking lot button, and we ride down without a word.

"My car better not have a scratch on it," Josh says when the doors open again. We walk toward the spot where Adam left his car, but instead of answering, I take out my phone and turn it on. I go straight to Twitter and punch out a message.

My dad isn't dead after all. #truestory

I don't check my messages or even look at my follower status. I shut off the phone and leave it off. When we get home, I go straight to my room, curl up in a ball on my bed, and let the sadness I've been holding off pour in and then back out. I consciously let myself feel. Instead of fighting it, I embrace and let it in. Remorse. Self-pity. So. Much. Fear. About the dad I don't know. For my mom.

I don't want her to die.

Finally when I'm emotionally and physically done, I roll onto my side, sit up, and reach for my phone. I turn it on and my phone pings with texts I missed. I have dozens of @ interactions in response to my last tweet. Notes from friends.

More new followers.

An @ message catches my eye. From @therealMcSteamy.

Do you want me to kick him for you?

I squint and look closer.

I click on the profile.

The user pic is Adam.

He's following me on Twitter.

I feel more exposed than I did when my video went viral.

chapter four

3. Rocking out to "Sexy and I Know It" in my underwear
    is a totally good idea. #thingsithoughtweretrue

Josh drives Jake and me to the hospital the next day, but Mom is cranky and insists we leave. She says she's tired and wants to sleep. The nurses assure us she's fine, and frankly we're afraid to disobey her, so we leave.

Josh and Jake both work in construction, at a development not far from Tinkerpark, so Josh drops me off at work. I end up walking through the entrance gate half an hour before my shift starts. I force myself to smile at a couple of girls setting up their entrance kiosk. One rolls her eyes at me but the other says hi. I have to pass the office on the way to the gift shop and pick up my pace.

"Morgan!" a voice calls out as I'm speed-walking to get past.

I sigh and slow my steps. Pretending none of the hospital stuff happened and ignoring Adam as usual is perfectly fine with me. I'm happy to go back to the boss/employee relationship. Honestly, I'm embarrassed, but he rushes out of the office and damn if my heart doesn't beat a little harder. I grab my phone like it's a security blanket and arrange my face into a suitable imitation of a smile as he jogs toward me. "Is your mom okay?" He sounds genuinely concerned. It cracks off a layer of my wariness.

"She's tired. Her surgery is in a couple of days. So. Yeah. Nervous, I think." I lift my hand to block the bright morning sun from my eyes.

"Understandable. Don't worry though. She'll be fine." He smiles.

"Hi, Adam!" a female calls. A couple of girls are walking toward us, and he waves without even glancing over, but I see them—two girls each with a perky ponytail, dressed in red Tinkerpark T-shirts. They're whispering to each other as they pass to go to the gaming area; they giggle and one of them wiggles her hips in an exaggerated dance motion. I glance back at Adam, but he's watching me and misses it.

"So," he says. "She told you about your dad?"

I blink, but my mind is on the girls.

"Your post. On Twitter last night." He gestures to my phone.

"Oh," I say, as if I haven't been tortured by the fact that he's following me on Twitter. "That's right. You're @therealMcSteamy."

He blushes, but he's the one who picked that name, so I smile. Suddenly I'm feeling slightly less vulnerable.

"You post on Twitter *a lot*," Adam says.

The sun disappears behind a bank of dark clouds that seem to be moving toward us. If it rains a lot, they'll shut down the park. I wouldn't mind a day off.

"If it weren't for Twitter, most of my best thoughts would be forced to stay in my head," I say.

"No Facebook though?" he asks.

"Not anymore." After the video blew up, I deleted my account.

"Are you stalking me?" I joke. Without thinking, I punch him on the arm as if he's one of my brothers.

"Ow." He rubs his arm, but I hardly put anything in it. And I'm a wimp. So I roll my eyes.

"Please," I say. "That didn't hurt." A day ago, I wouldn't have thought that I could tease him or have a real conversation with him. The sun emerges from behind a cloud and lights his face.

"You calling me a wimp?" he asks, smiling.

"You said it, not me." I glance down at my phone—another three followers. I smile.

"Can you go more than ten seconds without checking your phone?" he asks.

"I'm pretty sure I can go at least twelve." I tuck the phone back in my pocket and wait while he opens the gift shop door. He holds it while I walk inside. I remove a cloth cover off a row of breakable toys on a gift stand and head behind the counter to tuck it away. The checklist for opening the store hangs on a clipboard by the cash register. Each task has to be completed with times noted.

"Are they going to do the angiogram through her arm vein?" Adam leans against the other side of the counter, watching as I go through the motions of opening.

"Ugh. I have no idea." The thought of anything going through my mom's arm to get to her heart turns my stomach

"You know what they do? With an angiogram?" he asks.

"Well, she mentioned the dye, but I'm not sure really." I grab a feather duster from under the counter and run it over the glass case that holds crystal toys and other Tinkerpark souvenirs.

"They inject a dye to flow through her veins. It checks for blockages, like blood clots or thinning."

I stop what I'm doing and stare at him.

"I read up on the procedure last night," he says. "She won't even be put under anesthesia. It's not risky. The worst thing that can happen is usually an allergic reaction to dye."

I feel a little guilty for not doing more research myself.

Adam continues, "If they do find something, they can deal with it right away."

"I don't know if I want the details. I just want her to get better." I glance out the window to the clouds in the sky. They're getting darker and moving closer. It probably won't be busy at Tinkerpark.

"I guess you don't have a future in medicine."

"Not unless I become a drug addict."

He turns around and smiles, and it shines from the inside out.

"Why do you want to be a doctor?" I ask.

"Truthfully? I got hooked on *Grey's Anatomy* when I was a kid."

I'm at the cash register now and press buttons in a memorized sequence, and it opens. "You're joking, right?"

"No. Seriously. I had the same science teacher in my freshman and sophomore year. Mr. Stade. He was hooked on *Grey's* like me," Adam says. "Before classes, we'd talk about the medical stuff after every episode, whether they got it right or not. He took premed courses in college but switched to education. He's the one who encouraged me to think about a career in medicine."

I lean back against the counter, watching him. "Really? A teacher talked to you about stuff like that?"

"Teachers love me." He smiles, but it's fake, and he stares out the window.

My teachers never really encouraged me to do anything except hand in homework on time. I'm pretty sure most of them didn't even remember my name. Well, that's not true. I'm sure they know my name now.

"So. You're okay with blood?" I ask. "Cutting into flesh with a sharp knife? Pulling out organs with your hands?" I wrinkle up my nose and cringe. I've seen *Grey's Anatomy*, but I watched to see who was hooking up, not for the graphic stuff.

He nods. "I rock at dissections. You should see my mad skills taking apart frogs. And pig hearts."

I pretend to gag.

"Dissection is not for everyone."

He glances out the window again. "Here comes Theresa with your cash drawer."

I look up, almost sad she's coming to interrupt this. She walks inside the gift shop, holding the steel cash drawer in the air.

"Dissections? That's what we're talking about this morning?" She walks toward the cash register. "Hey, Morgan."

We perform the morning ritual of counting bills and coins as we place them in the till. When we're done, she shuts the cash drawer and looks at Adam. He's still by the window, but he's watching us.

"You done your opening?" she asks.

He shakes his head. "I'll be in the office in a sec. I'm talking to Morgan about something."

"Dissection?" She glances back and forth at each of us, raises her eyebrows, and then shrugs. "Okay. But hurry up," she says and stares at me for a moment and then leaves.

Adam walks to the front of the cash counter. He leans forward on his elbows, watching me. I grab a cloth and start wiping things down and glance at the clock. Ten minutes until the park opens. I want my phone now.

"So what about you?" he asks.

I glance over my shoulder, frowning. "What about me?"

"What are you going to do?"

I turn my body away and wipe a counter I've already wiped. "What do you mean?"

"I mean do you have a college you're dying to get into? Or are you going to go to take a year off and travel? Or get a job." He laughs. "I mean a real one. After high school."

"I'm thinking of taking child psychology or something. We'll see."

I wonder if he knows about the insurance coverage, if he knows I've been thinking about giving my mom my savings. "What about you?" I ask not wanting to dwell on me. "What school do you want to get into?"

"The University of Washington has a solid med school and seems the most doable. Columbia or Stanford are out of my price range." He shrugs.

"I'd love to leave Washington," I say with far too much passion and then scrub the already-clean counter even harder. "Go far away where no one knows me."

"Run away?" he asks softly.

I stop wiping and close my eyes, glad I'm not facing him. I have no idea why I said that out loud and wish I could snatch my words back. "You know, don't you? About the video? You probably saw it?" I wait, gripping the cloth in my hand.

"I heard about it." He clears his throat. "I never watched it."

I breathe out and slowly turn. "Then you're one of a few people at this park, heck, probably one of the few people in Tadita who hasn't."

He takes his elbows off the counter and stands straight.

"I don't want to talk about it." I bite my lip and glance purposely at the clock on the wall. He should be going back to the office now.

"You didn't post it. Did you?" His voice is low.

I bend my head and swallow and pick at imaginary fuzz on my T-shirt. It's the truth. I didn't post the video. But that's not the whole story. And it still haunts me. "It was my best friend." My voice breaks and I take a big gulp of air. "She did it without telling me."

We're both quiet. I can't look up. I don't want him to know the whole truth. I don't want anyone to know.

"Some friend," Adam says. "I'm sorry."

"I don't need anyone feeling sorry for me," I say softly and go after another surface with my cloth.

"Maybe you do. Need people, I mean," he says softly.

I look him in the eye then. "Every person I know has seen me in my underwear."

"I'm sure that's not such a bad thing," he says gently, as if he's trying to tease me.

"Morgan?"

I turn to see Amy standing in the door of the gift shop. She has on a pair of fingerless gloves and a long-sleeve striped shirt under her Tinkerpark T-shirt. I have an urge to run over and hug her for ending this conversation. "Are you two talking about your video?"

"Not anymore," I say quickly.

Adam smiles. "Hey, Amy."

"Hi!" She grins. "Are you being nice to me now?"

"Of course he is," I say. "Adam was telling me how bad he felt about yelling at you." I have the secret knowledge now that he's not as mean as he pretends to be.

He narrows his eyes but doesn't bust me.

"I was hoping we could be friends." Amy totally misses the non-verbal conversation between Adam and me. "I feel really bad about eating that popcorn. Maybe we could hang out sometime? If you want? If you're not still mad?" She glances at me and then back at Adam. "All three of us!" Amy takes a breath. "So did you want to? Hang out, I mean?"

"Adam has a girlfriend, Amy," I say to spare her feelings.

I glance at Adam, and his cheeks are red.

"He does? I mean, you do?" She tilts her head and studies him. "I didn't mean it like a date. I'm over that. I never thought tiny women and tall men belonged together. It looks awkward. And I hate heels." She turns to me. "Where did you take off to yesterday? You were in such a hurry and then both of you disappeared. I was worried, but no one knew anything." She pauses for a teeny second to breathe.

"Everything's fine," I tell her to cut her babbling short. "And Adam's not mad."

The look on his face makes me laugh out loud—like he's constipated or something. It's obvious he's trying not to get angry, and for that I give him silent props. I feel closer to him than I've felt to anyone in a while. He was so great handling the emergency with my mom.

Adam glances at his watch. "You should probably go start your shift. I have to get back to the office. Theresa's going to kill me."

"I know." Amy waves and wanders back toward the snack shop.

"Wow," Adam says. "I think she just broke up with me."

I laugh. "Sorry to interfere. I couldn't resist."

"Yeah. Way to undermine my authority." He laughs though. He doesn't sound so uptight anymore. I'm grateful to Amy for spinning in and lightening the moment with her whirlwind of energy.

"She's harmless," I say.

"A little. But it might be better if she came with a mute button." He glances at his watch again and rolls his shoulders back. "Okay. I really should get to the office." His cheeks turn slightly pink. "I wanted to make sure, you know, your mom is okay." He glances around the gift shop, avoiding my eyes.

"Thanks."

"And to let you know I'm stalking you on Twitter."

My turn for my cheeks to warm up. And then he grins and walks out, whistling to himself. It's very off-key. And it's a Taylor Swift song. I grin, but the notes disappear as the sounds of the amusement park opening up for the day swallow them up.

I'm tempted to check my Twitter feed, but I feel like I owe it to Adam not to since I'm technically now on duty. I replay our conversation in my head, and that's enough to get me past the urge.

• • •

A steady flow of customers keeps me busy for the next hour, and when there's a lull, I take a moment to sit on the stool behind the cash register to catch my breath. When I look up at a ruckus by the door, Adam is rushing inside and Theresa is with him.

I jump off the stool. Judging by the looks on their faces, I'm in trouble. "I just finished ringing through a bunch of customers. I'm going to fill up the gum machine in a sec," I say.

"Your brother called the office," Adam says, cutting me off. "Jake. There was a cancellation at the hospital and they're doing your mom's angiogram in an hour and a half. Your brother wants you to get right there."

Theresa is already behind the counter, and she pats my arm as she slides past me. "Go on," she says.

I don't move. I blink, trying to concentrate. I don't have a car. The bus will take at least an hour to get back to town and then I'll have to transfer to the hospital. I don't know what to do.

"Come on," Adam says. He's standing on the other side of the counter. "I'm taking you. Theresa's lending me her car."

My hands start to shake. Theresa puts her hand on my back and gently pushes me toward the exit. A customer walks in the store then, an old woman wearing a layered dress and an orange cardigan. Adam grabs my hand as I come around the counter and pulls me along, out of the gift shop.

"I'll get you there as fast as I can. You got this, Morgan. You can handle it."

chapter five

The elevator door opens and I stride through the now-familiar hospital corridor toward my mom's room. Josh is standing outside in the hallway, stroking his mustache between two fingers.

"You made it here fast," he says.

"Adam broke some speed limits."

"Is he here?" The ways Josh says it, he almost sounds hopeful, as if he wants Adam to explain things or take control.

"No, he was borrowing Theresa's car and had to get back to the park." Only his calm reassurances on the way over kept me from freaking out. "What's wrong?" I ask Josh. "Why're you out here?"

A nurse hurries past us with a stack of towels. "Mom wanted to be alone for a minute. Jake's in the chapel." He stands up straighter, stretches his arms into the air. "Mom asked for you to go see her as soon as you got here." He glances at the clock in the middle of the stark white wall across from him.

Mom wanted to be alone? Jake's in the chapel? This has "not normal" stamped on it on so many levels. I'm itching to run inside to her, but Josh looks absolutely miserable, so I put my hand on his shoulder. "You okay?"

"I suck at this. I freaking hate hospitals," he says. He brushes my hand off. "Go," he says.

"It's okay, Josh," I say, shuffling my feet, wishing I knew what to say to help him. "Lots of people aren't good at hospitals."

"Go," he says again, so I turn and go inside Mom's room.

One of the old men is gone, but the man with gas is still there. He's sleeping. Mom's privacy curtain isn't pulled around the bed. The bed is raised so that she's almost sitting up. She's staring into space and looks pale and fragile under the baby-blue hospital bedding. It would wash out anyone, but without her makeup on, she looks especially vulnerable. When I approach her bed, she glances at me, the corners of her mouth turn up, and her eyes brighten. She hasn't looked at me like that in a while.

"You made it," she says.

"Of course. You're my favorite mom." I step beside the bed and take her hand. It's seems lighter and bonier.

"I'm your only mom," she says and then sighs.

I stare down at her and, for a fleeting moment, get the sensation that our roles have been temporarily switched. I don't like it. I don't even like watching body-switching movies. They freak me out. This does too.

"Are you still mad at me?" she asks and turns toward the window. The blind is pulled down. The redbrick wall is hidden from sight.

"No. You're still number one."

She glances toward the door. "They're coming to get me soon. I don't have a lot of time."

"Mom." I squeeze her hand. "You're going to be fine. Okay?

You'll have plenty of time after the surgery to do whatever you want. Except smoke." The old man snores loudly, which I prefer to farting. "The angiogram will find it if something's wrong, and they'll get you all fixed up."

"I have a bad feeling. A dream."

"Mom..." I start to say.

She takes her hand from mine and waves her fingers at me in the air. "Let me talk. It's not about the dream."

I press my lips shut.

"I'm sorry." She blinks fast. Her eyes are bright and serious, and I see fear in them. She turns back to the blinds.

"The boys need you. They're going to rely on you to pull the family together. That's what women do. But first, you need to accept yourself for who you are." She sounds as if a death warrant in her name has already been written.

"Mom. You're not going to die. You're coming home in a few days. You're just going to have to make some changes to your life-style, that's all."

She doesn't answer me. She just sighs dramatically with her head turned toward the window.

"You need to know who you are first. I know that now. I wanted to protect you, Morgan." She sniffles. "That's why I never told you about your dad."

I look around and outside the door, see Josh still lingering around in the hallway. He's not looking inside. Tears plop down my cheeks. They roll one after another, after another. I want to keep my emotions under control, shoved down, but I can't. "Maybe you wanted to protect yourself," I say softly, knowing it's wrong to do this to her now. "That's why you never told me."

"You have no idea what it was like," she whimpers.

"So tell me," I plead. I want to know why she always made me feel horrible for wanting to know who my dad was.

There's a long pause, and she sniffles and gulps in air. Guilt pumps around my body, traveling through my veins. I open my mouth to apologize.

"The answers you might be looking for…who he is…"

I stop breathing. My heart pounds. The machines in the room whir and beep. The old man snorts and mumbles in his sleep. I push off the bed, get to my feet, stumbling a little as if I'm dizzy from low blood sugar or something. I fainted once in the hallway at school when I had too many Tylenol for cramps. It felt like this.

I reach out and touch the end of the bed to steady myself. "What?" I can't think of anything else to say, so I walk to the closed window and stand in front of it, my arms crossed, my back to her.

"I don't want to go to my grave knowing you never got a chance to find the truth. I'd feel guilty the rest of my life. Well—the rest of my death, I suppose." She attempts a laugh, but it fades as soon as it leaves her mouth. "I'd have to hang around the hospital as a ghost or something, unable to move on to the light."

There's a clatter from the hallway. Sounds like someone dropped a bedpan. I don't bother to look.

"Tell me," I whisper.

"I can't," she says.

My hands shake and I make fists at my side. I limp to the chair that's at the end of her bed and sit. Anger mashes with numbness. It feels cold.

"I'm sorry," she says.

I raise my head to look at her. She's staring at me and she clears her throat. I'd given up knowing long ago. I look away and study the picture on the wall above the bed. A cottage scene. Pastels. Boring. Tranquil. Exactly opposite to what's going on inside me. It's almost worse that she's only telling me because she thinks she's going to die. But I can't provoke her now. I have to keep her calm before surgery.

"You're not allowed to die to get out of this," I tell her. "You're not allowed to. We'll talk about this later."

She will have a later, and I'll save my anger for then. She's not allowed to die.

There's noise outside the room, and then a couple of nurses enter the room. One waves her hand in a shooing motion, telling me to get out of the way. She's young. Blond. Probably in her twenties. Pretty.

"You must be the daughter. Good. You made it. Now off you go. We're prepping her for her surgery. Go wait with Josh." I don't miss that the nurse knows my brother by name. She must like mustaches. The other nurse, an older one, starts unplugging and moving things around. It's a dance they've done a thousand times before with a thousand different patients.

"Wait," I say, and something in my voice must be extra desperate because both nurses pause. I step around the young nurse and lean forward so my mom's face is in line with mine. I take a deep breath.

"I love you, Mom," I whisper, and honestly I don't remember the last time I told her that.

She smiles, and the fine wrinkles around her mouth crease up even though I know she secretly gets Botox injections when she can afford to. *Thank you,* she mouths and then closes her eyes. "If you want the truth. Look at home. In my jewelry box. The answers are there if you want them."

The nurses are instantly moving again. I stand straight and move against the wall, out of the way, and before I know it, they're out the door, wheeling my mom down the hallway. There's so much in my head, and I can't process any of it right now.

"Take care of my mom," I whisper. I'm not sure who I'm talking to, but I think it might be God again. I hope He still listens, even if we haven't talked this much in forever.

The old man sighs in his sleep and then farts loudly again. I roll my eyes at him and leave the room. Josh is still standing in the hallway, staring off where Mom disappeared to. He calls my name, but I ignore him and keep going. I walk until I'm outside and then march straight to a cab waiting by the hospital exit. I give him our home address and then lean back against the seat.

Is this what I want? To find the guy who walked away from me? Do I want to rip off the scabs to those wounds? I feel fear throb inside me. What if I am left all alone? What if I need him? Will he even be willing to see me? Can I handle it if he won't?

Suddenly, I'm not sure I'm ready to find out who he is after all.

chapter six

J osh is leaning against the wall of the hospital room. He looks
as if he's been punched in the stomach. Jake is sitting, but his
eyes are closed. I'm standing beside my mom and staring down at
her, memories swirling around my brain—times I was in bed sick,
when she'd bring me soup and ginger ale.

The doctor spoke to us while Mom was in recovery, assuring us
she'd be out of the hospital shortly, within a day or two, and back
to her regular routine in a week or so. "She has to make some
changes, but she should be fine," she says. They found an artery
with 90 percent blockage and put a stent in.

The nurses brought her back to the room after they monitored her heart and blood pressure in the recovery room and
removed her catheter tube. They told us her puncture site has
been dressed and the bleeding stopped. My stomach rolled,
but I thought of Adam and how he'd explain it in a way I
would understand.

Her eyes flutter and then open and focus in on me first.

"Hey. What do you know, you're alive," I say softly and then smile.

Jake jumps to his feet and whacks me on the back of the head.
Luckily he whacks me lightly.

"Funny, Morgan," she croaks. "Always funny." Her voice is raspy and low. She'd make a good late night DJ on one of those call-in shows for lonely people, the way she sounds.

"How do you feel, Mom?" Jake asks, putting a hand on her forehead as if she's a child with a fever.

"Good. I mean…okay." She peers over at Josh. He straightens up, and his lips turn up in a shaky smile. "Hey, Mom," he says.

She squints, peering deeply at him. "I have a stent in my heart," she tells him. He pushes himself off the wall and moves closer.

She gazes at each of us and then down at her chest. "I had to stay awake. I guess I fell asleep after. I don't remember."

Jake takes his hand away from her forehead. "We know, Mom. It's all good. That stent will keep you going for a long time, like the Energizer Bunny."

"You okay, Josh?" she asks.

He nods but looks far from okay. He pulls on a corner of his mustache. Everything is droopy and lacks his usual swagger.

"I'm fine, Mom. This is about you."

"You should sit," I tell him and point at the chair.

Without argument, he pulls it up to the side of the bed and sits.

"The good news is I'm going to make it." Mom glances at me. "At least I hope it's good news." Her thoughts are almost visible as they bounce around her head. I hear her regret.

"You boys would have a hard time without me." She nods at me. "You too, Morgan?"

"Of course."

Jake frowns at me as if I've done something wrong.

She turns to Josh. "Would you mind going to see if I can get some ice to chew on?"

He nods and stands. "Sure." He hurries out of the hospital room as if he's grateful to have something to do.

"Poor Josh," she says when he's out the door. "This is hard for him. He doesn't like hospitals. You never know how you're going to react to stuff like this." She smiles. "Like you, Jake. You're handling this so well. I always said still waters run deeper."

He stares out after his twin. "Josh doesn't like the smells and…"

"The sick people?" I add.

"It's okay. George, your dad, is the same way," she says to Jake. "He almost fainted when I gave birth." Mom looks right at him. "Why don't you go help Josh? Give me a minute with your sister."

Jake looks at me, raises his eyebrows, then glances back at her. "Help him get ice?"

Mom nods.

He glares at me. "Is everything okay?"

"Fine," Mom says. "Just give us a minute."

"Sure. Okay." He slowly walks out of the room.

We both watch him leave.

"He was in the chapel during your surgery," I tell her.

She smiles. "Jake is my sensitive one."

I wonder which one I am.

"The nurse said they're going to send me home tomorrow," she says. "As long as my insertion site heals okay. In and out." She stares off into space.

"I wish they'd keep you longer. Just to be safe. It seems so fast," I tell her.

She turns to look at me. "That's the way it is, less expensive in the long run. I'll be seeing my own doctor regularly."

We're both quiet again. It's obvious we're thinking about the same thing—the elephant in the room. The name. Such a simple name. Such a complicated name.

"I found the papers," I tell her. "In your jewelry box. With his name. Bob White."

She sighs. "Morgan. I really thought...I didn't think I would make it. Maybe I shouldn't have said anything. Allowed you to find that document about your dad."

"You mean Bob White?"

She winces. I press my lips tight, wishing I had my ChapStick. He's not my dad. Dad is something you earn. "Well," I say quietly, "I didn't find him—not yet. But I can't pretend I don't know his name."

She sighs deeply. "I know."

"Why'd you never tell me before?"

She stares at me and I stare back. And then she pats the bed beside her. I half sit, not wanting to get too close. She reaches for my hand, but I move it away and scratch my head.

"I love you," she says.

I blink back a sudden flood of tears and look away. Now she says it back? I wait, but she doesn't fill the silence. "I know you do. But I still had a right to know. Even if he didn't want me. I had a right to know his name." My toes tingle. I feel it starting there. The anger.

I focus it toward him. I can hate him with much less guilt because I don't know him. It's harder to aim it at her.

"I can help you with what the insurance doesn't cover," I tell her. "I have savings."

"Are you crazy?" she asks.

I frown at the intensity in her voice. "Don't get worked up. It's okay."

"You are *not* paying for any of this. Your savings are for college. Do *not* worry about the insurance. One of my kids needs to go to college. Not that I'm not proud of my boys...but I want you to go. I'll manage. I spoke out of fear before. I thought I might not make it. I didn't want to burden you with bills when I was dead. I certainly won't when I'm alive."

"I can help," I say again.

She blows a feeble raspberry. "No. Absolutely not. The money you made is for your future, working with kids."

The anger in my toes rises a little. She had George to help with some of the boys' things. But there was no help with me. "What's wrong? What's with that face?" my mom asks. "Don't worry, Morgan. I can deal with this. It's going to be okay. It'll all get paid off."

I take a breath. In through my nose. Out of my mouth. She's not perfect, far from it, but she made sure I had everything I needed growing up. Well. Except a father. I stare down at my hands. I did a Google search for Bob White and it brought up a lot of images. It's embarrassing to not even know him to look at him.

"Bob White is a pretty common name," I say softly.

She sighs. "I know."

I sit up straighter on her bed. "I don't want to upset you, but I'm going to look for him."

She presses her lips together and stares behind me.

"Mom?"

She doesn't answer.

"Mom?"

A plump tear squeezes out of her eye and rolls down her cheek. She finally looks at me. "I know. I understand."

My insides ache because I'm adding pain to her recovery. The back of my throat throbs. "I wanted you to know. I don't want to go behind your back. Or hide it. I wanted you to know the truth." Even though she hid it from me for so long. It's the right thing to do.

She stares into space.

"I need to meet him," I continue. "I'm prepared for him to slam doors in my face. I mean, I know he's never even wanted to meet me. But I have to find him." I don't tell her my fear—that I might be left all alone.

Her face seems to pale even more. She picks at her blanket, looks up at me, but as soon as her eyes meet mine, she looks back down. She's terrified.

"Mom?"

She picks at the blanket. Her hand shakes. "What's it going to change?" she says softly. I stare at her, but she won't look up.

"Everything," I say, and the resentment in my voice makes it louder than I intend. "Nothing." I want to know who he is. How he lives. Does he have another family? Maybe I have a sister. Other people. Maybe, just maybe, if he meets me, he'll see that I'm not so bad—that I am a good person.

She glances up. "Just be careful what you wish for."

I hear her unsaid words. He's never looked for me. He's never tried to find me. But it's not his choice anymore. And it's not hers either. It's mine. I want to see him in person. I want to know what he looks like—maybe even find out why he left me. I'm ready to handle this like a grown-up, even if the two of them aren't.

"For the record, I don't want you to do this," she says, her voice flat.

I bite my lip to keep myself from backing down, telling her I won't. I inhale deeply and concentrate on breathing in and out.

Neither one of us speaks. The machines in the room whir.

"I'm sorry," she says after another moment of quiet. "I know it's not fair…it's just that…" She stops. Sniffles. Closes her eyes.

"It's okay," I whisper.

"No. It isn't."

I glance toward the door, hearing the boys chattering, their voices getting closer. "Victoria," Mom says softly.

I look back at her, wondering if she's drifted off or if maybe she's hallucinating that she's talking to an old friend or something.

"Mom?" I lean forward and pat her shoulder gently. "It's me, Morgan," I whisper.

"I know that," she says and opens her eyes. "I mean, Victoria, British Columbia. The last I heard, Bob was living in Victoria."

I slowly process that. "You mean in Canada?"

She nods.

"He's Canadian?" For some reason this strikes me as absurd. I giggle.

"When we met, he was working in the Seattle office of his company. He's an engineer. Before you were born, he moved back to Canada."

Of course he did.

God. This must explain my strange addiction to maple syrup.

"I'll be back in a minute," I manage, and then I rush out of the room. As soon as my toes touch the floor in the hallway, tears burst out of my eyes. The boys are close. Josh is holding a baggie filled with ice chips. My face must look bad, because they both rush to me as I bend over to catch my breath.

"What's wrong?" Jake says and pats on my back. "Is Mom okay?"

I lift my head, unable to speak. It's stupid, but it's the fact that he lives in Canada that slays me. He lives in a different country.

The boys run past me into her room. I start walking. My feet move quickly, until I'm running. Everything I've been holding is fighting to come out. The operation is over. Mom is okay. My dad is alive and his name is Bob White. And the thing that tilts me over the edge is that he doesn't even live in America, that he's Canadian.

And now, I'm a mess.

I jump on the elevator to the main floor, ignoring the smiles of an old man in a hospital gown pushing around an oxygen tank he's hooked up to. I don't have room in my heart for other people or their troubles. When the elevator door opens, I walk out quickly, avoiding people's eyes until I'm outside the hospital on the sidewalk.

It's dark outside, and I'm surprised the sun is down, though when I think of it, I can't tell when the day started and when it ended. I pull my phone from my pocket, turn it on, and walk to the path that leads behind the hospital. My phone beeps in quick succession, letting me know there are new messages. I ignore them and walk to a nearby bench and plunk my butt down. My heart beats triple time as I click on the Google icon. I type in Bob White + Victoria BC, take a breath, and press search. The connection is slow.

Finally the search brings up a few links. I scan down. One is a pharmacy website, another advertises a paint shop. I sift through pop-ups and see images of people attached to the name Bob White. There's an artist, a businessmen, even a politician. I wonder which one of them is dear old Dad. I'm furious I can't tell by looking.

I scroll up and down, clicking on links but nothing jumps out at me, nothing screams, *This is your father, Morgan McLean. You've come to the right place. Please call this number to speak with the man who made you.*

I'm disappointed. I'm angry. I want to eat carbs. How am I ever going to find him?

I tap my way out of Google, to the Twitter icon, and click on it. I think about tweeting my dad's name, telling my followers about him—asking for help tracking him down online. But no. I want to do this organically. I don't want anyone or anything to warn him that I'm onto him now. I want to go find him with the element of surprise on my side.

I scroll down, but my heart isn't in any of the things my friends are tweeting. I can't concentrate, and I'm close to typing a tweet to express my distress, something I vowed never to do. My online image is peppy. I don't want to drag people down.

I click out of Twitter and go to my phone. I stare at Adam's contact number, and then for the first time in my life, initiate a call with a boy. One that has nothing to do with work. Or school.

When Adam's voice mail picks up, I hang up without leaving a message. He has to have caller ID. He'll know it was me. If he wants to call me back, he will.

My phone beeps, letting me know a new text came in. I glance at it and frown. It's from my mom's phone. But how could she possibly send a text? She must have gotten Jake to do it. Or Josh. I glance at the message.

It's a picture of a man. I enlarge the image and look closer. It's a picture from a newspaper article. He's wearing a golf cap, but it's clear what he looks like.

There's a caption under the picture. Tiny. I enlarge it some more. "Bob White wins the Golf Tournament, for the Victoria Blues." I recognize him from Google Images, one of the less offensive look-ing Bob Whites. We have a match. I suck in a deep breath. After all this time, this is it.

I peer closely and disappointment settles in. He's an ordi-nary person, this Bob White, just a normal-looking man. Not too tall. Not too heavy or too slim. Not someone I can look at and automatically hate. I don't know what I expected, but it wasn't this. Just a man. It's hard to feel much of anything. It was almost better wondering if he was dead. Or really tall and handsome. Or maybe a famous celebrity who would never acknowledge me as his daughter because it would ruin his career. Not some guy in a golf shirt who looks like he shops at

Costco and pays all of his bills on time. He doesn't look evil. He doesn't look mean.

He is a man. But he's more. He's my dad. I try to imagine what his voice sounds like, what he likes to eat, if he has a new family. Mostly I wonder why—why he never wanted to know me. I stare at the photo. I have to go. Now that I know. I have to see him myself. In person. I'll find a way to go to him and see for myself who he is, and why he didn't want me. Maybe, just maybe, if he sees me now, sees I'm not so bad…

I shake my head and stop that train of thought. I wonder if he'll be underwhelmed and disappointed when he looks at me for the first time. I wonder for the millionth time why he left me. "Morgan," I say, speaking for the man in the picture, "I am your father."

chapter seven

4. Likeability can be measured by how many followers
you have online. #thingsithoughtweretrue

I'm working in the gift shop, ringing up a woman's purchases,
ignoring the shrieks of her unhappy baby. "Whoa," a voice says
from the entrance of the gift shop after she leaves. "That took com-
mitment." Adam walks in. "Ignoring a baby's cries." He walks inside.

I remember that I'm mad at him, so I fake a smile and act busy.
He never returned my call. He doesn't get off that easy. "So, your
mom's operation went okay?" he asks.

I don't glance up. "Fine."

"So…?"

"She'll be home in a few days." I bend down to pick up a pencil
I dropped on the floor. When I stand again, he's directly across the
counter. Frowning.

"Are you mad at me?" he asks. He's holding a brown paper bag.
Of course he would bring a packed lunch. It's mature and sensible.

"Why would I be mad at you?" Call display, dude. He didn't call
back. Text. Acknowledge my call in any way. I don't need to have
things spelled out. He's my boss, he felt obliged to drive me to the

hospital, and his interest about my mom is medical curiosity. I made up the connection between us.

"You have a break in a few minutes, and Theresa's on her way. Are you going to the staff room?"

"No."

He tilts his head. "Why not?"

"Break time," Theresa says as she walks in. "Hey. Is your mom okay?"

"Yeah. Thanks." I don't move.

"That's good." She smiles at me then turns to Adam. "You find your phone yet?"

He turns to me. "Someone stole it."

"Contact your carrier. Maybe they can trace it?" Theresa says.

I sneak a look at him. His phone got stolen. That's why he didn't call back?

"I called. They couldn't trace it. I have to buy a replacement." Adam turns to me. "I'm on my break too. I'll go with you."

"I wasn't going to go to the staff room," I tell him. I'd been counting down the time until I could go to the old abandoned washroom stall and catch up on my tweets. I grab my backpack and walk out from behind the counter.

"Don't worry," Adam says. "You can bring your phone."

"I know." I need to recalibrate. I can't be mad at him for ignoring my call since he didn't have his phone.

"Come on." He glances at my backpack. "You need to stop to buy something to eat?"

I shake my head. I took one of Josh's protein bars so I could have lunch in private. I hadn't planned on returning to the staff room again. Ever. I want to slip off to the path that leads to privacy, but I'm too chicken to admit it.

When we walk outside, two pretty girls in yellow shirts run up to Adam. One smiles at me, but the other looks me up and down and blinks in slow motion before turning to Adam. "So, I need to get off early this Saturday. Can I do that?"

"Talk to me later," he says to her and turns to me. We've reached the entrance to the staff room. It smells like dirty feet and cotton candy. It reminds me of my brothers when they don't shower after working out and try to cover their smell with cologne.

"Come on," Adam says, and we step inside. It's early for lunch, so there are only a few employees sprawled at one table. I avoid looking at the managers' table, closest to the far wall.

Some girls at the full table squeal with laughter, but Adam ignores them. "We don't have to sit over there," he says, gesturing to the manager table. "How about the couches?"

I shrug, kind of embarrassed he guessed my feelings about sitting at the manager table, and follow him to the grimy-looking couches that semicircle the vending machines. He walks to a machine and plugs in some quarters. "You want a Coke?" he asks me as he takes out a can.

I lift my shoulder and plunk down on a couch, trying not to think about how dirty it is. I put my phone on my lap.

"Sure, Adam, I'd love a Coke," he says in a high-pitched voice, imitating me. He puts in more change and pulls out another can. I turn on my phone to Twitter and scroll, but he stands right in front of me, holding out the can until I stop and take it from him.

"Thanks."

"How about talking to me instead of your phone?"

I put my phone down but glance longingly at it.

"So everything's okay with your mom?" he says and sits on the couch across from me. I dig through my backpack and pull out my bar, nod, and rip the wrapper open with my teeth.

"You sure you're okay?"

"I'm fine." I take a bite of my bar and pop open the can. Adam watches me as he unfolds his lunch bag.

"Did I do something to piss you off?"

"Besides forcing me to eat in this place?" I smile even though it's true and take a sip of the soda. It's awkward. I'm angry about things, most of which have nothing to do with him. I'm being kind of an ass and I know it.

He pulls a sandwich from his lunch bag and glances around the room, seemingly undisturbed by the other people or the mess. "Where do you usually eat?" he asks. "Outside?"

I shake my head, trying to shake off my mood.

He holds up his sandwich to take a bite. "Isn't anyone allowed to be nice to you?"

I put the soda between us on the table and lean back on the couch, sigh, try to explain. "Sorry. It's just. Since the video…"

He smiles. "I get it. And by the way, in case you didn't notice, I'm not exactly Mr. Popularity around here." He bites his sandwich and shrugs. "At least you'll be seen talking to me in public." He smiles again to show he's joking, but I wonder if he is.

The confession warms me a little. "I have to figure out things with my mom and my…birth father. And I usually use my break to get caught up with my friends, so I guess I'm a little edgy."

"Your friends on there?" He gestures at my phone and raises his eyebrows. "You have a lot of people following you. I have, like, twenty."

He has nineteen. But I don't say that out loud. And I try not to judge him for it.

"Stop me if this is a crazy idea," he says, "but I thought you might want to talk to someone, you know, in *person*."

I take a sip of soda and study the coffee table, trying to put my words together in a way that makes sense. It's so much easier to get things right on Twitter.

Adam watches me, his expression calm, not rushing me or trying to fill in the silence.

"Last night, my mom finally told me his name. My father." I stop and look up, waiting to see his reaction.

"Wow," he says and leans back on the couch. "That's huge."

"Yeah." I take another sip of Coke and smile at him.

"Why're you smiling?" he asks.

"Just that you get it's a big deal. I have a picture of him too. And I found him. He lives in Victoria, BC. In Canada."

He finishes off his sandwich, watching me. "Are you going to call him?"

"No. I'm going to go see him. I want to do it in person," I blurt out and wait for his reaction. I haven't told anyone that part. Not even online. And it's only when I say it out loud that I know I have to. I have a father. I want to show him that I made it, that his rejection didn't break me—not in a way that he'll be able to see, anyhow. I ignore the way my stomach twists. I ignore the little girl inside of me who wants to cling to his pant leg and cry and demand to be loved. I'm not that bad…am I?

Adam puts down his drink on the coffee table. I notice a carving in the table. *JM + LG.*

He pulls an apple from his paper bag and rubs it on his T-shirt. "So you're planning to go all the way to Canada to drop in on the father you've never met—without warning?"

I take an aggressive bite of the bar. "Yup. Pretty much."

He bites into the apple and some juice squirts out and hits my arm, but we both ignore it.

"Cool?" he says but phrases it like a question.

That makes me laugh. "I want to see his face when I tell him who I am," I say softly. I finish my bar and scrunch the wrapper up in my hand.

Adam watches me as he chews through the apple in big bites. "What do you hope to accomplish?"

I throw the balled up wrapper at the garbage and it goes in. I take that as a good sign. I believe in signs. Then I bite my lip, embarrassed. I don't want to tell Adam that I hope my dad will see me and change his mind. I pick at a hangnail on my thumb, and Adam leans forward to toss his apple core in the garbage. He misses and I hide a smile.

"He walked away," he says softly.

I sigh. "I know."

"Well," he says, "I guess anything can happen, but you should be prepared…in case…"

"Did you know it costs over two hundred thousand dollars

to raise a kid to the age of eighteen?" I interrupt before he can say more.

He sips his drink. "No, I didn't." He tilts his head, studying me. "Is this about money?"

I stare at him. He's looking at me as if he cares, and it's sweet. He's being rational. I know it. Of course it's not about the money. It's about me. Me. And Bob. And some stupid hope that I'm clinging to. That if he sees me…

"I can handle this," I say. "I just need to figure out a way to get there. To Victoria. It's not that far, but unfortunately, Josh is selling his car, so I can't borrow his. Maybe I'll rent one."

Adam leans back on his couch. "Don't you have to be twenty-one or even older to rent a car?"

"Really?" I unclench my jaw and roll out my shoulders.

"I can drive you," a tiny voice says from behind me.

Amy is standing beside the couch holding a paper tube wrapped in pink cotton candy. The corners of her mouth are bright pink.

"Amy," I say, "this is a private conversation."

She pulls a big chunk of cotton candy off with her tiny fingers. "You're sitting in the staff room, not the private conversation room. If you wanted privacy, why didn't you go to your bathroom stall?"

Adam looks at her. I narrow my eyes at her and shake my head. "Well, I heard. And I can drive. So that's probably a good thing if you really do want to go find your dad."

I glare at her. She doesn't even look old enough to have her driver's license.

She walks around the couch so she's in front of me. "I've

always wanted to go on a road trip." Her cotton candy sticks straight down, almost in my face, but she doesn't take her eyes off me. "It's at the top of my list, like the very top."

"How could you possibly drive?"

She puts her hands out like she's holding a steering wheel with her cotton candy and steers the air. "Um. Like that."

"I mean what car would you drive?"

Her mouth opens and closes, and then she takes a bite of her cotton candy and looks at Adam.

"She has a car," Adam says. "A new Mazda 3 hatchback. It's bright yellow. You can't miss it. I've seen her driving in the parking lot."

I glare at Amy. "You have a new car?"

She pulls off another chunk of cotton candy and looks around the staff room. "Actually, my dad bought it for me," she says, not looking at me.

"You have to give your parents your paychecks for rent. How could your dad possibly manage to afford a car? A new one?"

She makes a snorty giggle sound that's both nervous and awkward, and then she looks at me. "I may have exaggerated not being able to afford lunch." Her gaze darts off to the table of red shirts making a huge amount of noise as they snap pictures of themselves. "A little." She glances back at me. "Okay," she says. "A lot."

"What?" I ask.

She plunks her butt down on the couch beside Adam. She glances at him. "Um. I lied." She sighs. "I don't work here for the money, okay? I thought it might be a good way to make new friends. I was homeschooled until last year, and all the kids at my high school are so...lame." She picks off a strand of pink fluff but doesn't put it in her mouth.

"You don't have to give your parents your paychecks?" I repeat.

"No. My dad, well my mom too, since they're married and all, but my dad made lots of money. I didn't lie about him being an inventor though. He's a software designer. And he's good. Really good. He invented Sour Cats." She hums the theme song to the app that every person in the world seems to have on their phone or tablet.

"Your dad invented Sour Cats?" Adam asks. He turns to me. "I did hear that the guy who invented it lived in Tadita."

"Why? Why would he live in Tadita?" I ask.

"Where are we supposed to live?"

"Hollywood? Hawaii? Beverly Hills?" I suggest.

She shrugs. "My dad likes it here. And my mom grew up in Tadita."

Adam sits up taller and opens his mouth. I raise my hand up to stop him. "How do we know you're not lying again?"

She pouts a little. "I guess you don't." She holds out her cotton candy to me and makes a puppy dog face. "Want some?"

I glare at her.

She sighs and folds over a little in the middle. "I'm sorry. I was so embarrassed that Adam caught me eating from someone's popcorn, and you looked so *judgmental* when I told you, so I, uh, made that up so you wouldn't hate me. And then I had to take your money to go with the story. I meant to pay back the five bucks." She stands and digs into a pocket on her skinny jeans and pulls out a bill. "With interest." She holds out a ten, but I shake my head.

"Twenty?" She pulls out another bill and leans over the coffee table and puts it in front of me and then sits back down. "Yes. And I can pay for gas for the trip too." She grins and there's a glob of pink cotton candy stuck in her teeth.

I snatch the bill from the table and shove it in my pocket to spite her. "A yellow car? For real?"

"I like yellow. It's a happy color." She bounces on her butt, clearly excited. "Let me make it up to you. I'll drive you to BC. I can pay for the gas and the hotel."

She grins at me, a sparkle in her eyes. I frown at the excitement on her face, but it dawns on me—she might be the answer I've been looking for.

"Well," I say, "you wouldn't have to pay for everything." Am I actually taking this offer seriously? I don't even know if she's telling the truth for sure. I put my hand up. "Are you serious?" It's happening so fast. And while it's exciting, it terrifies me more than a little. "Would your parents even let you go?"

"My parents would totally let me go, trust me. They'd be thrilled. Me and a friend on a road trip? They'd be, like, orgasmic or something!" Her eyes open wider, and she's so honest with her enthusiasm and disbelief that this could happen that I have an urge to hug her close. I know what's it's like to be lonely. I know what it's like to have a parent who worries about me not having friends.

I chew my lip. "Are you really serious?"

"The sooner the better! Can you imagine? Me and you on the open road." She giggles.

"Are you old enough?" I say, not believing this is coming together so quickly.

She sits up straighter, like it will make her taller. "I'm eighteen. I can't help it that my parents gave me the short genes. Sue me. There are worse things." She glares at me and then taps the side of her nose. "Maybe we'll find out that your dad has a big nose."

I snort, even though I'm pretty sure she just insulted the size of my nose. I reach for my phone. I need to tweet this news. The road trip will happen.

"It's at least four hours to drive," I tell her as I type. I glance up. "Plus a ferry ride. And you need a passport to drive across the border."

"I went to Scotland last Christmas. Do you have a passport?" she asks.

"I got one a couple years ago, when we went on a school trip to Vancouver," I tell her.

"I want to come," Adam says.

I stop typing. We both turn to look at him. I'd actually forgotten he was sitting there for a minute.

"You can't come on a road trip with two girls," I say.

Amy bounces on her butt some more and makes a weird giggly sound. "Sure he can. Road trip! Road trip!" she chants. The girls in red turn to look at us, but I don't even care that we're drawing attention to ourselves. I've practically committed to going on a road trip with this tiny little person who sounds like an overactive mouse, and that makes me happier than I've been in a long time. I should be worried.

"Why not?" Adam asks. "Are you afraid you won't be able to control yourself around me?"

"Ugh," I say, and my cheeks warm. "Please."

Amy giggles a little too enthusiastically.

"Girlfriend," I remind Amy. "He has a girlfriend. He's kidding."

"I know. And I think I can control myself," she squeals to Adam. "But can you?"

I ignore her and frown at Adam. "Why would you even want to come?" The thought of being in a car with him for over four hours makes my insides twist up.

He ignores me and focuses on Amy. "Maybe you guys need someone to look after you. Maybe I need a vacation. Do you mind if I come along?"

She grins, and I see again how pretty she is when she smiles. "Not even a little."

"But why would you want to?" I repeat.

He laughs out loud. "Come on. You're not that bad. You'll have your face buried in your phone the whole time. Why do *you* care if I come along?"

"No," I say, determined to talk him out of this crazy idea. Immediately. My excitement is getting squashed down by his suggestion.

"Why not?" he asks.

"How about we don't want a bunch of male junk in the car? Never mind a room," I tell him.

"My junk?" He glances down at his crotch.

"God. Not that junk. Gross. Just, you know, junk. Boy junk."

"I like boy junk," Amy says.

"Now there's a tweet!" Adam says to me.

I roll my eyes. "You're not helping," I say to Amy. "And what do you know about boy junk?"

"What do *you* know about it?" she asks.

"I have brothers."

"Oh. Well," Amy says, "I figure it's like girl stuff, only different."

"Pretty much," Adam says.

I glare at both of them. "We wouldn't all be allowed to take vacation on the same weekend anyhow," I say.

"Who cares? I'll quit." Amy stands up, walks to the trashcan, and throws away a huge portion of her cotton candy. "I already came clean and you know I don't need the money. I'll quit. A road trip is better than working in the snack shop. And summer is almost over anyway."

A new group of kids storm into the staffroom, a mix of yellow and red shirts. They're loud as they gather around a nearby table, but for once I don't care what they're talking about or worry that they're all laughing at me. One of the boys walks over to the vending machine. "Yo," he says to Adam, "boss man."

Adam nods, and his happy expression changes just a little. I wait until the guy takes his chocolate bar and heads back to his friends. Maybe he does need a break.

"I can't quit. I need the money for college," I say and then stop and swallow, thinking of my mom, the bills coming in. I'd give it all to her without too much remorse. Shaking that off, I turn to Adam. "You can't quit either. It would look bad on your résumé for your fancy premed schools. Anyhow, you must need the money too." I frown, wishing he'd stop trying to ruin this.

"I do, but don't worry about that." He grins as if he didn't hear the negativity oozing from my mouth. "I can get the time off," he says. "For all of us."

"No, you can't," I tell him.

He frowns at me. "What are you? Work schedule patrol?" He gestures at the three of us. "Theresa is my aunt," Adam says and stands. "Nepotism is alive and well at Tinkerpark. She'll let us go. I'm her favorite nephew. Sort of. Anyhow, don't worry. You won't have to quit." He glances at Amy. "Unless you want to."

Amy is doing a little dance on the spot. She has no rhythm at all. None. But I smile at her, not caring if every one of those yellow or red shirts stares at us and makes fun of us.

"Not really. This is the best summer of my life." She grins.

"Huh," is all I can manage. Never saw that one coming.

"So," Adam says, "let's head to the office and book ourselves time off." Adam reaches for my hand to help pull me up, but I ignore him and stand on my own.

Amy stops her dance and pulls her phone out. "My fingers are sticky," she says, squishing up her nose.

"I wonder why," Adam says.

I glance at the phone she's holding. It's the newest model and is covered by a Hello Kitty bedazzled pink phone case. Why did I not notice that before?

"I'm calling my dad," she says. "This is going to be *epic*."

"Are you sure your parents will be okay?" I ask as I sling my backpack on my shoulder.

"My parents will throw a party. Trust me. They're always trying to get rid of me. I think they want to have sex in my bedroom." She smiles. "Joke. They want me to have friends."

Amy walks a few feet ahead of us, covers one ear with her hand, and starts gabbing loudly into her phone. Adam walks slowly beside me. "So? Road trip ready?"

I take a deep breath. "I'm kind of freaking out," I admit.

"It'll be awesome." He pushes his glasses up his nose. "Let's go do this thing," he says.

● ● ●

When Amy and I leave the office, we both have the next weekend booked off. We head back to our workstations together, and my mind is still reeling. Just like that, I'm going on a road trip. To see Bob White. It's actually going to happen.

"Don't you think it's weird that Adam wants to come along?" I ask her.

"No," she says. "The other day when I asked him to go on the rollercoaster with me, he told me his girlfriend lives in Vancouver. He went on and on about her. Blah blah blah. I'm over my crush on him anyway. He's too intense."

I try not to laugh. "He's okay," I say, thinking of how much he helped out with my mom.

"He'll probably meet his girlfriend somewhere. I'm sure that's why he wants to come," Amy says.

I ignore a twinge of something like jealousy in my middle parts. It doesn't matter. He's my boss. Maybe my friend. Not someone to get jealous over.

"You reach five thousand followers yet?" Amy asks as we walk through crowds of families.

I have this superstition. If I can reach five thousand followers this summer, things will turn around for me in my senior year. I know it. #superstitiousmuch

I stop in my tracks and stare at her. "How do you know about that?"

"Um. Twitter. Hello?" she says and keeps walking.

"You're on Twitter?" I ask and duck around a little boy running away from his mom. I smile at him and pull my phone out of my backpack.

"Um. Yeah. @5alive. I've been following you for weeks. You haven't followed me back."

"I have almost five thousand followers, Amy," I remind her, holding my phone up in the air and hurrying to keep up with her. She walks fast for someone with such little legs.

"Well, la dee da," she says. "The people online, they don't really know you, you know."

I start walking fast to get ahead of her. I am fricking popular on Twitter. I rock on Twitter. "For your information, I'm going to meet some of my Twitter friends at a tweetup in Seattle."

"Yeah? When?"

"We're working on it. It's hard to get everyone's schedules in sync." I have been talking about it with online friends, but doubt it'll ever really happen.

"Whatever," she says. "I'm going to pay for *our* trip to BC. Are your Twitter friends doing that?" She catches up with me and tugs on the back of my T-shirt. "Slow down, okay?"

I walk a little slower. She's offered her car and her money. She wants to be my friend. Is that so wrong?

"Amy," I say, "you don't have to pay for everything." I dig in my pocket and take out the twenty dollars she gave me. "Here."

She shakes her head and holds up her hands. "No. Keep it. I feel stupid for lying to you, taking your money."

I try again, but she steps back, so I shove it back in my pocket. "Fine. But we'll split everything on the trip. You're doing me a huge favor."

"Well, you're doing me one too." Her cheeks turn pink and she glances away from me. "More than you know. Anyhow, don't worry about me. I can afford it."

"No. We split it. But I'm going to book a hostel. Not a fancy hotel. It'll be cheaper."

"A hostel? Wow. Like world travelers. Poor ones." She sticks out her hand. "Deal. I will travel like the poor people."

I laugh but reach out and take her hand and squeeze lightly.

"Friends," she says. "I'd like to get more followers on Twitter, like you. I only have six."

My cheeks glow with pleasure. "I'll help," I tell her as we reach the spot where we go separate ways. "You really want to drive all the way to Victoria?" I ask.

"Totally," she says with a grin. And then she giggles. "With Adam too. And his junk."

I ignore that. "I have no idea how else I would swing this."

"Yeah, you don't." She grins and holds up her wrist, which has about twenty colorful bracelets wrapped around it. "I'm going to make you a bracelet for the trip.

I look at the bracelets. They're pretty cool. Some are string, some are beaded, and some have charms hanging off them.

"You made those?"

"I'm crafty. Since I was a kid. I make lots of stuff."

"Cool." I nod.

"I made one for Adam too. Do you think he's the type of guy who would wear bracelets?"

"I doubt it. But maybe he's the type of guy who needs to."

She grins. "Yeah. He is."

I wave and laugh and run to the gift shop, arriving a couple of minutes late from my break.

"You look pretty happy about leaving me one less gift shop employee next weekend," Theresa says when I rush behind the register to relieve her.

"You know already?"

"Who do you think gave the okay? Adam texted me."

"Thanks so much," I say.

She jokes around some more before she leaves me, which is kind of new and kind of nice. When she leaves, I find myself humming. I don't bother to pull out my phone. I don't even check for updates. My break is over and it doesn't even bother me.

And then, all of a sudden, that worries me too. If I don't reach five thousand, something bad will happen. I know it. I'm as superstitious as my mom.

chapter eight

There's no getting around the fact that I'm nervous. There are comfort zones and then there's this—traveling with two people I barely know. To Canada. My comfort zone resides in Tadita, most of it online. I don't let my mind wander too much to what's at the other end of the trip.

I can't believe I'm actually going to see my dad. It's something I've dreamt about my whole life. The thought of him as a real person makes me want to hyperventilate. My insides get quivery at the thought of what might happen. Maybe, just maybe, he'll see that I'm not so bad. Maybe he'll accept me, even after all this time. As much as I try to deny it, I can't bury my hope. Maybe he'll see that I'm worth knowing.

I tell myself that whatever happens, happens. That I'll deal. Secretly I'm a little proud. For the first time in my life, I'm doing something about this. I'm going to meet my dad. My father. I'm not going to hide. I just hope I can handle it.

Ten minutes before Amy's supposed to pick me up, there's a series of raps on the front door. I glance up from my Twitter feed, where I've been posting like crazy.

Ever feel like you're diagonally parked in a parallel universe?
#Ido #roadtrip

Josh is still snoring under his blankets, but Jake's out in the living room. I hear him answer the door. With a deep breath, I tuck my phone into my backpack and stand, slinging it over my shoulder with one last look around my bedroom. Next time I'm in here, I'll have met my father. I walk out, stopping in the hallway in front of Mom's, room and tap at her door. There's no response, but I push it open anyway.

"Mom?"

She's lying on the bed, on top of her covers. She's wearing a fitted T-shirt and the black velour shorts she bought me for Christmas last year.

She coughs, sounding fragile and tired. "How're you feeling?" she asks me.

"I'm good," I tell her. "How are *you* feeling?"

She coughs again. "I miss my cigarettes." She pushes her bottom lip out. The hospital stay seems to have cured her of her lipstick addiction. With her pale face and untidy hair, she looks like a little girl who woke up from a nightmare.

"You're doing great."

"I'm scared," she says with a sigh.

I don't know if she's scared because of her heart condition or because I'm starting out on a trip to finally meet my dad. I don't ask. She could have pulled out everything in her arsenal to stop me from going to Victoria—pity, fear, guilt, whatever it took. But she hasn't. I know she wants to tell me not to go, and I respect her restraint even though resentment swirls around my overactive brain. She hasn't brought up his name again. We haven't discussed him once—or why I'm going to Victoria. We're following family protocol by not discussing it.

"I want to smoke so badly," she says.

Jake's laughter floats into the room from the front hall.

"That's your friend with Jake?" She places her book on the bed beside her and slowly moves into a sitting position and then swings her feet over the side of the bed.

I almost tell her Amy's not a friend exactly, that she's more like a chatty coworker with a car. But it makes both of us happy to think I have friends again, so I nod.

"What about the boy? Adam? Is he coming here too?"

"No. I told you. We're picking him up after. He lives closer to the outside of town."

She sighs. "I'm still not happy about you traipsing off with two kids I don't know."

"Liar," I say lightly. "You're happy I'm going somewhere with real people."

She stares at me as she pushes on the bed and slowly stands. "It has been a while, but this isn't exactly the way I would want it."

I swallow the sarcastic responses that pop in my head.

She takes a shaky step forward. "Can you bring me my robe?"

"Sure." I put down my backpack and reach for the pink terry cloth robe on the door handle behind me. Everything about it is familiar, even the faint odor of smoke that clings to it. I hold it, proud of her for giving up her cigarettes even though she loves them so much.

For a fleeting moment, I wonder if I could give up the Internet if I had to. But that thought makes my head and stomach hurt, so I take a deep breath and hand her the robe.

She stares me down with her practiced Mom glare as she puts her arms into the sleeves, and when she pulls the belt around her, it emphasizes her tiny waist. She's incredibly thin, and I remember how physically fragile she is right now.

"It's going to be all right," I say softly and move to help her walk, but she shakes her head and wobbles forward.

"Just be careful." She touches the side of my face. "Be careful." She opens her mouth as if she's about to say more, but then clamps it shut, shakes her head, and clears her throat. "Well, come on, I need to meet this Amy girl."

I pick up my bag and follow her to the hallway. When we turn the corner to the living room and front foyer, Jake is leaning against the wall, smiling down at Amy. She's talking a mile a minute. He's watching her as if she's explaining the meaning of life.

Jake is handling Mom's condition and recovery well, but Josh seems to be dealing by ditching his '70s vibe and becoming more responsible. Before Mom came home from the hospital, he shaved off his moustache. He's selling his classic car and getting a more reliable one. I heard him talking to a girl on the phone and asking her to dinner—a girl he'd already taken out once. And yesterday he was talking to Jake about putting some money into the down payment of a condo.

Jake was the one who said he didn't want to move out yet or leave until Mom was feeling better. It's a role reversal. Josh was always a mama's boy. Josh is still the one who keeps the lawn trimmed so the neighbors don't complain, but it's Jake who doesn't want to leave me to handle Mom on my own yet. He has no idea how grateful I am.

Amy spots my mom and me and stops talking midsentence, but Jake doesn't take his eyes off her.

"Hey," I say. "Amy, this is my mom. You've obviously met Jake."

"How old do you have to be to cross the border?" Mom asks instead of saying, "Hi, Nice to meet you," like a normal person might.

"I'm eighteen," Amy says and straightens her back to stand as tall as she can. She barely comes up to Jake's armpit. He doesn't appear to mind, based on the goofy grin on his face.

Mom shuffles forward and stops beside Jake, leaving just enough room for me to squeeze by them in the hallway.

"Nice to meet you, Mrs. McLean," Amy says. "You look very good for someone who just had a heart attack."

Mom glances at me.

"It wasn't a heart attack," I remind Amy. "Just a blockage."

"Oh. Sorry. I knew that. I just meant you're so pretty and young. My mom looks like she could be your grandma."

"Well, that's the nicest thing I've heard all day," my mom says and smiles more genuinely than I've seen in a while.

She's so easily charmed, but I smile too because, as far as I can guess, Amy wasn't even trying to charm. She pretty much says whatever is on her mind. She's not one to lie. Well, except when she made me give her five dollars because she got busted for eating popcorn. There was that. But she did pay me back—with interest.

"It's true," Amy says. "My mom's hair is gray and she's round."
Jake laughs.

"I don't mean to sound mean. She is round. She calls herself that." She shrugs. "We don't care, my dad and I. She's big-boned." Her eyes light up. "Oh. I made you all something," she says. She reaches into her hoodie pocket and pulls out a handful of something. "Hold up your wrist," she says to me. I do as I'm told, and she slips a thick, colorful, rope bracelet on it. I turn my wrist over, admiring it. It's made of soft material, like a T-shirt or something.

Then she turns to my mom. "Wrist," she says.

"What?" My mom frowns but does as she's told.

"I had to make one for the whole family," Amy says and ties a beautiful bead bracelet with a heart pendant on it around Mom's wrist.

"It's really pretty," Mom says.

"It's my hobby," Amy answers.

She turns to Jake and puts two dark leather, knotted bracelets in his hand. "I didn't know if you would wear these, but I didn't want to leave the brothers out."

Jake grins broadly and slides both bracelets on his wrist.

Amy frowns at him. "One is for the other brother."

"Yeah. Well, we'll see if he deserves it."

Amy smiles and looks to me. "I thought you said your brothers were dorks," she says without a trace of irony. "He's not a dork."

Jake throws his head back and laughs like it's the best joke he's heard in years. Mom makes a sound in her throat like she's covering up laughter. I roll my eyes and step between Amy and Jake.

"I meant dork in the nicest possible way. Okay. We should go," I say to Amy and put my hand on her back to move her out the front door. I make a mental note to explain to her the concept of tact.

Amy digs her feet in, giving my mom a laundry list of the routes we're taking and how she's had the car inspected and her dad gave her his credit card. Amy tells her she's loaded up on snacks and drinks, and we're completely prepared for the trip.

Jake is watching us as if he's mesmerized. I wonder if someone took his brain out or if he's developed a drug habit. Jake doesn't stare at girls like that. And his cheeks are blotchy. I look at Amy and try to see her through his eyes, but all I see is a tiny, quirky girl with brown hair and a skinny build. She's pretty, but nothing like the girls Josh dates. Of course, part of the beauty of Jake is that he sees people from the inside. And whatever it is inside of Amy, he seems to like it.

"Come on, motor mouth," I say to Amy, and she laughs, but Jake gives me a dirty look and it makes me giggle inside.

"Text me," Mom says, and her voice breaks at the end of the sentence. I look at her pale face with her naked lips pressed tightly together, and my heart swoops. It hits me with a force. I'm going to meet my father. I wonder if the fear in her eyes is for me—or her.

"I'll be on roaming, so it'll be expensive." I don't want to chat with her while I'm doing this. It's too confusing. "But if there's an emergency, text me." I stress the word *emergency*. I don't want to deal with her drama, but I am worried about her health.

"I can give you my cell number," Amy says to my mom. "My dad bought me a texting plan for the weekend, and I have unlimited texting and calling from Canada." She looks at my mom and then at me.

"Nice of him," Jake says.

"He worries."

"I'll get a pen and paper," Mom says.

"No. Wait here. I'll be right back." Jake darts into the living room and trots back holding his phone. "Here, put your number in my contact list. Just in case." He hands her his phone. "I'll text it to my mom after."

"Sure. Yeah." She types in her info and then looks up at him, and they both smile. I watch the both of them.

"My dad invented Sour Cats," she tells Jake, as if it's natural she should tell him everything about her. Based on Jake's goofy smile, he doesn't mind.

"Did I tell you how she pretended to be poor and made me give her five bucks?" I ask.

"I did not make you," she says and glares at me then looks at Jake. "I got caught eating popcorn at work. It was the first excuse that came to mind. I felt really bad about it. She made me take her five dollars."

I barely resist the urge to tease her some more.

"I only got the job at Tinkerpark to make new friends. I was homeschooled for a long time."

"Yeah. People probably don't get you," Jake says. "That happens to me all the time."

I look back and forth between them and then glance at Mom. Her eyebrows are raised and she's trying to cover her amused smile with her hand.

Miraculously, Amy doesn't say anything—but she's beaming.

Jake glances at her. "So, um, text me. When you get there. Let me know how you're doing. Um. How Morgan is doing. You know, so we don't have to rack up her phone bill." I open my mouth then close it and put down my gym bag to slide on my laceless sneakers.

"Be careful, Morgan, okay? Don't let this guy hurt you." Jake reaches for my bag. "I'll carry it to Amy's car for you," he says.

"It's okay." I shake my head and take the bag from him. This guy is my dad, after all. I open the door and wait for Amy to follow me.

"Okay. I'll see you in a few days," I say to my mom without looking at her.

"Morgan…" Her voice is hoarse. I look at her, and her lips are pressed tight and her hand rubs her chin. "Whatever happens, whatever you find out…just remember that I love you." She blinks quickly.

I walk outside and Amy follows me. Jake slips on shoes and walks behind us, and the two of them gab all the way down the sidewalk to the street where Amy's car is parked. I glance up at the sky. Black clouds are swirling in the air and it's cool. Amy pops the trunk, and I throw my stuff in and walk to the passenger door. I'm about to jump in the car when the front door of the house opens and Mom runs outside. Her robe pops open and she grabs it and wraps it around her.

"Morgan?" she yells. Loudly.

I glance around to see if any neighbors are outside. Mrs. Phillips next door will have a great time with this. She thinks my mom is crazy already. She's mostly right.

Mom sniffles loudly. "I'm sorry," she cries. She drags a hand under her nose, clings to her bathrobe with the other, and bats her eyes, her mouth quivering. There's an instant ache in my chest. It was already there, but it's bigger now and it hurts my lungs. I inhale deeply as if I'm hollowed out.

"I'm sorry," she repeats.

The words slice through the wind and cut into me like the cold in the air. I want to yell and ask why she's sorry now, eighteen years later, but I lift my hand in the air, wave, and then open the car door.

Jake steps closer. "Don't worry, Chaps. She'll be fine. I'll take care of her." I get in the passenger side, and he walks around and opens the driver's door for Amy, holding it while she climbs inside. And then he steps back to the sidewalk, watching while Amy fires up the car. I wonder who is going to take care of me. And isn't that the point?

"Oh my God," I say as she checks over her shoulder for cars and pulls out. Jake is standing on the sidewalk, waving, and my mom appears to be freaking out and trying to run after the car. Jake is holding her back. "What the hell is wrong with my family?"

Amy lifts her hand to wave as she pulls away and toots her horn. "Nothing at all," she says. "They're awesome."

I close my eyes and try to let my mom's distress go. I don't want to take it with me. It is not mine to own. Not now.

Amy reaches across the console and pats my leg. "Don't worry. You're going to be fine. I had a dream." I stare at her to see if she's joking, and she giggles. "Chaps," she says. "You brother calls you Chaps?"

I start to laugh. She's sitting on a cushion to make her taller. It cracks me up.

• • •

Adam lives in the newest suburban area on the outskirts of town. Amy's got the address programmed into her GPS, and we find it without any trouble. As soon as we pull in front of a brown and black house nearly identical to all the others on the street, Adam comes running out the front door and up the drive. He's wearing black jeans with a plain white T-shirt and a green plaid shirt flapping open. His hair looks kind of frantic, sticking up in all sorts of directions.

"He's cute," Amy says as we watch him run to the car. I silently agree. "Like a nerdy band guy," she says.

"He looks like a young doctor," I say.

She tilts her head, watching him out the window. "Maybe a mad scientist."

He reaches the car and Amy pops the hatch, and he dumps in a small black bag, closes it, and then crawls into the backseat. He slides into the car. "Drive," he yells to Amy with a trace of panic in his voice.

She pulls out with a screech as he's still putting a seat belt across him. I turn around. "Are you being chased by the cops or something?"

"No." He doesn't smile or expand but he presses his mouth tight, so I turn around.

"Should we be concerned about our safety?" Amy calls.

"No. It's fine," Adam answers.

Amy raises her eyebrows and shrugs, not seemingly having any problem with whatever is going on with Adam. "So how old is Jake?" she asks me.

"Forty," I tell her, sneaking a peek back at Adam. He's frowning. "And he still lives at home with his mom." I turn back to her profile as she squishes up her nose and her forehead wrinkles up.

"He's not forty," she says, not playing along. "And he is pulchritudinous."

"Pulcra-whatinous?" I ask.

"Delightful to the senses. Beautiful," she clarifies.

"You're talking about Jake?" I pretend to stick my finger down my throat and gag.

Oh God, I think, *if Jake falls for Amy, they'll probably marry right after she finishes high school. She'll get pregnant and stall my imagined climb for him up the corporate ladder.* I imagine her babbling at family dinners. "And what are you, a walking dictionary?"

There's a grunt from the backseat. "You mean you didn't know what pulchritudinous means?" Adam asks.

I glance over my shoulder. He looks less stressed out. "You did?"

"No." He laughs. "Sorry 'bout earlier. My dad and I had an argument and I wanted to get away before he ran outside to have the last word," he says.

"Her mom ran outside in her bathrobe," Amy says.

"Amy's sitting on a cushion so she can reach the pedals," I say.

"Okay," Adam says. "Weird parents behind us, cushions underneath us. Road trip—ahead!"

All I can think about is the weird parent ahead of me, the one who left me behind.

chapter nine

Amy reaches over and pats my leg briefly again before returning it to the wheel. "I'm sure your dad isn't that weird."

I pull my phone from my hoodie pocket and check my followers. Ten
more since this morning. People have been RT"ing my call for followers.

#Road trip! I tweet.

There are immediate tweet backs from my friends.

@Morgantor Send us your road trip playlist #roadtrip #envy

I want to go on a road trip with my twitter best buds. #roadtrip #bucketlist,
I tweet back.

"Are you going to be on that thing the whole time?" Adam asks.

"Maybe." I punch out another message. Essential item for road-
trip? Earbuds.

"No way," Amy calls. "Front seat rule number one: you must
keep the driver entertained. You're responsible for changing CDs
and navigating. My dad programmed the Lynden border crossing
and ferry into the GPS already so that part won't be hard." She
comes to a stop at a red light.

"The Lynden crossing?" Adam calls from the backseat.

"My dad said it takes a little longer to get there, but the wait times are shorter."

@5alive Your dad is rad, I type.

The light changes and Amy drives forward, turns her signal on, and takes the ramp to the freeway. My heart skips as we leave Tadita behind. My text alarm rings and I glance at the text.

> Morgan? Text me, k? I need to tell you something.

It's from my mom.

Instead of answering, I send a text to Jake.

> Is mom okay? Health-wise?

A moment later, he texts back.

> She's fine. Worried about you meeting your dad, but fine. Don't stress.

> Let me know if she's not feeling well. I really don't want to talk to her, but I am worried.

> Yeah. I get it. I'll let you know if anything changes. She's good. This is about you.

Since she's hasn't had a relapse or anything dire, I put the phone down. If I talk to her, she'll make this all about her, but the truth is, this isn't about her. I don't want to hear what she has to say anymore, not until this meeting with my dad is done.

"I went to Amy's house and met her parents," I turn and tell Adam. "Her dad told me they used to drive back and forth to Canada all the time."

Amy's house was big but old fashioned. Everything looked expensive but kind of neglected, as if they'd bought it because they could but didn't really want to. Her dad didn't look like a software genius, with his big, protruding belly and wispy red hair, but he was sweet and nice, like a big teddy bear. It was obvious how close the two of them were. He listened to Amy like she was the most interesting person in the world and looked at her like she was the most beautiful. It made my heart hurt a little.

Her mom was sweet too but quieter. She was writing a book, she told me, and born without housework genes. I met Mary, their live-in maid, who they treated like an old friend of the family. Amy said Mary did most of the work and cooking, and her mom laughed and agreed. We ate dinner and then her dad took us for ice cream before he drove me home. Later, when I was alone in my room, I cried a little over how lucky Amy was.

"Amy's dad was a little worried when I told him I'd booked us at a private dorm room in the Stingray Hostel," I tell Adam.

"He's not a snob. He just wants me to be safe," Amy says, lifting her chin. "Adam. There are some bags on the floor with snacks in them. I got popcorn twists for Morgan because they're her favorite." I glance at her profile. I told her that a few days ago when she quizzed me about things I liked to eat. I didn't know she was going to buy them for me.

"That is really sweet," I tell her.

"I also bought different flavors of chips, since Adam said he likes them all. And pretzels and candy bars and Skittles. And Cheezies. The Cheezies are for me."

"Whoa. Selfish much?" Adam says, and we laugh. Amy makes a face.

"If anyone gets car sick, it will be rainbow colored," I point out.

Amy sits up taller. "There's a cooler bag on the floor too, filled with sodas. I'd like a Mountain Dew. There's water, Coke, and Gatorade."

"No root beer?" Adam says, but this time she glances at him in the rearview mirror and sticks out her tongue.

"You are officially the Queen of the Snacks," he tells her.

"Quit sucking up and pass me a Mountain Dew," she says.

Adam passes a bottle forward and I take it, twist off the cap, and place it in the cup holder for her. "Here you go, bossy pants."

My phone dings, signaling I've received a text, and I pick up my phone and read.

> I like your hair like that.

The text is from Adam. I glance back, but he doesn't look up from his phone.

I'm tempted to text back, *Let's send a photo to your girlfriend and see what she thinks*. But that's a little presumptuous. A boy can say he likes my hair without cheating on his girlfriend. Who do I think

I am? Sexy pants. Ugh. As if she'd be threatened by me. As if she should be.

I text back and then smile to myself.

> You should comb yours.

I hear him laugh.

"Put your phone away," Amy says to me.

"You said what?" I lay my phone on my lap but don't put it away. "My mom doesn't even make me put my phone away."

"Yeah, well, obviously she's not one of those parents who monitors her kid online."

I can't decide whether to defend me or my mom.

"Listen up, Chaps," Amy says. "Car rule number two: no phone face the whole drive time."

"Phone face?" I ask.

"Phone face: when one has their phone constantly in their face," Adam says. "Obviously. Do you want a Coke?"

"Is there diet?" I ask.

"No, don't you know all those chemicals are bad for you?" Amy says. "No aspartame." She turns her head slightly but keeps her eyes on the road. "Can you hand me the Cheezies?" she says to Adam.

"Because Cheezies are made with all natural ingredients?" I say. Then I turn to Adam. "Regular is fine."

He hands me the drink with an industrial-size bag of Cheezies. I pick up my phone. "My Twitter update from the Lynden border showed no lineup and only a ten-minute wait," I announce to prove my phone facing can also involve helpful travel tips.

I break open the bag of Cheezies and put them up on the console so Amy can reach it. "Just so you know, I'm all for you getting five thousand followers, but you don't have to do it on the road trip."

"Thank you, Amy," I say, but the sarcasm is potent.

"Suck it up," Amy says. "Try interacting with real people for a change. You might even like it."

"Amy, you're far too little to be my mother. Besides, the one I have is bossy enough."

"My car, my rules," she says and sounds happy.

I glance back at Adam. "Trade me spots?"

He raises his eyebrows and grins.

"Ha ha," Amy says, not at all offended. "You also have to arm pump all the truckers once we hit the highway."

"Clearly," I say.

"Wooooo," calls Adam from the back. "Arm-pump girl."

"No one is allowed to sleep, and that includes you, Adam." She glares at him with her rearview mirror. "I don't care if we do get stuck in long lineups at the border or the ferry crossing to Vancouver Island. No sleeping."

"Bossy pants is right," he says.

"My car, I'm the boss," she shouts happily. "This is not Tinkerpark. Shut up and hand us more snacks. Pass Morgan the popcorn twists. And I need Smarties."

It's noisy with paper and plastic rustling.

"You kind of take on a new personality behind the wheel," I say to Amy, but she's stuffing Cheezies in her mouth and ignores me.

Adam throws a bag into the front seat and it hits me in the head. I open the twists and stick my hand inside. With my other hand, I reach for my phone.

"Hey!" Amy shouts.

"Just one more tweet," I beg. "To sign out. I don't want people to think I'm ignoring them."

Adam leans forward and puts his hand over the seat. "Hand it," he says.

"No way." The thought of handing over my phone makes me hyperventilate a little. I hold it up so he can see and hold the power button down. "I powered it off. For now. See? I promise not to turn it on until…." I try and think how long I can hold out. "I'll need to check it again before we cross the border. In case there's any change with my mom."

Amy presses the volume button on the stereo and turns it up so loud that no one can hear my answer. It's a new pop song, and Amy knows every word and sings along at the top of her voice.

I turn and catch Adam's eye. He's munching on a bag of salt and vinegar chips, but he shrugs and starts singing too. I roll down my window, lift my foot up to the window ledge, and wiggle my toes in the wind. We've driven away from the clouds, and the breeze feels good.

I love the outdoors of Washington and, despite my fantasies of escape, can't imagine living anywhere else. Mountains and water are in my blood. I wonder if Victoria looks the same. I know that it's similar to Washington in climate, but that doesn't mean I'm going to like it.

Ahead of us, a semitruck approaches. I scramble to sit up and stick my arm out the window and pretend to pull a horn. When he honks at us, we all howl with delight.

• • •

Over an hour later, we're out of radio-signal range and the CD is on its second cycle, turned to low. The bags of popcorn twists and Cheezies are half gone, and we've polished off a monster-size box of Smarties. After a short bout of singing at the top of her lungs, Amy started talking. I think she'd saved up. She can talk about anything and does. I don't mind, really. She doesn't require much interaction, and it's about what my brain needs. Every once in a while, I grab my phone for an update and she ignores it.

"You're a good listener," she tells me.

I smile, but people always say that to me. I ask her about homeschooling, something I seriously considered when the video went viral.

"My dad and mom both taught me. Mom works on her book and Dad works on software projects in the home office. We had the best field trips. Plus, for one class project, I opened a shop on Etsy."

And then she squeals.

"What?" Adam sits up straighter in his seat.

"In my pocket." She points to her hoodie. "Adam's bracelet."

"I thought you hit a deer," he calls from the back. "What are you talking about?"

I lift my wrist and show him mine. "She made a bracelet for my mom too. And my brothers."

"What a suck-up," Adam says, but he smiles.

I dig inside her hoodie and pull out a couple of bracelets. "The orange one," she says. "That's the one for Adam."

It's braided with yellow and brown strings. It's cool. I hand it back to Adam. "Put it on," I tell him and tuck the other bracelets back in her pocket.

"I can't tie it myself," Adam says.

I turn around, and he holds out his arm and I tie the bracelet on his wrist for him. His skin is dark, smooth. I turn quickly back to the front window when it's done.

"My bracelets have magical powers," Amy says.

"Good to know," I tell her. She high-fives me as we pass a sign that tells us we're twenty-five miles outside of Lynden.

"Lynden once held the record for the most churches per square mile," Amy says. I don't know how she knows this stuff, but I'm too afraid of a long explanation to ask.

"Cool," says Adam from the back. They share a love of trivia apparently. I've learned all sorts of things listening to the two of them geek out, mostly about geography.

"Did you know the border between Canada and the United States is the world's longest border between two nations?"

I think hard. "*Juno* was filmed in Vancouver," I burst out. My favorite film of all time.

I'm met with silence.

"I never saw it," Adam says finally says.

"Me either," Amy says.

"Come on. You never saw it? *Juno* is the greatest movie ever made," I say. "I'm ashamed for both of you."

"Ever made? What about the classics?" Amy asks.

"*Juno* is far superior," I assure her.

"Did you know eighty percent of pictures on the Internet are of naked women? Think about that for a moment," Amy says.

The car is quiet as we all wrap our brains around that random fact.

"We're almost at the border. Are you afraid?" Amy asks.

I glance over. Her lips are orange. I look at the steering wheel and see that the fingers on her right hand are also orange.

"About crossing the border?" I ask. "Do I look like it? God, I have such a guilty conscience. Josh said they'll probably harass us at the border because we're young."

"Josh, the other twin? Does he look like Jake?" she asks.

"No. They're opposites in looks and personality. Jake is kind of introverted. Except with you apparently." She has the same effect on both of us.

"Well, my dad says I overcompensate—as in talk too much."

I laugh. "Don't worry. It's kind of your thing."

She nods. "I've crossed the border lots of times." She taps her fingers on the steering wheel. "Of course, that was with my parents. My dad said to take it seriously. Give short answers to their questions." She glances at me. "You should resist trying to crack a joke because you're nervous."

"Five miles." Adam points outside at a sign.

I reach for my phone but discover we're in a dead zone, out of

Wi-Fi range. It makes me kind of twitchy. I'm edgy without Wi-Fi but yawn, suddenly tired. I glance at my phone.

"They'll ask a lot of questions," Amy says. "Like how long will you be in the country? Why are you traveling to Canada? What's the name of the place you're staying at?"

"I wrote the address of the Stingray Hostel down. I'll grab it." I reach for my backpack, dig inside, and pull out a notepad with the info.

Adam leans forward. "What are we saying our reason is for visiting? Let's get our story straight."

"I'll say I'm going to see my dad," I say, "since that's what I am doing." I turn my head and narrow my eyes at him to show him his question sucks. "You have a guilty conscience too?" I ask.

"Maybe," he says. "Let's hope they don't have anything against teenagers or think we're drug dealers or something."

"We're driving her to see her dad—it's a dad-finding trip," Amy says. "We have nothing to worry about. My dad said I'm far too chatty to be a threat to Canada," she continues. "And I would never do drugs. Well, illegal ones."

I pick my backpack up and pat the pocket where my passport is. "You're the last person I would ever suspect of doing drugs." Reassured, I put the backpack back on my lap.

Amy glances at me and then back at the road. "You know, before? I wasn't asking if you were afraid of crossing the border. I was asking if you were scared about seeing your dad." She keeps her eyes on the road, but the empathy shines from her profile.

"I'm terrified." I glance behind me, but Adam is staring out the window, far away in his own thoughts.

I click the button on my window to filter in some fresh air.

"Ewwww," I say and wrinkle up my nose.

"Skunk!" Amy calls. I quickly roll up the window, but the smell is strong and penetrates the glass. Sure enough, we whiz by a munched up little black and white creature on the side of the road.

"Awwww. Poor little guy," Amy says.

"I think he got his revenge." I plug my nose.

"Can you blame him?" Amy says. She's quiet for a minute. "I can't even imagine what it must be like not to know your own dad."

"Yeah," I tell her. "You're really lucky. Your dad is awesome."

"I am," she says somberly. I'm glad she appreciates what she has.

"What do you think is going to happen?" she asks.

I don't answer and frown as the CD progresses to a happy song about summer fun.

"I guess I've tried hard not to really think about it too much," I finally say. "Like what if he slams the door in my face or calls me a liar?" I look out the window. "How do I handle that?"

Amy turns down the volume on the CD.

"Maybe you should call him," Adam suggests from the back. "Instead of just showing up at his door?"

"Surprise is the only element I have control over. I don't want to give him a chance to prepare. I want to see him react. I want to watch him recognize me. I want to hear an unrehearsed explanation for breaking my mother's heart and missing every day of my life."

Something flashes by the window and there's a sudden *pop* outside.

"OH EM GEE!" Amy shouts.

I glance over and her eyes are wide and she's gripping the steering wheel tight and sitting straight up in her seat.

"Amy?"

Her lips are pressed tightly together. I glance around, and there are no cars behind or ahead of us, but I hear a flapping sound

"Was that the tire?" Adam says from the backseat.

The car bumps a few times and then begins to slow. Amy steers the clunky car off to the side of the road. It's not a smooth transition to the shoulder as we gradually come to a stop. There's no one around, just open farmer's fields on both sides.

"It was the tire," she says. We sit in shocked silence until she flips on the hazards and pops the hatch open.

"Holy crap." I open my door and step outside.

chapter ten

5. Real girls don't change car tires.
    #thingsithoughtweretrue

Adam scrambles out of the car. Amy shuts off the engine and joins us at the front bumper. We all stand there and stare at the passenger tire.

It's completely flat.

"Let me guess," Amy says. "None of us knows how to fix this?"

"Boy fail," Adam says.

"Thank God my parents insisted on AAA." Amy looks around. "This is like a scene in one of those horror movies. Maybe we're going to get attacked by vampires or zombies."

"For God's sake, call AAA," Adam says. "You watch too many scary movies."

"There's no Wi-Fi or satellite," I tell them, holding my phone in the air. "No bars. We're out of range. My phone is useless. We're S-O-L."

"Totally flip flop screwed," Amy says. Her teeny voice sounds like Alvin from the Chipmunks. Adam and I glance at each other and burst into laughter.

"I'm glad you find this funny." She walks around the car and opens the driver's side door. "Maybe my phone has bars. Adam, get yours out too. Maybe we can get service." Suddenly she's the mature one in our little group. "We need to get this fixed before the border closes down. We'll miss the ferry to Vancouver Island."

The laughter in my throat vaporizes. Amy takes out her phone and Adam grabs his brand-new replacement phone, but none of us has service. We sit on the car and stare at the highway. The sun is shining. Two cars approach from the opposite way, and we all jump up and wave our arms around. Neither slows even though it's kind of obvious we're having car trouble.

I think about all the times I've seen people pulled over and considered stopping but kept going. I vow to stop next time. And then I think about my healthy fear of serial killers on the side of the highways. *Maybe not.*

"Come on," I say. "We might find a spot where we can pick up service. There has to be a farm or something around here somewhere. There has to be Wi-Fi. We need to find a pocket."

We walk along the shoulder of the highway, holding our phones in the air, watching for bars. Then we cross the highway to the field where cows are grazing nearby. Amy slips through the barbed fence. I shrug and follow her, trying hard not to get scratched by the barbed wire. Adam stays on the other side of the fence, staring at us.

"What?" Amy says. "Come on."

"There are cows in that field," he says, pointing out the obvious.

"So?"

"So what if they charge us or something?"

Amy stands on her toes and looks around. "I don't see any calves. If we walk quietly and respect them, they're not going to bother us."

"How do you know?" Adam doesn't move. "I've read about people being charged by cows."

"Are you kidding me?" Amy asks. "You're afraid of being charged by cows? This is not very bosslike."

"It's happened." Adam pushes his glasses up his nose and lifts his chin. "Maybe one of us should wait by the car, in case someone stops to help. And by 'one of us,' I mean me. I hate cows."

"So you'd rather have two girls get charged than you?" Amy asks him.

"No." He looks toward the car. "Like you said, you'll be fine. But cows freak me out. I don't even like eating hamburgers."

We both stare at him.

"Fine. Wait by the car." Amy throws her keys at his head. He manages to catch them. "Give Morgan your phone in case it gets bars first."

I'm surprised that he doesn't argue and just hands me the phone and jogs back across the highway to the car, the keys jangling in his fingers.

"What a mousetrap," Amy says, shaking her head in his direction.

I ignore her strange comment. "Do cows really charge?" I ask. I don't have cow facts readily available in my head.

"Rarely," she says. "Move calmly, don't make any sudden noises. Once they see we're no threat, they won't even care we're around."

I have no desire to make cows suspicious of my behavior. "How do you know these things?"

117

She shrugs. "I read a lot when I was a kid. I remember things easily."

She starts wandering the field, her phone held high in the air. I sigh and follow. We walk slowly, checking our phones. I keep one eye on the herd of cows as we get closer. The smell is obnoxious and there are piles of dung everywhere. When we're almost in the middle of the field and way closer to the cows than I want to be, Amy screams.

"I have two bars!" she shouts. "Hey! I got a text from Jake!"

I glance down and see my phone still doesn't have service. Neither does Adam's. I know her phone carrier is a different one than mine and make a mental note to switch. "Forget Jake. Call a tow truck!"

Amy calls 411 and gets a tow truck number in Lynden. When she reaches the tow company, she gives them her AAA number and our approximate location on the highway. She hangs up and turns, walking back toward the highway. "He said at least an hour, hopefully not more."

I glance at the time on my phone. If they're more than an hour, we might not make the ferry. It'll be cutting it close. Too close. I stomp behind Amy across the field and then slip through the wire and cross the highway to the car. My insides flutter with nerves, but I know what I have to do. I take a deep breath. Adam opens the door and steps out.

"Moo," Amy shouts at him and pretends she's going to attack.

"That's funny, said no one ever," he yells.

I ignore them, trying to psyche myself up.

"It's not illegal to be afraid of cows," Adam says.

"Not illegal. But kind of hilarious."

My stomach flips. I don't want to miss the ferry. I don't want wrinkles in our carefully scheduled travel plans. I pace up and down beside the car, arguing with myself.

"Are you freaking out because you can't use the Internet?" Amy calls out.

"No. I mean yes—but no." The truth is, Josh taught me how to change a tire, but I never intended to ever actually do it myself. And I'm scared I'll mess it up.

Adam jumps off the trunk and they both watch me pacing, kicking up gravel under my feet.

"What's wrong?" Adam asks.

"I know how to change a tire, okay?" I say. "But I've only done it with Josh helping me. I'm kind of chicken."

"Woo-hoo," Amy yells and jumps up and down, pumping her fists in the air. "Why didn't you say so, Chaps?"

I narrow my eyes. "Didn't you hear the chicken part?"

"Forget that. We're here. Tell us what to do. We'll help. Just do it."

"What are you, a frigging Nike commercial?"

She crosses her arms and glares at me. "You can do this, Morgan."

"Totally," Adam says. "And it only makes me hate you a little bit. I am made of lame."

I frown and fidget, kicking the gravel with my toe.

"Come on," Amy yells. In the distance, one of the cows moos loudly.

An excited feeling punches me in the stomach. I take a deep breath, close my eyes, picture Josh as he taught me. I'd been sure I'd never attempt it. I'm not sure I can do it.

"Step one…pull up the parking break. Adam, go find a big rock or something to put in front of the tires so the car doesn't roll," I say out loud.

I stand taller. While they run off to find rocks, I go to the trunk, take out the luggage, and lift the board up to find the spare tire, right where it's supposed to be. I reach for the jack. I close my eyes, think about missing the ferry. I can do this. I get to work.

chapter eleven

6. Everyone is embarrassed by the same things.
    #thingsithoughtweretrue

My hands are filthy. There's grease all over my shirt. The tow truck is canceled and there's a fiery orange explosion in my chest. I'm prouder than Michael Phelps's mom at the Olympics. The little donut spare is on, and I catch my reflection in the window and see the girl looking back at me glowing with pride.

When Amy pulls into the last gas station right before the border crossing, we pile out for a bathroom break and clean up. I check my follower status. 4444. All fours. I take that as a good sign.

Soon, we pull up to the border. There are only a few cars in front of us to cross, but each one seems to take forever to get cleared through. The car clock seems stalled; the minutes crawl by. When it's finally our turn, the officer stares down each of us while he checks over our passports. Amy starts to babble, but I poke her in the side and she stops.

"What's your purpose in Canada?" he asks me.

"I'm going to see my dad," I tell him.

"She's never met him," Amy adds. "He left her mom before she was born."

The officer leans in closer and studies me. "That true?"

I nod. He glances in the backseat at Adam. "We're here for moral support," Adam says and smiles bigger than necessary.

The officer writes something on his clipboard and then looks back at me. His expression softens. "I have a daughter your age. I don't get to see her much." He hands Amy our passports. "You kids drive safe." He steps back from the car and waves us through. We're quiet until we're a few minutes away from the crossing, and then I scream and woo-hoo at the top of my lungs. Amy and Adam join in.

After a car dance mini celebration, I check the GPS. "We're on 264th Street and it'll take us to highway 1. Then we head west to Vancouver," I tell Amy. "We're going to be tight for time."

"I don't want to get a speeding ticket," she says. "It's the one thing my dad would freak about." Amy drives for about five minutes and then sighs. "This scenery is exactly like Washington."

"You want more Cheezies? Another Mountain Dew?" I ask.

Amy shakes her head. "We could play table topics."

I reach for the popcorn twists and shovel a handful in my mouth. "Table topics?"

She glances over, as if I'm an alien or have grown a third eye. "Only the best game on the planet. It's a card game, like a conversation starter."

I shrug and glance back at Adam. He shrugs too.

"You seriously don't know? There are, like, thirty editions or something. We have more than half of them."

I shrug again. "Sorry."

"You wanna play? Adam?"

"Why not?" Adam says.

Amy bounces up and down on her seat. "Yay! Look in the glove compartment, Morgan. There's a set in there." I open the glove box and see a red, cubed stack of cards and take it out.

"How do you play?" I ask.

"It's easy. You just pick a card, read it, and then everyone has to share."

"How do you win?" Adam asks.

"You don't win. You talk."

"No one wins?" Adam says.

"Your family puts a lot of value on talking," I mumble.

She narrows her eyes into slits. "Yes. Unlike yours, we don't sweep everything under the rug and pretend it doesn't exist."

"How did you nail us so well?" I grin.

"Um, your mom never told you who your father was until you were eighteen."

"Point taken," I say.

"Sounds like a useless game," Adam mumbles. "No one even wins."

Amy gestures at the cube. "Just take one," she says to me.

I open up the box, take out the top card, and flip it over. I read it and frown, biting my lip. I reach in my pocket for ChapStick and apply it.

"What does it say?" Amy yells.

I clear my throat. "What is the most embarrassing thing that's happened to you and what did it teach you?" I read.

The silence seems infinite and obnoxiously loud.

"Well, I guess that's obvious," Amy finally says. "Everyone in

Tadita saw you dancing around in men's underwear. To that song."
She hums "Sexy and I Know It."

"Okay," I say. "We got it."

Amy nods. "But what did it teach you?"

My face burns. "Never to run out of clean underwear? God. I
needed clean underwear and my mom hadn't done the wash, so she
gave me an unopened pack of boys' underwear. She said it didn't
matter since they were brand new." I close my eyes, feeling humiliation heat up my blood. Tighty whities. People posted that they
probably belonged to a boy I'd had sex with, that I collected the
underwear from boys I slept with, like trophies.

"But why were you dancing for a camera? You should never put
stuff like that on video."

My ears burn. "Lexi and I were fooling around. She thought it
was hilarious that I was wearing boys' underwear. And while I was
shaking my butt around, she picked up my phone and taped it.
It wasn't supposed to be seen by everyone in the world." I glare at
her. "Especially you," I snap. And then I glance at her face and see
hurt in her eyes. She doesn't mean harm; she says out loud what
everyone else is thinking. Without the malice.

"I'm sorry. I didn't mean that." I reach over, touch her shoulder,
and steal a Cheezie from her bag.

"I know," she says quietly. "You didn't even know my name until
a couple of weeks ago, even though we worked side by side all
summer." She raises her eyebrows but doesn't look at me. Adam
is watching me though. I can see him from the corner of my eye.

"Well, I learned it sucks—to have something go viral online,"

I say. The car is quiet and the crunching of the whole Cheezie I shoved in my mouth is overly loud in my head.

"Well," Amy says after a minute, "at least you're not a terrible dancer. And it was kind of funny."

I close my eyes to black out images of me thrusting my pelvis at the camera in boys' underwear. With fake junk. I'm such a freak. Man. I glance out my side window. Canadian cows are clustered in a herd by the fence that runs parallel to the highway. I'd like to go out and stand in the middle of them. Disappear. I think of a great tweet and reach for my phone.

> Removing something from online is like trying to take pee out of a pool.

"At first I thought you must be an attention freak," Amy is saying. "But since we've become friends…" She glances over and then back to the road, as if she's waiting for me to say something. Which I should. But I don't. Her words burrow into my skin like a tick crawling in to suck at my blood, steal from my life source.

"Well, that's not who you seem to be at all." She stares at the road. "Or are you one of those closet exhibitionists?"

"That thing ruined my life!" The shame in me flares and I fight to extinguish it.

"Ruined your life?" She clucks her tongue. "I'll give you humiliating, but ruining your life? No way. There are worse things."

I'm kind of shocked she can act like it's not one of the worst things ever.

"Do you have any idea how many people saw that video?" I demand.

"Over three million, I think," Amy says as she takes out a Cheezie and bites the end off it. "Last time I looked. Completely viral. But it slowed down, right? Those things don't last."

"Like you're the expert on humiliation?"

"Well, you shouldn't have posted it," she says and nibbles on her Cheezie.

"She didn't," Adam says. I glance at him and then down at my hands.

"It was my friend," I say and turn my head to stare out the window. "Lexi. She slept over that night."

"Your friend?" Amy says. She smacks the steering wheel with her hand. "That's mean. Really, really mean."

"She posted it online. And for whatever reason, it caught on. It went out of control." I bite my lip, lower my eyes, forget the other part. "She doesn't even talk to me anymore. Lexi."

"She won't talk to *you*?" Amy yells, straightening her back and sitting up high on her cushion. "That sounds like a good thing," she says. "That's a horrible thing to do to your friend. To anyone."

"See?" I say. "I told you it was horrible."

"Embarrassing. Horrible is men who walk into schools and shoot innocent children and the teachers trying to protect them," Amy says.

"Horrible is the number of homeless people on the streets and mental illness as something we turn away from instead of trying to treat," Adam adds.

"Cancer is horrible," Amy says.

"Okay. Fine. I get it. My embarrassment wasn't life threatening. But it was…embarrassing."

"I'll give you that," Amy says.

"Thank you," I respond with as much sarcasm as possible and ignore a niggle that these two deserve the total truth.

A semitruck races up on Amy's side and passes us.

"Hey," Adam calls out. "You didn't arm pump the trucker."

I ignore him, staring out at the green hills that look like they stretch out for miles in front of us, wishing I could go back to that night and change it, knowing it will never go away.

"I hope you never talk to her again," Amy says. Another truck whips past and throws some stones; they sprinkle up on the car.

"Oh my God," I say. "They're going to hurt Honey Mustard."

"Honey Mustard?"

"Your car. Obviously." I don't admit that that deep down, I still miss Lexi. And don't blame her. Not entirely. I want to forgive her, be her best friend again. Go back to the way it was. "Okay. Enough of me. We examined that in enough excruciating detail."

"Want to hear my embarrassing moment?" Adam pipes up.

"Please," I say and turn around to face him.

He leans forward in the seat, his elbows resting on his knees. "So last year in biology class, we were studying the human body. We had a dummy with all the parts, all the body parts. Mr. Jackson, my teacher, was at the front of the class, pointing out things. And then, without warning, I sneezed and my gum shot out of my mouth and landed on the dummy's penis."

I cover my mouth. Amy and I look at each other and then I clap my hands. "Okay. That is awesome. Awesome."

"For weeks, everyone called me penis breath," he adds.

I swallow my laughter, trying to think how it must have felt for him. "Okay. It was embarrassing," I say. "But still, not viral…Okay, so what did you learn?"

"Not to chew gum in class?" he says.

"Maybe to aim your sneezes?" I turn to Amy. "Okay. Your turn."

"Hmm. Embarrassing? I don't know. I don't get embarrassed that easily. How about that people make fun of me for being small?" she says. "But I actually think it's worse to be ignored."

I study her profile, her cute, perky nose. "I don't know. I don't think being ignored would be so bad," I tell her. "Actually, I'd kind of welcome it since the video went viral."

"Not me. I hate when people act like I'm invisible," she says.

I sit up taller. "Toward the end of the year in my homeroom, I would have given anything to be invisible."

Amy frowns. "Why?"

"Right after the video went wild, my homeroom teacher was taking attendance, calling out names, and waiting for everyone to yell 'here.' He went down the class list and everyone yelled back, but when he got to me, I couldn't make myself yell. I said, 'here' quietly, but he kept calling my name louder and louder. Everyone in the whole class turned and stared at me. Finally a guy I've known since grade school says, 'Why doesn't she just yell it?' Mr. Todd stopped for a second and then got this really pissed off look on his face and started walking toward my desk yelling, 'Scream! I want to hear you scream.'"

I pause and swallow, and the horrible feeling returns to my stomach as I remember. "But I couldn't. I sat there staring at my desk, hating myself and everyone around me."

There's silence. A big uncomfortable silence hangs in the car. I wonder if I've gone too far. Sweat forms on my upper lip. I might as well be sitting in my seat naked. Picking my nose. I try to think of a joke or something to say to lighten the moment.

"What a jerk," Adam finally says, and anger drips from his voice.

"Totally," Amy says. "A big fat jerkolia on a jerk stick."

I laugh out loud and fall a little more in love with her.

"Me?" Amy says. "I can't remember one time in my life when I couldn't talk. I wish my brain didn't spit out everything, but sometimes it's like I have no control over my mouth. And I'm like blah, blah, blah." She reaches for a Cheezie and points it at me. "But remember, if the world didn't suck, we'd all fall off it."

Adam starts to laugh. The knot in my stomach loosens and I laugh too. Amy grins, and some of the shame I've been holding in for so long fades along with her stupid joke. It's a relief to share it. It takes away a little of its power.

"I have to pee," Amy announces, and without warning, she signals and pulls over to the side of the road. She leaves the car running, opens her door, runs to the passenger side, and squats right on the road's shoulder. I glance back at Adam, but he's laughing so hard he's holding his stomach.

When she hops back in the car, Adam says, "Apparently you don't get embarrassed."

"Maybe I have a clear conscience." She shrugs as she pulls on her seat belt, puts the car back into drive, checks over her shoulder, and pulls back out.

"Maybe you're missing the embarrassment gene," Adam says.

"New topic," Amy calls. "Adam. Your turn."

I pass the cube back to him and he picks a card. "Describe a situation where you did something you're sorry for," he reads.

"Is this game supposed to make us feel like losers?" I ask Amy.

"No. Not all the topics are sad. Go, Adam," she commands.

He clears his throat. "Really?"

"Really," she growls.

He's quiet for a minute. "Okay. Um. When I was twelve, my best friend, Dillon, had a birthday party. He decided to invite all the guys in our entire class, including the fricking asshole bully, James. He hated my guts. Dillon told me not to worry, so I pretended to believe him. The night of the party, we were in the basement waiting for pizza. We were playing video games and listening to music. James came over and started ripping into me and another guy sitting by the TV, Cameron. Cameron was a nice kid, just kind of overweight and quiet.

"We both sat there taking his shit, pretending not to mind, until James started punching Cameron in the stomach. Over and over and over. For no reason. And everyone just laughed along with him or looked away and said nothing.

"I tried to say something, but he turned and lifted his fist, so I shut my mouth. And then he grinned, knowing he was getting away with being a dick and I wasn't going to stop him. He loved that I didn't do anything. His expression was so happy. A few days later, I told my parents and they called Cameron and James's parents."

Adam presses the window down as if the story fouled up the air in the back of the car and he needs fresh air.

"So what happened?" Amy asks.

"James beat the shit out of me. He punched me and I bled. I'd never been beat up before. Or since," Adam says and sighs. "It wasn't very fun."

"That's terrible." My heart stings for twelve-year-old Adam. I watch him, trying to imagine what he looked like at that age.

"Yeah. No one, not Dillon, not even Cameron, wanted to hang out with me after that. I became the narc." He lifts his shoulder. "Whatever. I got over it. The next year we went to junior high and I made new friends. But the thing I was sorry for was that I never did anything while he was punching Cameron. I was just so glad it wasn't me at the time. But I ended up getting beat up anyway. I wish I would have stood up to him."

"Did you know that lots of famous people were bullied when they were young?" Amy says. "Tom Cruise was bullied for being dyslexic."

"Bullies smell out sensitive kids like spammers sense unfiltered blogs," I say.

Amy and Adam stare at me. "I thought of a time when I did get embarrassed. Want to hear it?" Amy says.

"Yes!" Adam and I say at the same time.

"My mom caught me masturbating," Amy blurts out. "She walked in on me in my room."

My mouth drops open. "Amy!" My hands fly up to cover my eyes. My whole face is on fire.

"What? It's not like you've never done it before."

I peek at her through my fingers, and she glances in the rearview mirror at Adam. "And especially you."

"What," he asks, "is that supposed to imply?"

I look back and he has his hand over his mouth, trying to conceal his laughter.

"You're a guy," Amy says.

"Why thank you," he tosses back.

"I heard four out of ten women prefer it to actually having sex," she adds.

"Well, thank God for the other six," Adam quips.

"Amy," I say, "is there any topic off limits to you?"

She's quiet for a minute, as if she's really pondering it. "Yeah. Maybe one or two," she says.

I can't even imagine. A giggle starts building in my belly. I try to suppress it, but the more I do that, the harder it is to stop. Amy looks sideways at me and frowns, but the urge travels up and bursts out of my nose and mouth. I laugh and laugh, as if I've been holding it in for days. I laugh until my stomach hurts and my cheeks are sore and I'm too weak to go on.

Amy and Adam laugh with me. And when it finally dies down, I close my eyes, smile, lean my head against the side window, and breathe; it feels like I've lost a few pounds of weight in my stomach.

"Holy fudgsicle sticks!" Amy screams.

My eyes open. I stare ahead and groan.

chapter twelve

7. The only thing crying the blues gets you is good lyrics
    for a country song. #thingsithoughtweretrue

The line of cars waiting for the ferry crossing is long and deep. Amy pulls up and sighs. "I hope we can get on."

"What do you mean hope? We might not get on? Are you serious? I thought you made a reservation with your dad's MasterCard?"

"I did. But we're late. Sometimes you miss the boat. Like, literally."

"No! We can't miss this ferry!" My leg bounces up and down. We have to get on. I can't be late. I hate bad omens.

Amy and Adam trade whale facts, oblivious to the freaking out inside my head. "Humpbacks sing to attract mates," Adam says.

"Good thing you're not a whale," Amy answers. "Your singing voice kind of sucks."

Adam throws a potato chip at her head. The space in the car shrinks, and I roll down the window, watching parents playing with a toddler outside the car, swinging her up in the air, each holding a hand. The dad is laughing and the mom's head is thrown back, soaking up sun. I hope they drop the baby on her butt.

We have to make this ferry. I can't deal with a blip in my plans. I can't handle it. I can't.

"You can see lots of humpbacks near Whidbey Island," Amy is saying. "My dad took me to Whidbey a couple of years ago. We took a day off work and school and went on a whale tour." She smiles for a moment, remembering. The image of her and a dad who would do something like that makes my eyes water.

"Have you seen the video of the humpback whale breaching in front of a fishing boat by Whidbey?" Amy asks me.

I glare at her, but she reaches for a Cheezie, takes one out, and then turns to Adam.

"A pod of orcas was spotted near Whidbey Island a while ago. I'd love to see that." She keeps gnawing on her Cheezie and I'm tempted to rip it from her fingers and throw it out the window.

"Do you know why they're called killer whales?"

"Is there someone we can talk to about the ferry?" I mumble.

"I think there's a guy over there talking to people," Adam says, and I look to where he's pointing.

"They're carnivores and great hunters, the best in the ocean. They'll eat almost anything in the water, even other whales. And they can weigh up to six tons." Amy's oblivious to the explosion gaining force in my head.

"Lots of seafood to keep up that figure," Adam says.

"They can live to be eighty years old."

I reach for the door. "I have to go and find out what's happening." I'm not excited about making waves but dread not getting on the ferry even more.

I hurry toward a youngish, uniformed BC Ferries attendant

with an unfortunate hairline. He doesn't even look at me when I ask about getting on the ferry and point at Amy's bright yellow Mazda in line. "Sorry, you're not making this one," he says, glancing toward her car. "You won't be able to board until morning. If you had a reservation, you won't lose your ticket. You can use it tomorrow, but the last car going on ends right there."

We're parked several behind the one he points at.

I stare at the car.

No.

"But I'm going to find my dad, and I've never met him and I don't have much time..."

"I'm sorry, miss," he says.

And then I lose it.

In seconds, I'm a big, snotty, wet mess. "We c-cccc-cccan't.... mmmm-mmmmisss." My bottom lip quavers. I can't breathe properly. The attendant looks around as if he hopes someone will save him and pats me on the arm, but the storm won't easily pass. Tears I've been holding in for years pour out.

"I don't know what I can do given it's past boarding time," he tells me but his voice breaks.

"My ddd-ddad..."

"Come on, miss." The attendant takes my arm and walks me back to Amy's car, holding me like I'm a little old lady he's helping across the street. He walks me to the passenger side, opens the door, and sticks his head down.

"I'll wave you through," he says to her. "Drive over to the left and I'll show you where to pull on."

"Thank you, thank you," I'm blubbering, but he pats my arm and runs, hurries off as if he can't get away from me fast enough.

Amy and Adam don't say anything, but Amy starts the car and follows his directions. As she pulls ahead, another attendant, an older and more important-looking one, steps in our path. The arm patter walks over to him and they chat, and then they both turn and look at me, and I awkwardly wipe under my nose and then wave. The arm patter walks back to the car.

Amy rolls down her window. He bends down.

"My supervisor doesn't want to allow you on."

I whimper, but he holds up his hand. "He's going to let you on this time because I said you had an emergency and I told you I'd let you proceed. Never again."

"Thank you, sir. You are very kind," Amy says and drives slowly around the other cars in line. When we reach the bridge to the boat and pull on, she toots her horn. I shrink down in the seat.

"Never underestimate the power of a girl in tears," she says.

I mop my face up with the bottom of my shirt as Amy parks the car in the last row onboard the ship.

"I'm going to see a humpback. This is on my list," she says as she puts the car in park.

I wonder how long her list is. I bet she writes things like that down and that she has awesome notebooks filled with her thoughts. I had a blog for a while but deleted all my posts after the video when viral. I climb out of the car and go to the trunk to get the windbreaker I tossed in. I wait while Adam and Amy grab clothes. Amy pulls on a bright yellow raincoat over her clothes. Her raincoat reminds me of a picture book that Jake used to read to me when I was younger. Jake used to read to me all the time. Josh and Mom prefer the television.

"I'm kind of a nutcase, right?" The stress from earlier is gone. "I don't feel as embarrassed as I should."

Amy turns to me. "It got us on the boat. And it's not like I haven't seen anyone cry before."

"Yeah, but not quite like that!" Adam teases, but he bumps his hip against mine as we head out of the parking area and up the stairs. We go all the way to the top deck and find an empty bench with room for all three of us. The seat gives us a great view of the dark water in front of us. It's spraying and chilly, and I'm glad I have the windbreaker on top of my hoodie.

Amy starts up a conversation with a little boy with auburn curls sitting directly behind us. He's sitting beside a woman I assume is his mom. Amy and the boy are debating whale sightings. I smile, listening to Amy's animated conversation.

"Have you ever seen a whale?" he asks Amy.

"Lots. Never a Canadian whale. But I will today," she tells him. "And so will you."

"A Canadian whale?" the boy says. "Whales don't have nationalities."

"When I see it in Canada, it's a Canadian whale."

"There's no guarantee we'll see a whale," the mom says. "It's best to go on an actual tour if you want to see whales. And we're going to visit Grandpa, not whales," she says to the boy, patting his arm.

"My grandma died and my grandpa moved to the island with his girlfriend," the copper-haired boy tells Amy. "This is our first visit. My mom doesn't like his girlfriend. She was Grandma's nurse."

"TJ," the mom says. "We don't have to tell everyone our family's business."

"She's my friend," TJ says and smiles at Amy.

Amy nods as if the two of them have known each other for years. She smiles at the mom and shrugs. "My dad always says the same thing."

"I don't have a proper set of boundaries," says the boy. "It's going to be the death of my mom."

"Mine too," says Amy.

The mom frowns at Amy, clearly not as charmed as her son is. "We won't see a whale from this ferry."

"Oh. We'll see one," says Amy, her voice full of conviction.

I lean back on the bench and stare off at the ocean, tuning out the boy and Amy. Even though there are people on almost every free space on this boat, with the huge ocean stretching out ahead of us, I feel alone. I'm getting closer. I tilt my head back, and chilly sprays of water land on my face.

"You okay?" Adam says softly.

I open my eyes but leave my head tilted back and nod once, not really convincing myself. I look into Adam's eyes, and I'm consumed by a huge rush of desire. I close my eyes again so he won't see it. Unrequited love may be my specialty.

"This is a huge deal," Adam says quietly.

"I know." I press my lips together. My courage is slipping as the ship takes us closer to the island.

"It's gutsy," he says.

I open my eyes, my misplaced lust dulled by the reality of

what we're approaching. "Not gutsy. I'm scared shitless," I admit. "It's stupid. What if this is the wrong way to do this? Confronting him in person? The signs seem to say maybe I should have called."

"I think the signs are saying it's the right thing to do. You knew how to change that tire. You got us on the ferry on time." He glances toward the ocean. "I don't think you're stupid at all."

The ship horn blasts, and Amy screams and then giggles hysterically with her new little friend.

We sit quietly and stare out at the water.

"Look! A whale!" Amy yells.

There's a flurry of yelling and pointing around us. I stare across the water. There's no whale in sight.

"No fair. I wanted to spot the first whale." The auburn-haired little boy starts to cry as the cool wind blows his hair around.

Amy turns to him. "Oh dear. I think I made a mistake. You keep looking!"

He sits up taller, and his mom's expression softens a little. He intensely scans the water and I watch with them, inhaling gulps of moist fresh air into my lungs. We're all quiet as we watch the ocean in front of the ferry, even Amy. There's nothing except waves. Once in a while, something catches my eye, but when I peer closer, there's nothing.

"LOOK!" the little boy yells. It's the most gleeful sound I've heard in a long time. "WHALE!"

My eyes scan the water, and there he is. A giant whale breaks through the surface, as if he's performing for us, and executes a turn in the air, and while my eyes widen and my mouth opens, he flips around and is back in the water.

"Wow!" Adam's the first one to recover his voice and he shouts and then laughs. The sound is as joyous and free as the little boy.

I smile, staring at the water, wishing I'd been able to get it on camera to post to my friends. The boy's mom claps her hands together while he bounces up and down, talking a million words a second. I glance at Amy. She's still. A tiny smile turns up her lips, and when she catches my eye, she grins. "I knew it," she says. "I knew we were going to see one, but I had no idea he was going to show off so spectacularly."

Her gratitude warms my shivering insides. I forget the picture I could have posted and realize that it's a gift. Real life doesn't always need to be posted online. I can remember this moment without a photo.

In some crazy way, it feels like this is exactly what Amy planned. "Thank you," I say to her and breathe out. In that second, I realize that even if my dad turns out to be a colossal asshole and a huge disappointment, this will not be a wasted trip. I'm going to make it through this.

Amy smiles as if she understands me, and I stare at her, drinking in her true beauty. It shines from inside all the way through the bright yellow hood she has pulled over her head. She's brave enough to be who she is. She embraces her inner weird and flies her freak flag with all she's got. And for once, I'm smart enough to see what a wonderful thing it is.

"It's amazing, isn't it?" Adam says.

I nod, knowing we're talking about different things, but knowing he sees what I saw too—Amy, wide-eyed and optimistic, exuding wonder and joy, and able to shamelessly be herself.

Everyone around us settles, and Amy turns to the boy and shares more whale facts from her head. I relax against the bench, allowing the views and the smells as we pass by the Gulf Island to fill some of the holes inside me. In spite of myself, in spite of the thoughts racing and competing for attention in my head, I am calm.

I don't speak again until the ferry lands in Saanich. Amy hugs the little boy who's staying on deck to catch a bus into Victoria. We stand to begin our rush to the car, back to real life.

"Bleck. It stinks in here." Amy opens her window to let air inside.

"It does," I say. My serenity floats off into the air outside the car. "Like junk food and feet."

Adam and Amy debate whose feet smell worse as we drive off the ferry and bump over the grated dock. My heart thuds hard when the car touches Pat Bay Highway. Amy's GPS announces that we have a twenty-minute drive to the hostel, and my stomach jumps and breaches and twists, like the humpback whale in the ocean.

Amy is talking, but I can't tune in or focus on what she's saying. My head is spinning and trying desperately to avoid where we are, yet at the same time, I look around me, drinking in the breathtaking beauty. The sun is shining and welcoming. Fresh air blows through the open windows of the car. It's visually and fragrantly delicious.

"We made it," I whisper. And once again, I'm a little girl looking for her daddy—a daddy who vanished on purpose and doesn't want to be found.

My phone bings that I have a new text.

> I really need to talk to you. Please text or call.

My mom again.

I text Jake.

> How's Mom?

He texts back a minute later.

> Fine. Ignore her.

I turn off my phone and tuck it under my leg. Jake said she's fine. This isn't about her, I remind myself. This is about me. Finding my dad. Seeing him in person. Whatever she has to say can wait until I get home.

Amy picks up my mood and stops talking and turns the radio to a local station. An Eminem song comes on and I reach for the volume and turn it up. Under his anger and aggressive rapping, I feel his desperation and hope, and it feels similar to mine. The song works with my mood. I lean back, staring out the window as we zip past colorful, vibrant flowers sprouting from green grass on the side of the highway. It's fragrant and lush. The island throbs with life. The cuss words contrast with the sweetness. It's perfect.

Eminem screams to a finish, and the car is silent with dead air.

Amy turns down the volume button as the DJ breaks into the silence with a falsely cheery voice tinged with panic.

"We're here," she says.

Reality crashes back.

chapter thirteen

8. You can tell by looking if someone has their black belt
    in karate. #thingsithoughtweretrue

We're in front of the hostel. It's an old house, painted burnt yellow and squished up beside a church. A Canadian flag sticks out the front along with a blue flag I don't recognize.

"It's small. No Hilton or Marriott," Amy says, peering over the steering wheel.

"Welcome to budget travel. It's cheap. And it'll be clean," I say. "It had great reviews online. I promise."

"You got great reviews online," she mumbles.

"I got a lot more bad ones than the hostel," I say. "It's really cute. It'll be fine."

"There's a parking lot at the back," Adam says. "Turn left." He's looking out the window, reading a sign. Amy finds a spot right away and turns off the car.

"Awesome driving," I say to Amy. "We made it!"

I have a sudden urge to forget about my plans, forget why I've come to the island. We could sightsee and be tourists and live for the moment. I could forget I have a dad who dumped me before I was born and a mom at home recovering from heart surgery. Forget both of them. I've been good at ignoring her texts. I could ignore him completely.

I choke on my own breath. My forehead beads with sweat. I can't ignore him. After eighteen years, I'm here to confront him. I'm about to meet my dad for the very first time. A huge, embarrassing sob explodes from my chest as loud and delicate as the foghorn on the ferry.

Amy reaches across, opens her glove box, takes out a box of Kleenex, and shoves it at me. "I get a lot of nosebleeds," she says.

I nod, swallow, hiccup, and use the Kleenex to wipe up my face. "Sorry," I say again and sniffle. Adam's sitting on the hood of the car. He escaped as I was losing my grip.

"I don't usually cry. I think I freaked Adam out."

"I think you did," she agrees. "But that's okay." She nods toward Adam. "He's a boy. They can't handle emotion. I, on the other hand, with all my lady parts, am good in a crisis. Jake says hi by the way. He's worried about you."

Her whiplash-quick ability to change the subject lightens the mood. "Amy." I wipe under my eyes and blow my nose. "You are awesome. Never change."

"Why would I change?"

"Why indeed." I put my hand on the door. "No wonder Jake likes you. Should we go and check in?"

"You're sure you're okay?"

"I'm totally fine," I lie.

"And Jake and I may become friends, but you came first."

I push the door open before I start blubbering again.

Adam jumps up when Amy and I climb out of the car.

"I'm fine," I call to him. "Fine." I put my hand up to cover my eyes from the sun, but mostly to block myself from him. "Let's go check in."

The hostel is clean inside and smells like fresh laundry detergent. An older lady greets us at the check-in counter and asks for ID. She checks it over while she explains the house rules. When she hands us back our ID along with a fresh set of sheets for each of us, I giggle at the shocked expression on Amy's face.

Adam glimpses at her too. "You don't make your own bed at the Hilton, Amy?" He laughs.

The woman ignores us and comes around the counter to take us to our four-person dorm room. She walks ahead of us and points out the community kitchen. Amy's eyes get even rounder. "We're not going to cook for ourselves, are we?" she whispers to me.

"Not if you don't want to," I whisper back.

Some of the heaviness on my heart lightens and floats off into air. "We haven't even talked about what we're going to do now that we're here," I say.

We plotted our route, looked at maps. I booked the hostel, and Amy bought an army load of car snacks, but we never really discussed the order of what we'd do once we arrived.

"We'll figure it out," Adam answers. Amy's too busy scanning the place with bugged-out eyes to answer.

"We have to share a washroom?" she squeaks.

I pat her on the shoulder. "Communal washrooms. You're roughing it, girlfriend."

We walk inside the bedroom. There are two bunk beds across from each other. Cheery paintings of different flags hang on the wall. There's a small window at the end of the room that looks out onto the street. The lady tells us a few more rules about curfew hours and then leaves. I glance outside, surprised it's still light out. It feels like it should be dark. It's been a long and eventful day.

I make up the nearest bottom bunk bed. Amy throws her expensive-looking luggage bag on the bottom bunk on the other side.

"Seriously. I have to sleep on the top?" Adam scowls but plops his gym bag on the bunk above Amy. I breathe a secret sigh of relief. I don't think I would get much sleep if he were right above me.

"You snooze, you lose," Amy says.

"Is your girlfriend going to meet you here?" Amy asks as she and Adam tuck in their sheets.

"My girlfriend?"

"Yeah. That's why you came, right? We don't have time to stop in Vancouver, so how else are you going to see her?"

"Uh." He glances at me as he tucks in the top sheet on his bed. "Not sure. Haven't figured it out yet." He presses his lips into a frowns and adjusts his blanket.

"You and your girlfriend have a fight or something?" Amy asks Adam as she unzips her suitcase.

"No." He pushes his glasses up his nose and throws his gym bag on the blanket.

"So? Do we get to meet her? I've already got her pictured in my mind." Amy makes a face.

"She looks nothing like that face you just made."

Amy ignores him and walks over to the window. "Hey, check out this guy." Amy points out the small window of the room. I follow her finger. Adam looks too.

A guy about our age is walking a black lab without a leash. He's shirtless and his chest is dark, smooth, and very defined. His face is beautiful, and he's smiling.

"Wow. I think that's the guy you're supposed to marry," Amy tells me.

I laugh. "Me? He's too perfect. Why not you?"

Amy shakes her head back and forth. "Nah. I don't really see myself getting married."

"Well, I do. You picked him. You get him."

"Yeah. 'Cause it's that easy," Adam says.

Amy takes out a cosmetic bag from her luggage and holds it up. "I need to go to the washroom. Do you think it's safe? Should you come with me?"

I cross my arms and glare at her. "You can handle it."

"This is so weird. There are other people here using it too. I saw a group of boys in the room down the hall."

She starts walking toward the door and then stops. "Wait, where do we leave our stuff if we go out?" she asks. "This is almost dangerous."

I pull a padlock from my backpack and hold it in the air. "We'll get a locker. Didn't you see them by the entrance?"

"Ugh," she says. "I didn't realize we were staying at a prison." She disappears out of the room.

"Too much?" I ask Adam.

"She'll survive. She may be a little pampered, but I sense she's very adaptable," he says.

I laugh again and take out my phone, realizing I've hardly had it out in the last few hours—and surprisingly, I didn't miss it. I snap a few photos of the room to post to Twitter later. I point the camera at Adam next. Instead of striking a muscle pose or something, he stares back at me, his face serious.

"Hey, Morgan," he says softly.

Goosebumps travel up my arm, and I lower the camera.

"That was not the guy you were supposed to marry," he whispers.

The blush starts at my toes and swoops quickly all the way up.

Amy walks back in the room then, her eyes on us. She narrows them and puts her hands on her tiny hips. "What're you two up to?"

"Nothing," Adam says, yanking his gym bag off the top bunk. "Want to go for a walk? Check out downtown?" He tosses the bag on the floor with a thunk. "You guys hungry?"

"Not even a little," Amy says. "I have enough Cheezie calories to keep me fueled the whole weekend." She plunks her little butt on the bunk she's sleeping on.

"Yeah," I agree. "I'm full of junk food too." Deep breath. "Plus, you know…I should figure out what I'm going to do. About my dad." I grin but hold it in place for about one second before it disappears.

"Yeah. What's the plan? You haven't said," Amy says.

"I have an address." I sit on my bed and search my backpack for my ChapStick. "For the dad guy." I try to laugh, but it comes out flat and fake, and neither one of them even smiles.

"So what's the plan?" Adam asks and sits down beside me. My legs stiffen.

"Well, I thought I'd do it tomorrow. At his home. Show up." I rub my lips with ChapStick and press them together, trying to ignore Adam's thighs.

Amy stands, takes a step across the floor, and sits on the bed on my other side. And then she reaches out her arms and hugs me so tightly I can barely breathe. My hands stay down at my side. When she pushes me away, she stares into my face, her nose inches from mine. "I totally understand why you're such an emotional mess," she says. "It even explains some of your exhibitionism."

The earnest expression on her face breaks some of my tension, and I giggle. "I know. Right?"

Adam laughs too. "Amy, you're growing on me."

She leans across me to smile at him. "I am? Really?"

"You are."

"Well"—she leans back—"I don't have a crush on you anymore, just so you know."

"My loss," he says.

She grins. "Plus, you know, you do have a girlfriend, even if you are afraid to see her in person."

"I'm not afraid." But he develops a sudden interest in his sneakers and bends over to re-tie laces that look perfectly tied to me.

"No? Well, you don't seem excited. Maybe you like the *idea* of a girlfriend? That's what my dad says to me. That I like the idea of a boyfriend but I don't want the emotional implications."

"You mean, like sex," Adam says and then pulls in his chin and ducks to avoid smashing the top bunk with his forehead as he stands.

"Sex is physical. Not emotional," Amy tells him.

"Yeah. Keep telling yourself that." He walks over to the window and looks out. "You'll find out."

"How do you know I haven't had sex? Maybe I'm a closet nympho who happens to look young."

"Amy." I untangle myself from the bed and stand, holding out my hand to her. "You don't have to pretend to be all jaded just because you look young."

She narrows her eyes at both of us, ignores my hand, and flops on her back, staring up at the top bunk. "Whatever. I'm so a virgin."

"I'm shocked," Adam says. My evil glare is directed his way, and he shuts his mouth.

Amy sits up and hugs her knees in a yoga-like movement. "You need to do it. Tonight. Do it now."

"I'm not a virgin," I say, wondering if she's trying to foist me off on Adam.

She bats her eyelids slowly and claps very slowly. "I'm happy for you. But. I was talking about going to see your dad tonight."

"Oh." I pretend to laugh, but it sounds like a baby's cry.

She crosses her legs and ticks off a finger. "You're not hungry." She ticks off another finger. "And you're not in Victoria to sight-see." She scrambles off the bottom bunk and grabs her bag. "You're not going to relax until you do this."

"What? Now? No. Not now."

"Why? Why wait? It's not like you'll sleep a wink until it's done." Amy grabs her car keys and throws them. My hand automatically shoots out to grab them. She throws her arms in the air when I catch them and jumps up and down like a cheerleader in the final play of the game. "Go. Take my car!"

I flex and unflex my free hand, jiggling the keys up and down in the other. "I can't."

"Why not? It's not like you made an appointment to see him," Amy points out.

My heart pounds. I spin the key chain around and around on my finger.

"I think she's right," Adam says from where he's leaning against the windowsill. "The sooner you do it…the sooner it's done."

"As painless as tattoo removal," I mumble.

"It's not going to be any easier if you wait," Amy says.

"But I don't want to strand you guys. You should, you know, go downtown, see some sights." I glance at Adam. "Call your girlfriend."

"Forget my stupid girlfriend," Adam says.

"Stupid girlfriend? Why is she stupid?" I welcome the opportunity to bounce to another topic.

"Seriously. Forget my girlfriend." He moves his hand back and forth, close to his neck, in a slicing motion and then clears his throat. "We can walk to lots of places from here." He walks to Amy and drapes his arm across her shoulder, and she sags from the weight he puts into it. "Right, Amy?"

"We could come with you if you want," Amy says to me and scoots out from under him, punching him on the arm.

Adam rubs it. "What is it with you women and your punching?"

"You just told me I looked ten. And now I'm a woman?" Amy asks.

I bat my eyelashes to keep in the tears stinging behind them, but this time it's happy tears for the two of them arguing and keeping things real.

"I think you should do it, Morgan," Adam says, still massaging his arm. "And we could come with you."

"No!" My voice cracks and I clear my throat again. "I need to do this alone."

"You don't have to," Amy says softly.

"Thanks. But I need to." They've already seen enough of my humiliation. This is the type of thing meant to be experienced solo. I lick my lips and taste the cherry wax and then squeeze the keys tight, and the teeth of the keys make an impression on my skin. "I don't want to drive. I can't drive. I'll get in an accident. I'll be too distracted. I'm going to call a cab. That was my plan anyhow." I lift my arm and throw the keys back to Amy, but she misses and they clatter on the ground.

"Are you worried because you're a bad driver?" Amy asks.

"I'm not a bad driver!" My temperature flashes up and then smolders down a second later, and I laugh. As usual, Amy has a knack for taking my mind out of the dark place.

"What? I'm not one of those people who would get all freaky about a scratch or something. It's just a car. A pretty little bumble bee car. But still, just a car. The GPS is in the glove box. Go." Amy bends down to pick up her keys and holds them up.

I shake my head. "No. I'll take a cab."

Amy sniffles and then wipes underneath her eyes. "But what if he's a total jerk?" she says and sniffles, walking over and trying to give me her keys.

"We can at least drive you. I don't think you should do it alone," Adam says softly. "You don't have to."

"What if he throws you out?" Amy wipes under her eyes some more.

"Why are you crying?" My heart melts but I put the keys back in her hands.

"I don't want you to get hurt." She sniffles loudly. "We should come." She sits down on her bed and drops her head in her hands.

I slide onto the bed beside her. "It's okay, Amy. I'm going to be okay. I planned to take a cab. I've prepared myself for the worst." Deep down, I know it's not something I can prepare for, but she doesn't need to know that.

She leans over and puts her head on my shoulder. "But your dad abandoned you when you were a baby. Face it, he's not a really cool guy."

I gently push her head away but slide an arm over her shoulder.

"We should come," Adam says. He walks over and sits on the other side of me. I'm sandwiched in the middle of them again.

"I have to do it alone," I repeat. I swallow a few times. "I'm scared," I tell them. "I am. But it helps, knowing you guys are here." I stop, tapping my finger up and down on my leg. Not so long ago, they were strangers. Now they know me better than anyone—even Lexi.

"No matter what…no matter what he says…" Adam shakes his head and jumps to his feet, smacking his head on the side of the upper bunk with a loud thunk. "Ow." He rubs his head and scowls. "I will *kick* his ass if he hurts you." And then he glances down with a half smile. "Well, I'll risk getting my ass kicked again anyhow."

"I have my black belt in karate," Amy says. She gets to her feet and does some fierce-looking roundhouse kick thing. Then she makes a loud sound and jumps, kicking her leg surprisingly high.

Adam and I stare at her, our mouths open. "You have your black belt? For real?" I ask.

She shrugs and sits back down. "It's not all about the black belt. It's about the training. I trained hard. I focused. What?" she asks. "I trained with my dad for five years." She shrugs. "He doesn't have his black belt yet."

"Seriously?" Adam shakes his head and pushes away from where he's leaning and paces at the end of the bed. "Ninja Amy. That is seriously awesome." He frowns then, stops pacing, and turns to me. "You sure you don't want us to come along? For backup? Amy might come in handy."

I shake my head and swallow. And swallow again and swallow again. "I can handle it." I still have hope though, that it's going to go better than I fear—than they fear. Scooting off the bed, I take out my phone and the small purse I brought along so I don't have to haul around my backpack and all my stuff. It holds my wallet, my phone, and my ChapStick. Adam glances at Amy, and they both shrug as they grab their bags. I grab my backpack to lock it up and walk slowly behind them. After we put away the bags, I flip to my Twitter page and click on recent tweets.

"How many new followers?" Amy asks. I glance up; she's peering over my shoulder.

I look at her. "Only a few."

"We'll work on it," she says.

"Thanks," I say to both of them. "Here goes nothing."

chapter fourteen

The cab smells faintly like cologne. I glance at the cabby with his shaved head and black leather jacket. I wonder if Adam wears cologne, and then shake him out of my thoughts and tell the cabby the address of Bob White.

"How long will it take to drive to the Rockland district?" I ask.

"About ten minutes," he supplies in his growly voice, low but not unfriendly.

Exactly what Google Maps predicted. My stomach rolls around.

"You visiting relatives?" He's polite in a nice-uncle way.

"Sort of," I tell him.

"Fair enough," he says and that's it. He doesn't say anything else. He must sense my desire not to have a long conversation. Cabdrivers must be like doctors or bartenders. They read people's cues. Some want to talk. Some don't.

I lean back against the seat and stare out the window. There's an epic battle inside me, but when I catch my reflection in the window, my face looks calm and void of emotion. Years of practice.

I grab my phone from my purse and click to my Twitter page but can't read anything. I don't know what to tweet. This isn't something I feel like being pithy about. It's okay for now to know my friends are near.

My eyes turn back to the world outside the cab window. We turn down a street, and it's easy to tell we're in a very well-to-do area. The houses are surrounded by beautiful trees and rock paths and stone fences.

The further we go into the neighborhood, the bigger the houses get. My heart aches. It's not that he couldn't afford to have helped out. He didn't want to. He just didn't want to.

We're not destitute, the twins and Mom and I, but this area is in a different league. The majors. I try to breathe and, for the first time, understand how awful it must be for Josh when he has an asthma attack. I can't seem to get in a big breath.

"This is it," the cabby says as he pulls up to a big brick house. I wonder if my mom has seen the house. It's old but it's obviously been well preserved or renovated. The front yard is huge, filled with beautiful trees and big decorative rocks with pebble paths. The house faces the water and mountains.

"Nice place. You have to pay for views like this," the cabby says as I stare at the house. He turns to me. "Everything okay, miss?"

"Fine," I manage and almost tell him to drive on. Just leave and take me with him. Instead, I lean forward to see what's owed. I pull my wallet from my purse for some of the funny Canadian money, hand him a green, slippery twenty, and tell him to keep the change even though it's less than fifteen dollars for the fare. I try to catch my breath, but my heart is pounding fast, like I've been running. I sit completely still, staring at the house, wondering what I'm doing—why this even remotely seemed like a good idea. I could have called or started off with an e-mail. But no.

No. I want to see him. I want to meet him. And I want him to meet me.

"You sure you're okay?"

"Yes, thank you," I whisper to the cabdriver and reach for the door. He watches me, his face wrinkled up and worried. I open the door.

I pause, considering whether I should ask the cabdriver to wait for me. Instead, I slam the door and fight an urge to puke from fear. I'm all alone. On a strange sidewalk. In a strange town. A strange country. I can't swallow but take a deep breath. My hopes seem sillier now.

The cabby drives away slowly, and I lift my hand and wave but don't move from where I'm standing. I think about tweeting, but Adam and Amy will probably see it and know I'm stalling. They've got Twitter eyes on me.

Instead, I lift my phone and take a picture of the house to show them later. The long brick driveway runs parallel to a stone path that leads up to a huge wraparound porch. I glance around to see if anyone noticed me snapping shots, but there's still no one on the street. It's quiet. Too quiet.

I take a deep breath and wipe my clammy hands on my pants. Maybe I should have changed or at least put on some makeup. Then again, why should I try to impress him?

Yes, get angry, I tell myself. It's better than being afraid. "Okay," I say softly to myself. "You can do this."

I stare at the doorbell, trying to force myself to push on it. I imagine pressing the buzzer and running. I lift my chin and close my eyes.

I reach out and press the bell.

chapter fifteen

9. Parents only lie to their kids about Santa and the Easter
Bunny. #thingsithoughtweretrue

Hello?" calls a woman's voice. The tall door is half shut and blocks most of her face. I only see dark, curly hair.

I'd hoped no one else would answer.

I can't tell her age. Is she a wife? Daughter? Maid?

I straighten my back, refusing to feel bad for his family if he has one. I try to smile but my mouth quivers. I'm not the bad guy here. I didn't do anything wrong. The choices Bob White made weren't my fault.

"I'm looking for Bob White," I manage, and my voice sounds husky in my ears.

I wait for her to slam the door or send out a pit bull to chase me away.

"Yes?" she says and the door opens another crack. I see her whole face. She's slight, almost fragile, with thick, puffer-fish lips, bloated and kind of fake looking. She's wearing a black turtleneck that touches her chin. She's older than I thought. Dark chestnut hair cascades down to her shoulders in waves. I wonder if she recognizes me—if she hates me.

"Bob White. Who used to work in Seattle?" I prompt.

"My Bob lived in Seattle. A long time ago." She tilts her head and narrows her eyes and she opens the door fully, leaning her hip against it. *My Bob*. She's not a housekeeper then.

"Do you work with Bob?" She sounds polite but cautious.

Taking a deep breath I say, "I'm Morgan McLean," as boldly as possible, as if my name is something to be proud of and not the name of the girl in men's underwear dancing on a video that went viral on YouTube a few months before. It suddenly occurs to me he may have seen the video.

She smiles, but her eyes don't flicker with recognition. My stomach drops as if I'm riding the rollercoaster at Tinkerpark. It's both a relief and an insult. Unless she's faking it, she's never even heard of me. This woman. Bob's person.

"Um. Is he home?" God. It sounds ridiculous. Soon I'll be asking if he can come out to play.

"Bob's working." She stands taller and she looks at me with narrower eyes. Suspicion crinkles the corners of them. "Can I ask what this is regarding?" She glances down at a silver watch on her wrist. "He doesn't see solicitors."

My face heats. "Um. I'm not a solicitor." Am I? "It's, um, personal." I fidget, shifting my weight from one foot to the other.

"Personal?" She takes a deep breath, looking me up and down with her nose twitching a little, as if I smell. Bad. I might because my underarms are soaking and there's sweat on my upper lip despite the cool night air.

"What's this about?" She glances out past me and frowns as if she must notice there's no car. "Has Bob done something?" She glances behind her. There's a meow and a fluffy long-haired black cat swirls around her leg and swishes its tail at me.

"No," I say, watching the cat. "Nothing at all." He hasn't. Not in eighteen years. I glance up. "Do you expect him soon? Or is there a number I can reach him at? I'd really like to talk to him." I didn't plan for him not to be home when I rang the bell. I really should have thought this through more, but I'm good at blocking things—years of practice from a good teacher. My mom.

The woman bends down and picks up the cat. The size of the cat in her arms makes her look even smaller. The cat stares at me with big, round, yellow eyes. They're judgmental and find me lacking. The cat owner looks me up and down too. I see a flicker of suspicion in her eyes.

"I don't even know for sure if he's the right Bob," I say quickly. "I need to ask him some questions."

She strokes the cat and watches me. When the cat purrs, she pushes her hip off the door. "It's important, isn't it?" She's studying my face. I wonder what she sees.

"Very."

She stares at me so hard, I wonder if she's peering inside my head and reading my thoughts. Uncomfortable and lost, I wonder if I should just turn and leave when she steps back and opens the door a little more.

"Fine." She steps away from the doorway and drops the cat to the floor. With a mew, he scampers off and runs down the hallway behind her. "Come in. Wait here. I'll go check on him. Bob is working and asked not to be disturbed, but he's in the office downstairs." She blinks. "Who do I say is calling?"

"Morgan McLean," I repeat.

"That's right." She nods as I step inside, and she gracefully rounds me and closes the door behind me. "I'll be right back."

Her feet glide along dark hardwood, and she disappears down the hallway, out of the front foyer, around a corner. I glance up. The ceiling is high, and a huge chandelier hangs right over my head. I step off to the side, suspicious of the bolts. Down the hallway, a door opens and footsteps traipse down the stairs.

My body starts to shake. Inside and out. Even my bottom lip quivers. And then my mind trips. I want to run but force myself to stay still and calm.

There's another mew. The cat is back, sitting close to the corner wall, watching me. Staring. Disapproving. He's close to a dining room with French doors, which I only know because the twins talk about construction and house design. The doors are thrown open, but instead of inviting, it has a premeditated and staged aura. Dark hardwood flows into the dining room without a trace of dust or even cat hair. The furniture inside looks unused; everything about the house suggests lots of dollar bills. I shuffle my feet on the plush entry mat, breathing deeply to keep myself from keeling over. I'm tempted to take out my phone. I wish I were all alone, chatting with online friends or transported through time to the tweetup we keep talking about but never seem to make happen in Seattle. I wonder if I've gotten new followers. I wish this stupid plan had never occurred to me.

A low hum travels up the stairs from the basement. Voices meld together and muffle, and it's impossible to hear actual words. And then footsteps. Two sets. I breathe deep. Deny. Deny. The power of denial is my superpower.

I wipe my hands on my jeans. The door opens. A tall blond man steps out, around the corner to the hallway. The cat purrs and prances toward him. My eyes don't leave him. His nose has a bump just like mine. He even has a dimple on his cheek where my cheek puckers in. Our eyes are the same shade of brown.

He's wearing jeans and a golf shirt, trim and fit for an older man. I can't take my eyes off him. He's so familiar looking. He's a stranger. There's no doubt I've found my dad. I swallow and fight an urge to cry.

"Yes?" He walks a few feet in front of me and stops. Stares at me.

My face burns. "I'm Morgan." I cower, just a little, but shake it off and stare at him.

I wait for it. His anger. Maybe some excuses. A reaction to having me show up on his doorstep without warning. Eighteen years later. His daughter.

"Morgan?" He glances back, and I realize his wife followed him around the corner. She stoops over and scoops up the cat. His gaze returns to me. "Have we met?" he asks.

There's an audible breath of relief from her mouth, and it softens the crow's feet in the corner of her eyes. She stands taller and touches his back for a moment and then goes back to stroking the cat.

He hasn't told her. About me. She doesn't know. To me, keeping quiet is the same as lying. I frown. Apparently she doesn't know him as well as she thinks she does. Her boyfriend? Her husband? I squeeze my fists together.

"We haven't officially met. But you know that already." I speak methodically, trying to mask the anxiety in my gut. My mind is black. I want to punch him in the gut. He doesn't even care enough to acknowledge me? Not exactly what I was hoping for.

"You do look familiar." His eyebrows crease and push together, and then he crosses his arms.

Familiar? I clench my teeth to keep my damaged pride pouring out. "What exactly can I do for you, young lady?" His tone is less amicable now.

The hairs on my arm stand up. "Well, you haven't done anything so far." How can he look at me like that? He has to know I'm the daughter he abandoned. Even I can see myself in his face. He has to see himself in mine.

"What it is you want?" He uncrosses his arms and steps in front of the woman and cat, as if he's protecting them from me. Me? Unbelievable.

"It's me," I say. "Morgan." My voice cracks on my name.

Nothing.

"Morgan McLean." My fingernails press into my skin as I wait.

He shakes his head and glances at the woman beside him, and their eyes speak without words. He's suggesting I'm a lunatic.

"Maggie McLean's daughter," I spell out.

"Maggie? Maggie McLean?"

Ah-ha, Einstein. Catching on now?

I brace myself for his outburst.

"From Seattle?" He frowns and reaches into his pants pocket and takes out a tube of ChapStick. I stare at him, kind of shocked, almost laughing, while he smears it on his lips. Nature versus nurture debate teams would have a blast with this.

"The one and only." The clock in the dining room ticks loudly.

"I haven't talked to Maggie in years." He tilts his head, studying my face. "How is she?"

"She just had heart surgery." I unclench my fists and lift my chin so he won't see how much it's quivering.

"I knew your mom a long time ago. I haven't seen her in years." He glances at the little woman with him, as if he wishes she'd rescue him. "She's okay?"

I stare at his face—the face that was never there for me. The face that never wanted a child, never wanted me—still isn't embracing me now. "She's fine. She actually thought she was going to die. And that's when she told me how to find you. She's protected you all these years."

"Protected me?" He glances at the woman. The cat stares at me, not blinking.

I put my hands on my hips, hating the cat, wanting to hiss at it.

"Your mother broke up with me over eighteen years ago. I haven't seen or talked to her since. I'm sorry she's been sick, but...?" He raises both eyebrows and glances at his watch, but his face is getting visibly paler by the second.

My stomach hurts and my hands shake but it's impossible to tell if it's from anger or fear. I could easily throw up. "She's not," I tell him, "going to die."

"Um. That's good?" He rubs his lips together and looks at the woman, his eyebrows raised.

I stare at him. This isn't what I'd braced myself for. I expected excuses. I hoped for regret—but not disinterest or impatience. It's actually worse.

"I'm eighteen," I say.

He stares at me long and hard, and then his eyes wrinkle more in the corners and his back straightens.

"When were you born?" he demands.

"December."

He presses his lips together, frowns, and rubs at the back of his neck. The woman puts her hand on his arm.

"My mom raised me. Alone. Well, me and my older twin brothers."

"Jake and Josh," Bob says.

"Yes," I reply, though I want to shout *Obviously!*

There's a sudden awful taste in my mouth and a whoosh in my ears as my body goes ice cold, as if the heat has been sucked out with a vacuum. "You were aware that she was pregnant?"

He blinks, clears his throat. "Pregnant?"

Oh my God. What has my mom done? An urge to laugh tickles at my stomach and then my breath is sucked out again. "You didn't know?" I manage, and it's both a statement and a question. Heat rushes through my body and I sway with dizziness.

"What are you saying?" His words sound as though they've been dipped in horror and fear.

"She was pregnant." The cat mews. The clock ticks. I can barely breathe. "With me."

"Camille," he says, not taking his eyes off of me. "Camille?"

I'd almost forgotten the slight woman. I'm afraid I'm going to pass out. Drop and fold to the ground. He's got a hand on his heart. Camille quickly puts down the cat. "Bob, are you okay?"

"She says she's my daughter." He doesn't take his eyes off me.

"Bob?" She looks back and forth between us.

"Maggie McLean. You remember? The American who sent me off with no explanation. About a year before we met." He looks away from me to Camille and his eyes are wide.

"You didn't know?" I whisper again, but I don't even know if they hear me. The realization punches me in the gut. I wipe my eyes with the back of my hand. This is worse.

"Why're you here? Why now?" Camille says. Her voice isn't angry, but it's firm. Bob blinks and blinks with his mouth hanging slightly open.

I focus on Camille. Someone rational. A stranger. I want her to help me. Intervene. Tell me what's going on. "I never knew who my dad was. I never even knew his name. My mom never told me. Then she had heart pains. She thought she was dying. So she told me where to find the info. So she wouldn't go to the grave feeling guilty."

"Oh dear," Camille says softly. A phone rings but no one even glances toward the noise.

Oh dear is right.

"Your mom knew I was here?" Bob asks, blocking the real issue. My mom had his baby eighteen years ago. Me. And she didn't even bother to tell him.

"Apparently she's good at keeping things to herself." I'm able to breathe by concentrating on it. In. Out. In. Out. I remember getting punched in the stomach in sixth grade. By Kim Stevenson. I can't even remember why, but I remember how it felt—exactly like this. "You didn't know?" It comes out in a whisper.

"You think you're my daughter?" His voice is higher pitched and creaks at the end. The phone rings again. My phone beeps, letting me know I've received another text.

My nose tickles as if I need to sneeze. The sensation that my chest is being crushed gets stronger. "I thought you knew. I thought you left us."

I realize that I'm an idiot for believing my mother in the first place. Truth has never been her thing. And it hits me with force. He didn't even know about me. I've been beating myself up for being unlovable, unwanted, and he didn't even know I existed.

How? How could she do this?

And then I begin to lose the grip I've been holding on to since I found out his name. I came here to see the man who gave me up without a fight. But he didn't fight because he didn't even know. I think of her frantic texting. That's why she's been trying to get ahold of me. This truth is worse. He didn't reject me. He didn't have the chance.

My eyes spill tears and my nose leaks. How could she do this? For so many years.

Camille slides over and puts an arm around me. But even now, even in this, I can't shake the feeling that somehow I'm the one who caused this mess.

"Shit, shit, shit," Bob says and then spins on his heels and stomps out of the hallway. The sounds coming out of my body get louder. I shrug Camille off and hug my arms around myself, wishing I could disappear. She pats my arm then gently leads me into the den.

It's carpeted and cream colored and thick under my shoes. I try to protest that they might be dirty, but there's no way for me to talk like a rational person. Camille looks like the sort of person who would care about dirty carpets, but she doesn't say a thing or even seem to notice.

She guides me to a chair, takes my purse, sits me down, and then puts my purse on my lap. I take out my phone. A text from my mom.

> Call me. Please.

She's fine. It's not her health. It's this. She's been trying to stop this. Too late. I delete her message.

"Bob really had no idea," Camille says softly. "It's a shock. Give him a few minutes, okay?" She slips out of the room.

My hysteria dies down. My cheeks burn with humiliation. I'd been judging him for being a man who would abandon his own daughter. But he didn't even know.

When Camille returns a few minutes later, she's holding a glass of water and a box of Kleenex, and she hands both to me. "You okay?" She sits on the chair beside mine and smiles ever so slightly. Her legs are slim, tinier than mine even.

I move my head up and down and blow my nose into a Kleenex. "So where do you live?" she asks.

"Tadita. Outside Seattle. Where my mom met…Bob."

My voice is scratchy and high-pitched. I think about standing and walking out, walking through the front door and continuing on until my feet bleed. Maybe walking all the way home, but my butt is Velcroed to the cushion.

"Is she here with you? Your mom?"

"No. I came with…friends." And then, in spite of everything, a tiny smile tugs at my lips. Amy and Adam are friends. Real friends. And I know, when I return to the hostel, they're going to be there for me. They're going to help me get through this. "They're at the Stingray Hostel. That's where we're staying." I should have let them come along.

She nods. "Are you in college?"

"No. I start my senior year of high school in September."

We stare at each other.

"I didn't know," I say, "that Bob didn't know about me. My mom…" It sounds stupid. I sound stupid. I am so over my head here, it's not even funny. I stand up. "I should go."

I have the real story now, and it's certainly not the story I thought it was. I've seen him. But the truth is, you can't leave someone you don't know about.

She scoops up the cat and stands. "No." She touches my arm. "You shouldn't go. Let me talk to Bob for a minute. I'm his wife, by the way. I'll be right back. Sit." She points at the chair, and as if I'm a puppy in obedience school, my butt drops back in the seat. She walks out again, and I hear a low buzz of voices outside the den.

I have no idea what to do. I wring my hands together and

glance down at my purse. I want to take out my phone. Tweet this moment. Make it funny, less traumatic. The stupidity of it all. My mom and her lies. Omission is lying. Only bigger. Way bigger. Now I know why she's been frantically texting me. But she let it go too long. Again.

I imagine ways I can turn this horrible, embarrassing encounter into a tweet my followers will enjoy. Camille pops back into the den. Her face is impossible to read. She walks over and sits in the chair beside me. "How long are you here?" she asks.

"We're leaving Sunday."

"He's going to want to talk to you, to see you. But…" Her lips press tight and something flashes in her eyes. Anger? "He's gone for a run."

I stare at her, blinking. "Pardon me?"

She sighs. "He runs when he's stressed. He's pretty overwhelmed." She laughs, but the sound is tinged with bitterness. "I have no idea how long he'll be gone. Could be half an hour. Could be four hours. He does marathons, so he can run a long time."

"He left?" I shake my head. It makes no sense. I stand up, put my purse over my shoulder, squish my eyebrows together. Bob White just found out he has a daughter so he's leaving to go for a run. It's perfect. Exercise to Bob must equal wine to Mom. He may not have abandoned me when I was a baby, but he certainly did just now.

"Can you leave me some contact info so we can call you later? I know he's going to want to talk to you. He just needs…to process."

An inappropriate giggle tickles the inside of my nose. Maybe my mom was right to not tell him about me. Maybe he would have run off the first time. It's ridiculous. I'm more than a little freaked out myself, but I'm not running away. "No," I tell Camille, and the urge to laugh vanishes.

"Morgan," Camille says. "He'll come around." She walks closer, puts her hand on my shoulder. "This is a big deal. Leaving wasn't the best idea. But this is how he deals, with exercise." She shakes her head. "It's a shock after eighteen years. He needs to process it. Neither one of you is the bad guy here."

I duck away from her hand and retrace my footsteps toward the front door. She's implying my mom is the bad guy, and that's certainly what every arrow is pointing to. But despite what she's done, despite it all, she's still my mom. How am I going to deal with that? Everything is mixed up. This scenario is so different from anything I imagined or even tried not to imagine, I don't know how to process it.

"Maybe she had a good reason for not telling me about him," I say to Camille. "Maybe he would have taken off like this the first time."

"No. This is different. He's not gone forever. He's gone to think. Listen, he's not perfect. Who is? But he's not a bad man."

I hurry toward the front door. She's right behind me. "The twins' dad is in their lives. So why did my mom choose not to tell Bob?" My mom stayed. She raised me without any help. I put my hand on the front door handle.

"There is nothing about Bob that should worry you. I promise you that." I turn the knob. "This wasn't his fault. Morgan? Can you leave me your number? Please?"

I push the front door, wanting to say no, but I can't. I ramble off my cell number but she doesn't write it down, she only nods.

I wonder how she'll remember, if she'll forget or mess it up. I'm hopeful she will and worried she will at the same time.

"I'm sorry," she says, and there are tears in her eyes. "For both of you. He's a good man, Morgan. And you seem like a nice girl."

"Thank you," I manage and close the door behind me. I pull out my phone and write a tweet.

My dad didn't even know I was born.

And then I glance up and stop on the sidewalk when I see what's outside.

chapter sixteen

10.   Never rely on a backup system.
#thingsithoughtweretrue

A horn blasts. Amy's bright yellow Mazda is parked on the opposite side of the road from Bob White's car. In this neighborhood, it looks like a kiddie bumper car from the amusement park.

I hurry down the pebbled walk. The front driver's window is unrolled. Adam's arm is resting on it. His glasses are slipping down his nose a little. He looks like a complete and total nerd, and he's exactly what I didn't know I needed. But I do.

I run across the street toward the car.

"Hey," he says as I get closer.

"What're you doing here?"

"Thought you might need backup," he says.

I look at the passenger seat and peer into the back. "Where's Amy?" I walk around to the passenger door and climb inside the car. It still smells like Cheezies.

"I asked Amy if I could take the car and go see my girlfriend," he says. "I lied."

"What're you doing here?"

He glances down at his crotch. My eyes follow his. His phone is in his lap. Thank God. "I was worried about you. And I saw the tweet about your dad a second ago."

There's a loud honking in the sky. I glance up at a flock of Canada geese flying in the sky. In a *V* formation. I watch them, envious of their ability to fly wherever they want to go. I wonder if birds stick with their families or if the parents abandon them. How do they decide who leads?

"What happened?" he asks softly.

I blink and forget the birds, turning back to Adam. I sigh. "What are you doing here?" I repeat.

He lifts his shoulder and gazes straight into my eyes. "This is a big deal. Meeting your…father for the first time." He reaches for my hand, but I pull away and tuck it in my lap and turn my head. It's dark outside. Finally. It's been one of the longest days of my life.

I bite my lip. "Why did you come alone? Where's Amy?"

"I thought Amy might be, I don't know, a distraction." He pushes up his glasses. "She's in the common room at the hostel. She made friends with two old ladies from England. When I left, they were talking about tea. I thought you might, you know…need someone. Either way it went." He blinks, and his eyes are round and shine with sympathy. He lifts a shoulder unapologetically.

I sigh and it's so big and so loud that it seems to suck up all the air in the car. I open up my window a little, and a night breeze blows in. Bob White's house looks different in the dark.

The big, stupid house of the man who didn't even know I existed until a few minutes ago. I imagine how much it must suck for him and try to think how it would make me feel. But it's hard. I feel so alone.

"What about your girlfriend?" I ask Adam. "You came all this way for her, didn't you?" I half wish a boy would come and rescue me. I try not to wish it were him.

He lifts his chin. "What happened with your dad?"

"Adam," I repeat. "What about your girlfriend?" It suddenly has more importance than it should. Even in the darkness of the car, lit only by the outside streetlights, I can tell his cheeks are red.

"Well." He glances at me and then grins. "Technically, I don't really have a girlfriend anymore. If you must know the truth, she dumped me."

"She dumped you? When did you talk to her?" My knee bounces up and down, up and down. A tiny bit of happy leaks into the puddle of sad and confusion swirling inside me.

"Um. At the end of school. She's actually dating some guy who's a shoo-in for Stanford Medical now."

I stare at him. "You haven't had a girlfriend all summer? You've been pretending?" I have an urge to laugh—and then to punch him hard because I'm so sick of lies.

"Well, it sounds worse when you say it like that. It was just easier to pretend to have a girlfriend at work. Some girls at work are super stalky. Like Amy." He snorts, but when I narrow my eyes, he stops. I stay silent, my lips pursed, waiting for more. I'm good at silent treatments, taught by a champion.

"But you told me you had a girlfriend at the hospital."

He looks out his window and clears his throat. "That's because I, um…I was embarrassed. You were all worried about your mom and I was acting all weird, so I blurted out the fake girlfriend thing. It was dumb, I know…" He stops and doesn't look at me.

I can't believe I'm sitting in front of my father's fancy house, talking about this. It's hard not to laugh. It's also hard not to be a teeny bit happy, despite everything.

"You *made up* a girlfriend?" I'd much rather talk about this than my dad.

"I may have exaggerated my girlfriend status by a few months but she's real. We broke up." He lifts a shoulder and meets my gaze. "It seemed like a good idea at the time. Then it got too awkward to admit the truth."

I sigh. "I'm sorry. It's not like I've never done anything stupid."

Adam doesn't say anything.

I stare at the house Bob lives in. On the outside, it's so beautiful. "He didn't even know about me," I say quietly. "My dad. As in… my mom never told him she was pregnant. Eighteen years ago. And nothing since. He had no idea."

Adam gasps. "No way."

"Yup."

"That's really, really crazy."

"You think?" I say and attempt a smile.

"I'm sorry, Morgan," Adam says after a long silence. "You've been through a lot."

We look at each other. "Thanks," I tell him. "You're a good guy."

Adam reaches over and pats my leg. I should be embarrassed, but under the circumstances, it's too much effort.

"So now I have to process this, that my dad didn't really ditch me. My mom ditched him—and never told him she was pregnant. He didn't even know." I laugh, but it sounds like a sour burp. "You know what he did when he found out?"

"What?"

I stare down at his hand where it rests on my leg. He has a silver ring on his thumb. I've noticed he always wears it. "He went for a run," I tell him softly. "He left me with his wife, slipped on a pair of sneakers, and ran away as fast as he could."

"He shouldn't have left you like that." He leans across the console and half hugs me. Our faces are inches apart. I smell chips and soap. He stares into my eyes. I stare back. Blinking. Confused. Emotionally naked.

"No one should leave you like that," he whispers.

There's some crazy chemistry in the air. I wonder if he feels it or if it's just me. I hold my breath. I'm filled with an absolute certainty that I must kiss him and I must do it now. I don't care if he lied about his girlfriend. I don't care about my dad. Or my mom. I tilt my head, and next thing I know, his lips are pressed against mine. It's incredible and crazy and real and...Oh. My.

"Holy," he says, pulling back for a second, and then with one hand, Adam rips off his glasses and throws them on the dash and then his arms are on my back and he's kissing me harder. I'm leaning into him, over the console, pushing on it to get closer to him.

Everything else disappears. My mom. My dad. Amy's car we're steaming up. All I want is this.

Adam.

I never want to stop. His hand reaches under my shirt. My head is arching back and he's kissing my neck and I'm so into this I could rip off all my clothes and toss them.

Tap. Tap. Tap.

There's knocking on the driver side window. We pull away from each other and stare up at the man outside—the one my mom ditched without mentioning she was pregnant.

Daddy-o.

Apparently he went for a short run.

"I need to talk to you," he says.

chapter seventeen

11.   Personal lives should always be kept personal.
#thingsithoughtweretrue

The next morning, we take the car to the shop to get a real tire put on for our trip home. We're all at Melody's Tea Shop in downtown Victoria.

After Bob interrupted the make-out session the night before, he asked me to join him and his wife for tea. I told Bob there would be five of us for tea. He didn't argue. Adam was the one who recovered from the embarrassment first, and Bob kept his thoughts about our groping in the car in front of his house to himself.

Afterward, Adam and I drove back to the hostel and talked about my dad and not about what happened between us. We found Amy in the common room with the English ladies. One look at my face and Amy said farewell to her new friends and followed me back to our room. When I told her what happened with my dad, she cried and sat beside me on my bed, holding me tight, refusing to let go. She never even asked why Adam showed up at my dad's.

So I brought my friends to tea and here we all are.

Bob and his wife, Camille, are tucked on one side of the table;

Adam, Amy, and I sit across from them on the other. Bob is wearing a golf shirt and Camille is wearing expensive jeans and a sweater with beautiful accessories. They look rich and classy.

Camille and Amy are having a conversation about tea as they sip from delicate china cups. I'm staring at a coffee mug in front of me but feel Bob's eyes on me, checking out my features the way I check out his, trying to verify his part in my existence. Adam's leg is pressed up snugly beside mine. Camille and Amy are nibbling at pastries and chatting, but I couldn't eat for a million dollars. Adam isn't eating either and is sitting almost as stiffly as me. I wish Bob would try to make conversation. He's the grown-up after all. I want to ask a million questions but I'm afraid.

This is so not how I pictured my family reunion.

"My dad started giving me tea when I was about ten, only decaf though, herbal teas," Amy is telling Camille. "He says they're good for lots of things that ail us." I look over, and Camille smiles at me but nods her head at Amy as she continues on.

Melody's is a warm and cozy teahouse and restaurant. The old building is rustic with dark, delicious wood, and under most any other circumstances, I'd love the ambiance. The smells wafting in the air are incredible—teas, coffees, and pastries.

"I need to call your mom," Bob blurts out, breaking the awkward silence at our end of the table. "Can I have her phone number?" His voice is loud and barky, as if he's used to people doing what he asks. Amy stops talking and we all stare at him. Adam presses his leg closer against mine, takes off his glasses, and cleans them with a paper napkin. All eyes turn to me.

"Uh. Sure. I guess." I write out the number on a napkin and hand it to Bob.

He takes his phone from his pocket and, with his back to us, dialing as he goes, steps away from the table.

He walks off into the teashop connected to the restaurant. I don't take my eyes off him. The phone stays on his ear and his mouth opens and shuts, talking. She obviously answered. I wonder what she's saying. His eyebrows tilt down as he listens, and his lips are pressed so tight they almost disappear. He stops walking, and his foot taps up and down on the tile floor.

"It's going to be okay, Morgan," Camille says to me. "He's going to make this right."

I want to ask how she thinks he can do that. Time travel? Amy blinks and looks as if she's about to start crying. I struggle to keep my emotions under control, pretend my whole world hasn't shifted.

Soon Bob strides back to the table and stands in front of his empty chair. "It's all true," he says to his wife. "She was pregnant when she left me. She says she'll submit to testing. But I don't have to, do I? Look at her." He lifts his hand and finally looks at me, really looks at me. "How could Maggie do this to me?"

I know what you mean, I think. It's hard to tell by his tone if he'd be happier if he had never known. Is he sad? Pissed off? Impossible to read.

Camille stands and wraps her arms around him, her head resting on his shoulder. He puts his chin on her head and closes his eyes. Under the table, Adam puts his hand on my knee and squeezes. I close my eyes, pretending it's all okay, that this is under my control.

"Well, this is really nice for the two of you," Amy blurts out.

"That you have each other to lean on and all. But what about Morgan? How do you think she feels?"

I open my eyes and see a tear roll down her cheek. My own eyes are scratchy with the ones I'm holding in.

She glares at Bob. "She drove all this way to find a big mess." She's quivering with anger on my behalf.

"It's okay, Amy," I tell her and swallow again and again over a new lump increasing in size in my throat.

"No. She's right." Bob lets go of Camille and they sit. He leans on his elbows and stares across the table, studying my face. I want to look away from him, but it's pointless. I can't. We stare at each other in a deep intimate way, and a shiver runs down my back. "Where do we go from here?" he asks.

A waitress walks close to us, but she pauses. She must pick up the tension in the air because she turns and wanders in the direction of another table.

"Are you a nice person?" I ask softly. It's a stupid question, but I want to know. I want to know so badly it scares me. Because he still has the power to hurt me. He is the one calling the shots here. I'm just a kid with my heart on my sleeve.

"Not always," he answers with a small smile. He picks up his tea and takes a sip and then goes on. "I'm kind of a workaholic and I have a temper. And I go running at inappropriate times." The hint of a smile reappears at the corner of his lips but disappears quickly. "What about you?"

"There's a viral video of me dancing in my underwear online," I tell him.

"But the video wasn't her fault. Her friend posted it. Ex-friend."
Amy sighs. "And at least Morgan's a good dancer."

I squirm, and Adam reaches over and puts his hand over her
mouth. She makes strangled sounds, and for the first time since I've
ever thought about the video, I laugh. Adam laughs too.

Camille's eyes open wider and Bob watches me. "Nothing like
jumping right into the rebellious years," he says. I can tell he wants
to ask more, but he doesn't.

"No. You missed those too," Amy tells him with a sniffle. "They
say the worst years for teen girls' parents are between thirteen and
sixteen. After that, they become human again."

Bob and Camille exchange a glance, and then Bob catches my
eye and we both smile. Amy is a gift.

"Morgan's really popular online you know. She'll have five thousand Twitter followers by the end of summer," she adds.

We all look at her. It sounds silly in this context, but I love her
for it.

"She's quite the tweeter," Adam says.

"I don't even like Twitter," Bob says.

I realize I'm glad for that. Last thing I need is a parent monitor-
ing me online after this long. *Parent?* I realize I thought of him as a
parent and it makes me want to cry again.

"So." Bob turns back to me. "How are you feeling about all
this?" Camille reaches for his hand on the table, but Bob pulls
away, focused on me. There's a tiny surge of satisfaction in my belly
at her hurt expression and I frown at my reaction. I reach for my
purse and dig for my ChapStick.

"I don't know," I tell him as I take the cap off.

He watches me. "Why did you come all this way to see me?" he asks softly.

I jab my ChapStick at my lips, stab at them. I glance at Adam and Amy, feel a blush in my cheeks.

"Tone, Bob," Camille says, and he glances sideways at her and then back to me.

"You must have been angry," he says in a quieter voice. "Thinking I abandoned you," he prompts, a trace of impatience in his voice. I guess he's not used to dealing with teenagers.

I shrug again. He's right. I must be angry, but it's impossible to feel much of anything.

"Of course she's angry. All this time she thought you ditched her as a baby," Amy pipes in. "She didn't know you had no idea she existed. This is a huge turn of events. Huge."

"Amy." I glance at her. "Don't speak for me, okay?" I say softly.

Her bottom lip juts out, but other people's words don't belong in my mouth. Not now. Not again.

"I only want to help," she says.

"I know." She's being amazing, but I need to do this on my own.

"It's huge for both of us. We have to figure things out," Bob says. "I have no idea where to begin—or if we even can at this point."

Those words land hard, a direct hit. My heart stings. It's one thing to be rejected when he'd never even met me, another entirely to be rejected all over again. I drop my head down and study my cup of coffee, cold, forgotten. More weight settles on top of my already-heavy chest.

"Yes." I force myself to sound harsh and uncaring. I lift my chin, narrow my eyes, as if this whole thing isn't ripping my insides apart. "Maybe I don't want anything to do with you either."

Bob clears his throat and coughs. "That's not what I meant."

"Morgan!" Amy says.

Tears squeeze out of the corner of my eyes, and embarrassed, I wipe them away. "I don't know what to do—or what to say."

I will myself to stay strong. I want to keep the hurt from my face. From my voice. From my heart. I may think I'm brave, but deep down, I'm afraid he'll still leave me. Now that he knows about me.

"This is hard for me too," he says.

"Congratulations," I blurt out, and then my cheeks burn at my rudeness. "Sorry," I add softly, without looking up.

Amy makes a funny high-pitched noise and clamps her hand over her mouth. I feel Adam's eyes on me but don't look at him.

"It's okay. But this is difficult. You live in Seattle," Bob says.

It's not a question, but I correct him. "No. Tadita. You should know the geography. After all, you lived there too, long enough to get my mother pregnant." I drop my eyes so I don't have to look at him. I hate that I sound so bitter, so defiant. But I can't help it. I'm so afraid—and emotionally naked. I want to cover myself up.

"Morgan," Amy says. "You're being mean. All you ever wanted was a dad."

My cheeks fire up and I glance over at her. "Amy, I never said that." I frown. I don't want Bob to know the truth. I want a dad. So. Much.

"You didn't have to," Amy says. Her face crumples up and she hiccups as she starts to cry, but she manages to do it at a low volume.

"Oh, sweetie," Camille says to Amy and reaches across the table to pat her arm.

I push away from the table. There's sweat on my top lip and behind my knees.

"Sit down," Bob says in a voice that's used to being obeyed.

Adam stands too and reaches for my hand. His fingers press against mine and it's reassuring. It grounds me.

"Please?" Bob says in a softer voice. "I'm trying to figure out the right things to say. I have absolutely no idea what that is."

"Me neither," I whisper.

I look at Adam. I sense that no matter what I decide to do, he'll stand by me. "It's your call," he whispers. I wish he would tell me. But this is my life. My decision. There's no way to hide from this. I squeeze Adam's hand and sit. He slowly sits beside me. Amy glances up, no longer making noise but still sniffling and wiping at her eyes.

Everyone stares at me. I feel more exposed than I did the first day of school after the video went viral.

"Why did you come?" Bob finally says as if he's choosing his words carefully. He nods his head toward Adam and Amy. "You brought friends and drove all the way to Canada to see me. Why?"

I stare at him and blink, trying to remember the feelings that brought me here. "I just found out who you are," I remind him. "She just told me," I whisper. "And I thought you were aware of me. If I'd known earlier who you are…the truth…well, I would have come sooner."

"Okay." He picks up his tea. "But why like this?" He takes a tiny sip, puts his cup down. "You could have called." He has a wary expression.

I almost smile and put my hand over my mouth. I can't tell him what I wanted. Him. I wonder if he thinks I'm a parasite, there to suck things from him. Like, like money. I glance at Adam. He's watching Bob, his eyes narrowed, his hand in a ball at his side.

"What are you implying? She wants a father!" Amy squeals.

Camille puts a finger to her lips and makes soft shushing noises at her.

My stomach turns, and I'm glad I haven't had anything to eat. "I wanted to see you," I say. "In person. But things haven't turned out the way I planned," I admit.

"And what did you plan?" Bob's voice is slightly challenging.

Camille puts a hand on his arm. Amy covers her mouth again and makes a squealing sound. Adam makes a sound in his throat, and anger shoots from his eyes toward Bob. It's tangible across the table.

"None of this is her fault," Camille says. "Her mother lied to her as much as she did to you."

My mom's image seems to hover over the table like a ghostly apparition. For a moment, I hate her. I really and truly hate her— for lying to me. And for a moment, I hate him too—for getting her pregnant in the first place. But most of all, I hate me—for being a person who would let this go on as long as it did. I should have fought harder for the truth from my mom. I should have found out the truth long ago.

"This kind of brings up a new argument for abortion," I say, and it's awful and tears leak out again, and I drop my head, ashamed.

"Oh, Morgan," Camille whispers.

Amy gasps and Adam puts an arm in front of me, as if to protect me. I glance up. Bob's face is white.

"Morgan!" Amy yelps. I glance sympathetically at her. She's going to need therapy after this, but this is not about her. I don't want to need anyone. I don't want to admit part of me hoped for more from him. That I still do.

Bob crosses his arms.

"I thought it was your choice to abandon me. I was angry. Maybe I'm still kind of angry," I admit. But I'm sad too. So sad. How could I be anything but sad? "I don't know why I'm here. I don't know what to do now," I tell him.

His body visibly deflates and I see tears in his eyes. "The truth is, I am your father."

I sigh. "I know."

We stare at each other for a moment, and I drop my eyes first.

"I think what I really wanted was to meet you," I'm finally able to admit. A different waitress holding a pot of hot water and a pot of coffee in each hand approaches the table, but Camille shakes her head and the waitress turns quickly and veers off in another direction.

I sigh. "I kind of thought you owed her too, you know? I thought you knew about me and, knowing that, you still never contributed a thing," I confess. "A part of me thought you should pay her back for those years." I think of her bills—and then watch as my college years drift out of my reach. "But now, the way things are, you don't owe her anything."

"I don't?" he asks quietly.

I lean forward. "No. None of this is your fault. "

Despite everything, I'll give my mom my college money. I won't let her go broke over her hospital bills. No matter what the circumstances, she raised me all alone. It was her choice. I don't agree with it. But I still owe her for all she sacrificed for me.

I glance at Amy and Adam. Concern bounces off their faces and lands in my chest. They're on my team. At least I got them out of this: the road trip. And I'm keeping them when it's over.

"So that gets me off the hook?" Bob asks. I think there's sadness in his eyes. But I wonder if I'm imaging it.

I press my lips tight. "Yes."

"I'm your father," he says, but he looks at Camille when he says it. Not me.

"Biological," I say.

He winces, but there's that truth thing again, sticking its neck out.

He rubs at his chin, his eyes still on Camille. "I don't know what the right thing to do or even say is."

"I know," I say. "Me neither."

"We don't have to figure it all out this second," Camille says, her eyebrows tight and a worried tilt to her lips. "You are his daughter though, Morgan. And that means something. To both of us." She wipes under her eyes.

"You better know that Morgan is awesome," Adam says to Bob. His voice is louder than usual and it breaks. "You're lucky you got to meet her."

Bob coughs. "I kind of noticed how you felt about my daughter," he says.

I drop my eyes to my lap. The memory of Bob standing outside and peering into the car window while Adam and I groped each other is not a picture I want to recreate in my mind.

"He said *daughter*," Amy loud-whispers, oblivious to the subtext floating around the table.

Bob and I look at each other and drop our gazes at the same time, as if we're on an awkward date. A father-daughter date.

"How long have you two been married?" Amy asks Camille.

"A long time," Camille says with a smile.

"So why don't you have kids of your own?"

There's a pause. Noticeable. "Things don't always go as planned," Camille finally says, and then she slides off her seat and picks up her purse and adjusts it on her shoulder. "Excuse me, I have to go to the ladies room."

Bob watches her leave and then turns to me. "Camille and I weren't able to have children," he says. "It was really hard on her."

"Oh. Fudgsicle sticks. I'm really sorry," Amy says.

Bob doesn't look at her. "I loved her," he says to me.

I glance at Camille. "Camille?"

"No," he says. "Your mom. In case it matters. It was a long time ago. But I loved her. If I'd known about you, I would have married her."

"I guess she didn't think you would," I say. "All she told me about you was that you didn't want children."

He sighs, and it's deep and heartfelt. "I did say that. God. I was so young. I didn't feel ready to take on a whole family. She probably sensed it." He picks up his teacup and swirls around the remains in the cup and then puts it down. He glances around the restaurant. "She never gave me a chance." The regret in his voice makes my heart hurt again—for him this time, not only me.

"Even if it didn't work out with your mom, I would have been there for you." He smiles at something in the distance, and I look over my shoulder and see Camille returning to the table.

I stare at him. If he had married my mom, taken care of me, maybe his life would never have led him to Camille. And he loves her. So what does that mean? If he had to go back and make a choice, would he change things? Would he pick her over me?

Something burns my stomach. Is it wrong I want it to be me?

Bob waves over the waitress and pays for the bill for the entire table. I make no move to stop him. When the bill is covered, we all stand. He walks over, looks down at me. I stare up.

"Dad?" I say softly, trying out the word on my tongue. He stares back at me, blinking. His eyes look moist. "Dad," I say again, without giving the word any meaning or emotion. "I don't know what to call you. I don't know what to say. "

"I know," he says. And that's it. He turns to Camille.

The good-bye is awkward and clumsy, and I have to resist an urge to bolt. Bob reaches out and shakes my hand. I cringe as I hear myself say, "Nice to meet you," as if we finished a job interview and I know my chances are slim to none because I didn't get the answers right.

I feel as if I failed, that somehow I didn't measure up, that I didn't pass an invisible test—was found wanting.

I shuffle my feet as he reaches for Camille's hand and then, without a look backward, he leaves. He makes no promises to see me again, to be my dad. He just waves. I watch his back as he walks away, expecting him to turn and say something about the future. I wait. He doesn't.

I duck my head. I'm exhausted. I can't shake the impression that I did something wrong, that I failed—that he's leaving me.

chapter eighteen

12. I'll never dance again. #thingsithoughtweretrue

Even Amy is quiet on the walk back to the hostel.
It's a bright, shiny day, but a cool wind blows off the water. We walk past old brick buildings mixed with modern buildings, and some of my negativity whooshes away with the breeze. The older buildings remind me of parts of Tadita, but almost every old-fashioned lamppost has a hanging basket of colorful flowers on it. The colors and fresh air take a little more off the edge. It's hard to stay angry and dark when Vancouver Island is so beautiful and vibrant, as if it wants to cheer me up. We decide to take the long way back to the hostel, so we can stroll through the Inner Harbor by the water. Amy's chatter restarts as we reach streets filled with tourists. People are selling food and beautiful paintings. Everywhere, there's music.

Amy stops in front of two cute guys playing guitar and singing a lively song. Without warning, she begins to spin and dance with her hands up in the air, her head back, pure joy on her face. She has absolutely no rhythm, but it doesn't matter. I smile, soaking up her happiness. When she grabs my hand and pulls me to her side, I decide to surrender to the music and dance with her. People around us stop to watch, but it doesn't stop me. They clap and cheer, and the musicians smile, encouraging us. The dancing turns into something so much more than beats—a deep soul cleanse. When I dance and move, I feel free. I remember this. I love this and realize it was stolen from me. Dancing to music. Right there, I close my eyes and I take it back. Around us, people pull out their phones and cameras to take pictures of the musicians and Amy and me dancing, but it doesn't embarrass or shame me. For the first time in a long, long while, I don't care about anything but losing myself in the moment. Screw Bob White. Screw my mom. Screw Lexi. And screw me.

When the song ends, Amy hugs me. The crowd claps and yells for more, but hand in hand we run back to Adam's side. He's smiling and clapping and whoops for more along with the musicians.

"I have always wanted to do that," Amy pants to me. "Thank you!" Her eyes shine and we hug again.

"No. Thank you," I tell her. I dig into my purse and throw some coins into the musician's guitar case filling with bills and coins from the crowd. We drift off with leftover giggles that fade as the singers begin a new song. I twirl and walk and my exhilaration starts to fade, but I won't forget it. This moment. The beauty of music and dancing is back.

Amy buzzes and chatters as we walk, until finally our hostel is in sight. "What time do you want to leave in the morning?" Amy asks when we reach the front walkway.

"The earlier the better for me."

Adam nods.

"Are we still driving to Butchart Gardens this afternoon after we pick up the car?" Amy asks.

Adam shakes his head and mumbles about going to a flower garden, but we ignore him because we know he wants to go too and is only pretending to protest for his male ego.

Inside the hostel, we take turns using the washroom and getting ready. While Adam is out of the room, Amy comes over and sits beside me on my bed. "I'm really sorry about what happened to you."

I nod. "I know you are, Amy. Thank you."

"He doesn't seem *too* bad. Your dad, and Camille's real nice."

I wince when she says the *D* word. I'm still processing. Disappointed, like it's Christmas morning and I unwrapped all the gifts and didn't get the one I wanted. It makes me feel like a jerk—unappreciative of what I do have.

She pats my leg. "Do you think it's better this way?" she asks. "That you know the truth now? Or do you wish that you'd never found out?"

I pick up the pillow and hug it close to my chest. "I don't know."

"I'd want to know." She hugs her knees in tight so she's a little ball. "I think it's better to know the things we have to deal with."

She stares off into space, seeing something that I can't.

"Is everything okay, Amy?" I ask her.

She shakes her head back and forth and unwinds herself from the ball. "It's fine." She swings her legs off the bed and stands up. "Thinking about you is all. I mean, your mom committed to a big lie a long time ago, and I wonder why she didn't just say he died or something and leave it like that. I think it's because she knew it was wrong. Deep down. And she left it open to fixing."

I shake my head. "I can't even begin to understand."

She looks around the room and is quiet for a minute and turns back at me. "Where's your phone? Let's check your followers. Think of some new hashtags to tweet."

I pull my phone from my hoodie pocket, and Amy sits down again and looks over my shoulder, squealing when I show her how many new followers she has. Earlier, I tweeted out a follow request to her Twitter name.

"Write something true," she tells me.

Some days you're the dog, some days you're the hydrant. #true, I type.

She laughs. "I like the true hashtag, but I like 'things I *thought* were true' better."

I smile.

"You're going to be all right," she says. "You know that, right?"

I punch her on the shoulder. She chews her bottom lip and it quivers for a second, and then she smiles and lifts her knuckle and we fist bump.

• • •

The afternoon is nice. The gardens are beautiful. We go for dinner and talk about everything except things that matter. I keep a lid on the things bubbling inside until we get back to the hostel. After I crawl under the covers, I start to shiver. I tuck up my legs and wrap my arms around myself. I make myself as small as I can. I hold my breath until my lungs ache, but I'm unwilling to let anyone hear me cry.

My body is stiff. I continue holding my breath until forced to suck in a breath. My eyes are squeezed tight, and for a moment, I see an image of myself as if I'm floating over looking down. My inability to do anything except squeeze myself into a fetal position troubles me. I have to deal with this.

The girl I was before this trip is dead. I'm worried who will take her place. It frightens me. I'm afraid my bitterness is bigger and will never be contained. I'm not sure I want to meet the new me.

chapter nineteen

13. Statistics don't lie. #thingsithoughtweretrue

Adam gets shotgun for the drive home. I didn't actually give him a choice and took the backseat without asking.

Amy pulls out of the parking lot, giving Adam the rules for front seat passengers. I don't want to listen. I want to be left alone. I don't want to drink in beautiful scenery. I don't want cheering up. As if we're on the same page, the weather is hazy and gray. I approve. Even Amy gives up and lifts the car rules, and they leave me alone.

There's no line at the ferry, and we're able to pull on right away. We park and wander to the seats on the top. Clouds drizzle. I hunker down under my hoodie, half listening to Amy telling a family of four about the whales we saw on our trip out. Adam sits behind me, and I feel him watching me.

I'm glad Amy's able to carry the conversation because I'm not ready to be pulled from my mood. I want to stay the center of my own universe for a little while longer, relishing my negativity, bathing in it. I make up speeches to say to Bob and my mother—words I worry I'll never be brave enough to deliver.

"You okay?" Amy says.

I stare at her. Bob didn't call or anything before we left. My mom even stopped texting. "No."

"Well, say something then," she says in a voice that implies she's fed up with me. "Get it out." Adam nods in agreement.

I squint at her. "I hate him!" A blackness that's nibbling at my soul pours from my mouth. People turn to stare. I sound ridiculous, but Amy is right. I don't want to keep the negativity inside anymore, afraid it will take over completely. "I hate him. I hate that he didn't even bother to call me before we left. " I shake my head. Why didn't he bother to call? Am I really that bad?

A mom sitting close on the bench opposite us puts her arm around her little girl, pulls her closer, and narrows her eyes at me. A breeze fills my nose with the smell of salt water. "He's an asshole," I say.

The little girl peeks out from under her mom's arm to stare at me. Her eyes are wide.

The rush of anger dissipates, and I'm left with disgust. Even this little girl can see the blackness in my soul. She's right. It's me. It's always been me.

Adam reaches for my arm but I pull away.

"You okay?" he asks softly.

"No. I'm not."

I have to get my head clear somehow. I have to face my mom. There's a lot I want to say to her now. But for the life of me, I don't know how to say it without being swallowed by my own self-loathing.

• • •

"Hey!" Adam shouts.

My eyes pop open and I'm surprised drool is gobbed up on the side of my mouth. I sit up and glance outside. I didn't even realize I'd fallen asleep. We're surrounded by familiar Washington scenery, trees and grassy hills. The windshield wipers are on, but the rain is more of a dribble. There's a country song playing low on the radio.

"Did you see that guy?" Adam is saying to Amy.

Amy's eyes are on her rearview mirror. "You mean the creepy hitchhiker."

"He didn't look creepy. He looked like he was in trouble. And it's wet out there. We should go back and see if he needs help." Adam turns to me. "Are we in a dead Wi-Fi area?" He glances at Amy. "Maybe he can't use his phone for help. He could be in trouble."

I sit up and look around for my phone. "I don't know." It's on the floor beside an unopened bag of salt and vinegar chips, so I reach for it.

"You don't know?" Amy says. "I thought you were on the phone since we passed through the border crossing."

"I haven't been on my phone at all," I say, and it's a shock to hear those words come out of my mouth.

"Never mind that!" Adam shouts. "What about that guy?"

I frown at his profile. Maybe it's not a big deal to him, but it is to me. I turn my phone on. "I've got one bar," I tell him.

"One? I don't have any. We should go back and help that guy."

"What if he's a deranged murderer?" I ask and reach for the bag of chips. I'm not hungry but something salty can't hurt. I rip the bag open with my teeth and the smell of vinegar immediately fills my nose.

"What if he's not?" Adam says. "What if he's just a dude who needs help?"

"Adam," Amy says. "There is absolutely no way we are picking up a hitchhiker. Have you not watched any scary movies? Do you not know that three teenagers on a remote highway are not supposed to pick up hitchhikers? Like ever. He's probably a serial killer. I'm not about to die now after all of this."

I nod agreement, dip my hand into the bag, and pull out a handful of greasy chips.

"What are the statistical probabilities that guy is a serial killer? How many serial killers are there, really? Maybe thirty out of three billion people? What's the likelihood he's one?"

"We are not picking up a hitchhiker!" Amy shouts.

My mouth stops right in the middle of chewing chips. Adam and I both stare at her.

"Wow." Adam says after a silence. "You seem a little bitter, Amy. I didn't know you were so against hitchhikers."

She waves her hand in the air. "Chips."

I hand her the bag of chips.

"I hate statistics," she says. "And I don't believe you should put yourself in danger if you don't have to." She puts the bag on the console and scoops out a handful and dumps the pile on her lap. Then she takes one and shoves the whole thing in her mouth.

"What about people who look away?" Adam says. "So many crimes are committed right in front of people and they don't even help or report them. It's a frigging epidemic. No one wants to get involved."

"People always think it's not going to be them," Amy says, "that things only happen to other people. Well, life doesn't happen that way. Look at Morgan. What's the statistical probability her video would go viral? How many people try and never succeed to do that? It's like winning a lottery, only for Morgan it was a bad one."

"True story." I wipe my greasy hands on my pants and reach to the floor for a Coke. Amy's not done though.

"What are the statistical probabilities that Morgan would never know who her dad was until she was eighteen? And never mind the statistical probability that I'd live past my survival rate."

Boom. The words bounce with physical force. A bee splats against the windshield, leaving behind a streak of bright yellow. Adam reaches for the radio, turns it off. The hitchhiker is a distant memory.

"Survival rate for what?" Adam asks.

I lean forward so my face is in the middle of them in the front seat.

Amy's cheeks are red, and she keeps her eyes on the road and swallows the last of her chip. "Nothing." She presses her lips together. "I didn't mean to say that."

"Amy," I tell her in a gentle but firm voice, "pull over."

"No." She shoves another chip in her mouth. "Forget it. Forget I said anything. I didn't mean to."

She's clearly flustered. There's practically smoke coming off her cheeks.

"Amy," Adam says. "As your boss, I insist you pull over."

"You are not the boss of this road trip," she says, but the car is already slowing down, and she puts the signal on, moves to the shoulder of the road, and puts on her hazard blinkers.

"I really don't want to talk about it," she says with both hands gripping the steering wheel tightly.

We wait.

"Cancer, okay?"

I point at the field beside us. "Come on," I say. Someone has to take charge. "We're going for a walk." It's not drizzling anymore, but the shoulders are muddy.

"There's a herd of cows over there." Adam points to a herd of black cows in the field beside the road. The only thing keeping them from crossing onto the highway is a wire fence.

"Screw cows, Adam," I say. "The girl had cancer. You can face down some living steaks."

"I don't want to make a big deal about it." Amy is still gripping the wheel. "I only wanted to make my point that my mom and dad refused to believe the stats. Because they were pretty grim."

I open the back door. "Well, maybe you did a little, 'cause it came out. And I'm glad it did." I climb out and bend down, holding the door. "How come you can casually mention masturbation, pee on the side of a highway, but forget to mention you had cancer?" I slam my door then and walk to the driver's side and open her door. I'm shocked Amy's kept such a big secret.

She stares at me without moving. "I made it past the five-year survival mark a couple of years ago. So technically I'm considered cured."

I put out my hand, and she stares at it and then sighs and takes it. I pull her from the car, and chips from her lap fall to the ground. "Bird food," I say. "Come on. Let's go stretch our legs. Or you can pee on the side of the road again." Amy snorts as we walk to the shoulder of the road.

Adam comes out of his side of the car. "I still hate cows," he mutters and slams his door and hurries to catch up to us.

"Suck it up, princess," I tell him. Amy giggles.

Adam walks with both hands in his pockets and mumbles something else about cows.

"So I'm flipping out about my stupid life, and you don't think to mention your much bigger problems? You totally win," I say to her.

"I don't win." Amy pushes me hard and I stumble. "I don't want people treating me like I'm fragile or creepy. Which they do—if they know." She waves her finger in front of my face. "And my problems don't make yours less. It's not a competition."

"I know." I lift a shoulder. My troubles seem pretty shallow, no matter what she says. I'm seeing a whole new dimension of Amy. And her eternal optimism and sweetness only add more layers to her personality. I can't even imagine what she's been through.

"What kind of cancer?" Adam steps up so he's alongside us and stares down at Amy as if he's X-raying her insides.

"Leukemia. They found it early. I was lucky."

"You had a good doctor?" Adam intently studies her from behind his glasses like an investigator or something.

"Only the best. Perks of a rich daddy—chemo, radiation, stem cell, blood transfusions."

Adam whistles. Amy stops walking. She stares out at the cows. "I've been clear for almost seven years. But two-thirds of survivors will face chronic health issues."

"I thought you hated statistics," I say.

"Sometimes they're hard to ignore," Amy answers.

We all silently acknowledge that.

"So what about now?" Adam asks. "Are you still being monitored? Do you still see an oncologist?"

"Why do you care?" Amy asks.

"He wants to be a doctor, remember?" I remind Amy. "Plus, we're your friends."

"Yeah. You've kind of grown on me." Adam bumps a hip against her and she loses her footing.

She steadies herself, puts both hands on her hips, and glares at each of us. "Why do you two seem like you have some weird thing going on. Did you make out?" she asks.

My mouth drops open. Adam looks at me and then looks away. "Um, change the topic much or what?" he mumbles.

"I knew it!" She claps her hands together. "Wait, what about the girlfriend?"

"She dumped me," Adam says, "after Morgan threatened to kick her butt."

"I did NOT! It was before the summer. He's a liar, liar pants on fire, ahhhh," I shout and run toward the field and scissor jump across the barbed-wire fence. Unfortunately, the seam of my jeans snags on a barb. There's a long rrrrrrrrrip sound.

"Oh my god!" I scream and try to pull my leg off the wire, but I'm off balance and drop over half the fence from the waist, hanging off the barb by the ripped hole in the butt of my pants.

"*Eeee!*" Amy screams, pointing and laughing. "You're wearing your 'Sexy And I Know It' boy underpants!"

"I am not!" I shriek. "I threw those out. Get me off, get me off!"

Amy's laugh erupts into an almost hysterical sound, bursting from her tiny body. "I'm ssss-sorry," she tries to say, but she can't stop giggling.

Adam's deeper laugh joins hers, and neither one moves to help me. They're losing it over my split pants while my butt hangs out over the fence for a cow to come along and chomp.

I manage to unsnag my leg and drop to the ground, roll, and then pull up what's left of my pants. Both of them hold their stomachs with tears rolling down their cheeks. I try to stay mad, but their laughter is contagious. Soon my own giggling starts and I'm holding my stomach, getting cramps along with them.

Finally when we manage to get our senses back and start walking toward the car, we're splattered by a truck driving in the opposite direction. It zooms too close to us and the back tire hits a mud puddle. It only makes us laugh harder.

I try to hold on to the comical break as we drive on, but reality settles in over me like dark clouds once we reach the city limits of Tadita. I listen as Adam tells Amy the truth about his girlfriend and why he lied to her, but I can no longer participate in conversation. The chips I ate no longer seem like a good idea.

I still have to face my mom.

chapter twenty

14. Dear old Dad ditched the family before I was born.
     #thingsithoughtweretrue

A my drops me off on the sidewalk in front of my house. "You can do this," she calls out the window. "Good luck."

There's a humming in my head. I'm home. And I still haven't heard from Bob. Does that make my mom right? He didn't want kids. And that's all I get from him? Tea?

Instead of facing that or her, I turn back to the sidewalk and walk, but my knees are stiff and my gait lopsided. Mrs. Phillips from next door is working on her garden and waves and stares a little too long at my bare legs. I walk on, trying to figure out what to say to my mom. My fear bothers me. Should I really be the one who's worried? She knows that I know. But no matter how irrational it is, I can't stomp the feeling that I'm the one who messed things up.

All my life, I believed that my dad left because of me, that he wanted to have nothing to do with me—that I was too flawed to love. I clench my hands into a fist and my fingernails press into my skin.

This is my life.

It's time to deal.

. . .

Mom is perched on the couch in her pink robe, her head in her hands as I yell. She hasn't said a word since I launched into my tirade.

"How could you have made that choice for him?" I pace in front of her. "And for me? You had no right to do that."

She says nothing. Her silence is worse than shouting. "Talk to me," I beg. "Tell me why."

She lifts her head and presses her knuckles against her mouth and stares at me. I stare back, and then her gaze darts back to the carpeted floor.

"Mom? Say something! How did you keep this up?" I shout. "How do you not talk about it for eighteen years? That takes a lot of dedication." I narrow my eyes. "And alcohol."

I've crossed the line and I know it, and she glances up then, her quivering chin and watery eyes showing I finally hit a mark. Jake and Josh hurry in from where they've been hiding out in the kitchen, proving they've been hovering and waiting to swoop in to her rescue. The synchronicity in their steps and the expression on their faces irks me. It's not fair.

"All right, Morgan. Stop yelling. She just got out of the hospital," Josh says. His face is still clean-shaven; it appears his '70s phase was cured by mom's heart condition. He walks over and sits beside her on the couch. It makes me crazy, and my head pounds with resentment. Always her over me. Always.

"She got out of the hospital over a week ago. I think the discovery she lied to me about my father for eighteen years deserves a little yelling. I've been holding in my shouting for eighteen years." The ugliness inside me is turning inside out. "Why don't you go run off with one of your little groupies, Josh? Stay out of it!"

"Morgan," she snaps, because heaven forbid I insult her precious Josh.

"What?" I snap back.

"Morgan," Jake says in a lower and calmer voice. "Settle down, okay? It's not helping either one of you to be screeching." He sits on the loveseat across from Mom and Josh and leans forward, running his hand over his closely cropped hair.

"She was trying to protect you," Josh says. "She wanted to warn you after you went running off on your trip, but you wouldn't answer her texts."

"That was too late." I shake my head. I'd known in my gut that she had something to say when she kept texting. But it was too late. "How would *you* feel if some girl appeared in your life eighteen years from now saying she was your daughter and her mother didn't want you to know?" Heat flushes my face.

"Let her explain," Josh says.

"I'm waiting! I've been waiting but she won't say anything."

"That's because you're not talking; you're yelling," Josh says.

"I've been holding things in for a long time. You guys, you precious twins, you were allowed to make noise and complain but not me. I've grown up feeling not good enough, that if I did something wrong, I'd be sent away." And then my body deflates. It's the closest I've ever come to understanding the truth about myself. I sink down on the chair closest to me and drop my head.

"I wanted to protect you from being hurt," my mom says, repeating Josh's excuse quietly, and then she sniffles loudly. For effect. For the boys. It's not for me. Or for my dad. Or what she did.

I glance up and she's wiping under her eyes. "You were protecting yourself," I say.

Part of me feels like I'm inside my body watching myself. I've read all the books about how hard it is for girls to grow up without fathers. I checked half of them out of the library.

Josh still has his arm protectively around her. "Morgan," Jake says, and he glances at Mom. "She had to have good intentions." He stares at her as if he's waiting.

Mom doesn't say a thing.

"You did what you thought was right," Jake tells her. "Right?"

"Lying about something so major?" My head swims in the understatement.

"She didn't lie," Josh says, but the expression on his face doesn't match his words, and he takes his arm away from around her shoulder.

"Lying by omission is still lying. That, I believe, is a direct quote." We all know it.

Mom jumps to her feet. "You have no idea what it was like for me," she cries.

Her robe opens at the waist, revealing pajamas underneath. She looks tiny and vulnerable. I think of her heart and want to get up and re-tie her belt for her, tell her to calm down. But I don't. "So tell me," I say instead, "why you never told him about me."

Mom puts her hand to her mouth, and her eyes open wider. Jake and Josh jump to their feet and each one takes an arm, but she shakes them off.

"I loved him, okay?" she says quietly. Her eyes are cold and hard. "I loved him, but he didn't want a child. The day I found out I was pregnant, he told me he was going back to Canada, to get his MBA, for God's sake. He never asked me to come. He never invited me and the boys. He certainly wasn't about to go back to school with me and three kids to look after." She grabs each side of her robe and pulls it tight around her and belts it.

"But you never even gave him a chance," I say in a low voice.

"And if I did? He would have done the right thing. And how long until he would have resented me? I would have been the one responsible for ruining his life, his dreams. He would have left eventually, and I couldn't deal with that. I was young, pretty. We had fun. He never wanted my family. He wanted me as I was." She laughs but it's bitter. She wipes her dripping nose on the back of her terry towel bathrobe sleeve and sighs. "I didn't tell him about you. I told him it was over. No long distance thing. And the truth is, he never came after me. He never tried to fight for me. Not once. Maybe if he had, I would have told him. I let him go, and he never looked back." She sits back on the couch and puts her head in her hands. The boys each take a seat beside her and pat her back.

I jump to my feet. This wasn't supposed to be about her, how hard it was for her. She had years and years to make things right. It took a lot of stubbornness to keep that up.

"You were scared, Mom," I yell. "You made the choice for you.

You never thought about me, what I might want—or need." I sweep my arm out. "My whole life, I felt like it was my fault, that he wanted nothing to do with me. But he didn't even know! I deserved to know that."

She buries her head in her hands, but I spin on my heels. "I will never forgive you," I tell her as I walk out the front door. It's not true. It's horrible and I hate myself for saying it, but I want to hurt her. I want her to feel some of the pain I've been feeling. I don't know what to do with all the emotions swirling around my head, competing for attention. I head to the front porch. The clouds aren't hiding the sun anymore. It shines bright, mocking me. It's a waste. What could have been mocks me.

"Hey!" a voice yells to me.

I lift my hand to block the rays. Adam is standing at the end of the driveway.

chapter twenty-one

Adam smiles. "I tried to call. Text. Tweet. But you weren't answering."

My phone is still in my backpack. Inside the door. "You lied to me too," I say, as if he's been part of the conversation I was having with my family. "You lied to me too." I walk down the steps of the porch toward him, and he raises both hands in the air as if he surrenders. I march on, open my eyes wider, and tug on the bottom of the cotton shorts I'd changed into. My cheeks warm. The overexposure suddenly matters.

"You okay?" he asks.

"No," I say. And it's the best I have right then. His hair is wet and combed back. He's got on a black T-shirt and black jeans, different clothes from when I was dropped off not so long ago.

"Thank you," I say and glance down at the dirty T-shirt I'm still wearing. The greasy stains on the front. The splotches of mud from the side of the road. "For coming. But you lied about your girlfriend."

He tilts his head as the sun zips behind a cloud, and we look at each other without squinting. "I told you, Morgan. It was an excuse. For work. It's not always easy being in charge of people our age. And I was going to tell you the truth…"

"I know." I gesture my hand to the house behind me. "It's not you I'm mad at."

There's a spraying noise, and I glance over and see Mrs. Phillips at the bush growing between our property with a hose in her hand. Doesn't she realize it just stopped raining? She sprays the bush but makes no attempt to hide her curiosity.

"You look good," Adam mumbles.

I look down. I'm a mess. The breeze has turned cool and the sun has slid behind a cloud. I wrap my arms around myself, wanting to lie down and sleep.

"I guess I don't need to ask how it went?" Adam asks.

I shake my head. "Not really." I walk forward until I reach his side then stop, looking up at him. "What are you doing here?"

"I thought you might need someone to talk to." His cheeks are blotchy and he avoids my eyes. He's making it a habit, showing up when I need him. I don't want to like it. But I do.

"Do you want to go for a walk? Or a drive?" He points at a truck parked in front of Mrs. Phillips's house.

"That's yours?" It's an old red truck. A small one, rusty on the bottom.

Adam nods. "Sort of. I use it when my mom doesn't need it."

"Hmmm. I wouldn't have pegged you for a truck guy," I say.

"I wouldn't have pegged you as someone who would dance around in men's underwear." His mouth turns up, and under his glasses, his eyes shine.

I relax a little and laugh, like I know he intended me to. "Sorry,"

I say again, shrugging my shoulders and rolling my neck around to get out some of the kinks. "It's not you."

"Yeah. I kind of guessed that. So? Walk or ride?" he asks again.

I press my lips tight, wishing I had my ChapStick handy. Something flitters by my face and I glance up and see a black, orange, and white butterfly. It flaps its wings gracefully and flies up over my head and quickly out of my sight.

"How about a ride?" I tell him. "I already went for a walk. In these shorts, my neighbors might make a call to family services."

He laughs. The sun comes out from behind the cloud. "Come on, cheeky," he says. I tug the bottom of my shorts and join him to walk down the sidewalk to his old truck. He opens the passenger door. It feels like a date. He stands, holding it and waiting for me to climb in.

"Uh. I can get in on my own," I tell him, worried stepping up in front of him will expose way too much of my rear end. He already thinks I'm an ass—I don't have to show it to him. I make a quick decision. "Wait," I say.

He stares down at me, still holding the door.

"Are you in a rush? Can you wait while I go and change?"

He shakes his head. "Uh. No. Not if you want to. But you don't have to. You look fine to me."

"I want to."

He steps back and holds out his hand. I pull down my shorts again and run back toward my house. "I'll just be a minute," I call.

I run into the house, past my mom and brothers sitting in the living room. Mom is sipping from a wine glass. I stop and glare at her. She puts the glass down on the table beside her.

"You sure you should be drinking that?" I can't help asking.

"Don't judge," Josh says. He's got a bottle of beer in his hand. "She's allowed one glass a day."

I shake my head and start walking down the hallway.

"What're you doing?" Jake calls.

"Changing," I yell and open the door to my room and go inside.

"Into a nicer person?" I hear Josh say, but I ignore him and close my door behind me.

I hurry to my closet and stand in front of it, staring at a sundress hanging in the middle. It's never been worn. It's so pretty, with greens and blues. I bought it with Lexi last year. On sale. We were going to wear the sundresses to a dance. And then the video went viral, she stopped talking to me, and I stayed home from the dance. I've been saving it for a new special occasion. I take a deep breath. This is it.

I pull off my dirty shorts and T-shirt and chuck them on the floor beside my bed. I carefully remove the dress from the hanger and pull it over my head. Then I slide on a pair of sandals that are on the floor of my closet, go to my dresser, and take two seconds to finger comb my messy hair. There's permanent frizz in it from the damp air, so I fluff with my fingers, decide I don't have time for makeup, and sigh.

I run back in the hallway, past the living room.

"Hey," Jake calls. "Where you going in a dress?" He stands up and follows me to the front door. I bend down to dig through the backpack I left there, grab my purse, and shove my phone inside.

"Was that a boy out there?" my mom asks from where she's sitting in the living room. I hear hope in her voice and frown.

"Seriously?" I force myself to look at her.

"You look pretty," she says softly.

I press my lips together, say nothing, and turn away.

"We're going to take Mom to a movie," Jake says, "if you come back later and we're not home."

Do they think I'm over this? That all is forgiven?

I reach for the door. "Fine," I tell him. "I think I can handle it."

"You going out with a boy?" Jake asks.

"Yes." Without saying bye, I run out the door, trotting up the driveway and up the sidewalk to Adam's truck. He's sitting inside, so I climb in and put on my seat belt.

Adam turns the volume button down on the radio. "Wow," he says. "You look like a real girl."

"As opposed to a fake girl?" I say.

"No. A real girl. Real pretty."

I make an embarrassing scoffing sound and realize how transparent I am, trying to impress him with a dress.

"I like it," he says.

I dip my head to hide my smile and force myself to say what I'm thinking. "You look nice too."

He revs up the truck and pulls out on the street.

"So, you want to go somewhere in particular?" he asks.

My tongue's suddenly thick and I shake my head.

"How about I drive for a while?"

"Sure."

"So," he asks after we pull out of my neighborhood and onto the main road, "how'd it go with your mom?"

"Probably about how you think." I glance out the window as we pass by a row of lavender trees. I press the button to unroll my window and inhale the scent. "I love that smell. Lavender."

Adam doesn't respond.

I press the window closed and sigh. "There was screaming. And tears. But that was from my mom."

"Hmm."

"I'm mad. So mad. So mad I don't know what to do with all the anger. I don't want it to take over or control me. But how do I forgive her?"

"I don't know," he says honestly. "Time?"

"I need a lot of that," I say and glance at his profile. His slightly turned-up nose. The strong cheekbones. "Thank you."

"For what?" Adam asks.

"For coming."

"How could I not?"

I look into his eyes, and my anger begins to fade until it's more of a low-grade headache dulled by medication—I'm aware it's there, but it doesn't need my attention anymore.

We're quiet as we drive through the familiar streets of Tadita, until my phone beeps in my purse to tell me I have a new text. I think about ignoring it but then I reach for it. "It's probably Amy," I tell Adam.

When I see the message, my heart speeds up.

Adam glances over before returning his attention to the road. "What? You okay? Amy okay?"

"It's not Amy."

Hey. What's up? I miss you, the text says.

"Who's it from?"

"Lexi."

"Lexi the video girl?" Adam asks.

My lips turn up in the corner. "Technically I think I'm the video girl."

He makes a raspberry sound. "She's the one who posted it. I'd like to put up a video of her dancing on YouTube."

I glance at his profile. He's pressing his lips tight, scowling. It makes me smile. "She's a terrible dancer." It's true, but I never said that about her before. I never would have. But she is a terrible dancer. And she ended things. And never told me she was sorry. I can't blame her completely for the video going viral. Maybe I could have stopped it. But she started it in the first place.

"Figures," Adam says. He glances at the phone. "So what'd she say?"

"She said she misses me," I say softly, staring at the message. I think of how many times I'd hoped to see a message from Lexi, how much I'd wanted her friendship back—how I wanted us to be friends again. But no matter what, she didn't ask my permission to send out that video. And then I think of Amy, driving all the way to Canada for me, furious with my dad on my behalf, crying on my behalf. In the short time I've known Amy, I know that she would never ever do what Lexi did. And maybe, just maybe, that's what I deserve. Amy.

I stare down at my phone and then press delete.

Adam pulls his truck into the parking lot of the high school.

"Getting in line early?" I say. "Beating the rush, Dr. Adam?"

He rolls his eyes at me. "Let's go for a walk," he says, turning the ignition off.

We hop out of the truck at the same time, but Adam walks to my side and reaches for my hand. "This okay?" he asks. I bite my lip and nod, and his bigger hand closes over mine. It feels like heaven.

We walk to the playground without saying anything, but when I spot the swings, I drop his hand and run and jump on one. Adam gets on the one beside me and we start pumping our legs. We laugh, racing to get higher faster. For a while, we are in sync, and I remember swinging like this with Lexi. "We're double dating," I yell, like I did when our swinging matched. It's more fun with Adam.

I drop my head back, and my hair blows in the wind while I pump my legs, going higher and higher.

"You're beautiful," Adam shouts.

A cackle rings from my throat. "You're only saying that because you can see up my dress on the swing." My insides like being told I'm pretty.

"Not from where I'm sitting," he calls. "But I could move."

I laugh, feeling free and light. Adam jumps off his swing, and I scream and jump off too, afraid he really will see up my dress.

We both laugh, and he grabs my hand and pulls me toward the grass, and we sit.

I flop onto my stomach and pick up a white wildflower. A beautiful flower among weeds on the schoolyard. I study the flower, watching the petals fall and blow away. Some of my anger floats away with them. Adam's eyes watch me.

"I don't know how I'm going to forgive my mom," I say without looking up. The grass underneath me is damp, but not enough to soak my clothes. It feels cool and smells fresh.

"I bet," he says. "But she's still your mom. That doesn't change."

"How I look at her has." The sadness drags my body closer to the ground, and I flip over onto my back so it doesn't crush my lungs. It erodes some of the layers of anger that have been protecting me from hurt. So much hurt.

"What about Bob?" Adam asks.

I breathe in deeply and close my eyes, splaying my hands out on the grass like I'm going to make an angel. A grass angel. "I don't know. I haven't heard from him since we had tea. I think I'm getting ticked off."

"What a mess," he says. "You're handling it amazingly well."

"Not really." I roll up so I'm facing him, crossing my legs and adjusting my dress to make sure everything that's supposed to be covered up is.

"What's your dad like?" I ask him.

Adam stretches his long legs out in the grass, resting back on his hands. "My dad? He's okay. We get along okay—except when he's pissed off."

I pick a wildflower and start shredding it, wondering what it would be like to have Bob pissed off at me. Not normal and almost natural, like it must be for Adam.

"Like the day we left for Victoria," he adds.

I glance up. "Why? What happened?"

"My brother was having a bad day, and my dad was heading out of town. My mom was fed up, so he wanted me to stay home and help her. But I knew Mom would settle down and be fine, because I've seen it a million times, but my dad was overreacting. That's when you guys showed up. I ran out in the middle of his rant, and I was afraid he was going to race out on the street and cause a big scene. Or drag me back inside."

I laugh and then cover my mouth. "Sorry. I'm not laughing at you. It's just that my mom did run out on the street. Remember?" And then I frown. "There I go again. Talking about myself. Ugh." I stick out my tongue and groan.

"You've got a lot going on."

I frown and shake my head, focusing back on him. "What's wrong with your brother?"

He pushes himself so he's sitting up straighter. "He's autistic and he, you know, needs a lot of attention. But he's all right though. He's a good kid. He's young. Only seven."

I process that. I realize that the more I talk to people, the more I see everyone has something going on underneath the surface.

"My mom doesn't work anymore. Not since my brother was born. That's when my dad started driving a truck. Before that, he was home. He worked for the State Department, but he makes more money driving a truck and I think he really likes it. The only thing that bothered him was that he had to quit coaching my baseball team. I quit too, a couple of years later. That's when I started working, to save money for college."

"You played baseball?"

"Yeah." He rips out a bunch of grass and throws it up in the air and watches it blow away. "Pitcher. Believe it or not, I was pretty good."

"Why wouldn't I believe it? I suck at sports," I tell him.

"So what's your thing then?"

"You mean besides Twitter?" I grin to show I'm kidding.

He rolls his eyes. "Hardly. Like when you were growing up? What'd you like to do?"

"Well. I was a Girl Scout. And later on I started hanging out at the YMCA. My brothers did sports there and I got suckered into volunteering, babysitting. Lexi thought it was lame, but I actually like working with kids." I lower my eyes.

"Well, I can lend you my brother anytime. He'll teach you lots."

"How come you didn't say anything about him before?" I ask.

"Well, it's not like I go around telling everyone my brother is autistic. I mean, I'm not ashamed of him. But people…they judge, you know."

I press my lips tight and nod. "I used to think everyone else had it so easy. Like if I had a dad, my whole life would have been perfect."

Adam laughs. "Perfect is not a real state of being, dad or not."

"I'm getting that."

He stares off into the distance. On the street across from the schoolyard, there's a group of kids playing, and every once in a while, a shout or a laugh blows over in the wind. "Ever since my girlfriend, my ex-girlfriend, dumped me, I've been kind of, you know, steering clear of girls. Like I don't want to get involved. I'm going away to school at the end of high school, so I didn't really see the point."

I hug my legs tight.

"And you know, I didn't even really like you at first. I'd heard things about you. I mean the video. You were a wild girl who danced around in her underwear. And all the guys talked about your butt, how smoking hot it was."

I open my mouth to protest but he keeps going. "And you kind of have this thing, this air, that you don't need anyone. Like aloof or whatever. "

I squish my face up. *I do?*

"And you're so pretty."

My cheeks heat up, with pleasure and embarrassment.

"But then, that day at the hospital, I saw who you really were. Not a snob who thought she was better than everyone else, but a girl trying to be brave. And you were trying to be tough, and I knew then you were nothing like I thought. And I wanted to get to know you better." He stares off at something not visible to others. "I'm leaving Tadita after high school. And everyone at Tinkerpark hates me. I get moody sometimes."

I look at him for a long moment and bite my lip. "A year is pretty far away. I don't care what anyone at Tinkerpark thinks. And you should see me when I have PMS."

He laughs and the tension between us lifts.

"People whisper behind my back wherever I go," I tell him. "I can never escape what I did, what got posted. Not in Tadita."

He laughs. "Are we really sitting here trying to convince each other why we shouldn't be together?"

I hold in a girly giggle—and an urge to shout *Let's not!*

He doesn't take his eyes off me. "I don't care so much what other people think. That's one of the blessings of having a brother like mine." He scoots his butt closer so he's right beside me, and then he reaches up and tucks a long strand of hair behind my ear. "I really want to kiss you again," he whispers. His head moves and my head moves and then his lips press on mine. Soft, full lips that make me shiver. I stop for a second and pull back, staring into his dark eyes. Watching him watch me. Seeing his pupils grow larger under his glasses.

I surprise both of us when I lunge at him, wanting those lips on mine again. I land on top of him.

"Whoa," he says with a laugh and gently pushes me back a little. He stares into my eyes and then his gaze lowers. He lifts his finger and slowly, gently brushes a fingertip from my throat to the middle of my chest. I close my eyes and swim in the wonderful sensation. Immediately, all my blood rushes down.

"You're so pretty," he says again, and he makes me feel like maybe I am a little bit. He bends his head down and his warm lips touch my neck. I tilt back my head to give him access and groan as he traces his way back to my mouth. When his lips find mine again, I attack back with zest. I feel like he can see into me, and it doesn't embarrass me or make me ashamed. I lay out my soul. I've never felt the desire to share everything. I cling to his neck as he pushes me gently back on the grass. Interesting. So this is what everyone was talking about.

I move my hands down and feel the muscles and knots along his back and breathe deeply. "You smell so good," I tell him, and my thoughts turn naughtier.

"I like you, Morgan McLean," he says as he leans on his elbows, balancing himself over me.

"I like you too," I return shyly.

He places his hand along the side of my face. "So beautiful."

I turn my head away.

"What?" he asks, staring down with eyes that are almost black.

"I may be many things but not beautiful."

He traces his finger over my chin. "Trust me, Morgan. Some girls are cute and some girls are pretty. But to me, you're beautiful."

My breath stops momentarily before entering my lungs. Our mouths are so close. I hope my breath is fresh. It's doubtful, so I hope he doesn't notice.

"I don't need to be saved," I tell him.

"I wasn't offering," he says.

His lips press down on mine and nothing else matters. Nothing but this. I want to be this girl, the one who gets the guy, the one who walks down the hallways at school holding hands and has automatic plans on Saturday night. It's not me, not who I've ever been—not even who I wanted to be. Not really.

Until now.

A throat clears.

I open my eyes. Adam's open as well. We glance over and there's an older woman standing on the grass, not so far away from us. She has a little black dog on a leash, a Chihuahua, and he's staring at us like we are slutty exhibitionists.

"I'm all for young love," the woman says, and her eyes twinkle with merriment. Adam flips himself into a seated position and I sit up. "But maybe you should take it somewhere private. You're giving a free show to a group of boys on the street." She points off and I see the boys with skateboards on the street. But they're indeed all holding them under their arms, their eyes on us. When they see us looking over, they start whooping louder.

I smooth out my dress and pat down my hair, pulling a few blades of grass from the back. "Oh my."

"Oh my, indeed." The old woman giggles as if she finds our teenage hormones amusing. "Come on, Fredrick. Our work here is done."

The Chihuahua gives a little woof, but it sounds more like a burp than anything else.

She waves and giggles again then walks away with the little black dog.

Adam stands and holds out a hand to me. I reach for it and he pulls me up. "Whoa," he says. "That's embarrassing."

"But fun," I say and giggle at my forwardness. We start running as the boys on the street make catcalls behind us. We run fast, holding hands all the way back to the truck.

"We can go to my house," I tell him when we climb back inside. The boys are little blips we can barely see, but they've gone back to skateboarding off the curbs.

Adam glances sideways as he fires up his truck.

"My mom is out. My brothers too. They took her to a movie. They'll be gone awhile."

"Really? You want to do that?" He backs out of the parking lot and heads up the street.

"Yeah," I tell him. "I do."

"Okay." He smiles and reaches for my hand over the console. We hold hands all the way back to my house without saying too much.

All I can concentrate on is the feel of his fingers and his thumb as he rubs it over mine. When we reach my house, he shifts the truck into park in the street in front of Mrs. Phillips's house and pulls out his keys. He leans across the middle panel and lays a scrumptious but short kiss on me. "Wait here."

He hops out, walks around the truck, and opens my door. Then he grabs my hand and pulls me out, closing the door behind me. He bends down and kisses me and it alters my brain chemistry. When he comes up for air, I'm too tongue-tied to say a thing, but he takes my hand and pulls me toward the front door. Well, I float. When we reach the porch, he stops, turns to me, and smiles.

"You make me want to be a better person," he says softly. "To deserve you. I want you to know how right you feel to me."

I swear the birds in our neighborhood sing brighter. His lips are perfect. Soft. Warm. Thrills run through me. All over me. I could stay like this forever. Freeze time. Stand in front of my house and kiss Adam for the rest of my days.

"Keys," he demands. I stumble, still connected to his lips, trying to rummage inside my purse to find the keys. I concentrate on his fingers stroking my back. I'm incapable of thinking straight, but my fingers locate the keys and I hand them over. We step apart and he unlocks the front door and holds it open and we both step inside the front foyer. The lights are off and it's dim, and he pulls me by the waist until I'm pressed up against him, and I drop my purse, slip off my shoes, and he steps out of his.

We walk into the living room, not speaking as we move to the couch. We kiss and my head rides through wave after dizzy wave. A throat clears.

"Um, Morgan?" says a squeaky voice.

We both snap our heads up.

"Oh my God. Amy?" It's the equivalent of a cold shower. I sit up and move away from Adam. He coughs and sits up too. Amy's on the couch opposite ours, pulling on her shirtsleeves and looking at the floor.

She gets to her feet. "I'm totally sorry. I tried to get your attention but you were kind of busy." Her face is scrunched up and her chin is quivering and she rubs at her forehead.

"What are you doing here?" I ask.

"I wanted to talk to you." She glances at Adam, and her bottom lip quivers even more. "I've been texting and tweeting, but you haven't answered."

"I'm so sorry—I didn't have my phone." I can scarcely even believe the words I'm saying. When have I ever gone so long without my phone?

"When I came by to see you, Jake was here. He told me you two went out but that you wouldn't be long, and I could come in and wait. I guess I fell asleep. When I woke up, you two were all…" She sniffles and hiccups another sob. "I'm sorry. I'll go."

She's shaking and obviously upset as she hobbles toward the door. I stand and go to her side, taking her arm. "Amy? What's wrong?"

"Amy," Adam says. "It's okay. We can all talk."

"No," she says, fluttering her hands around and then stopping in the front hall to slip on pink Uggs with a sparkly design of Miss Kitty on the side. "I wanted to talk to Morgan. No offense." She runs out the front door. I watch as she hurries down the walk, wondering how Adam and I missed the yellow Mazda parked down the street.

Something is wrong. I glance at Adam and then run out after her in my bare feet. I catch her pretty easily and grab her by the arm.

"Amy," I say. "Please. Something's obviously bugging you. Come and talk."

She folds against me. "Would you ever lie to me?" she asks me.

My breath catches. After all this time, has she found out what I've been hiding? About the video? My part in it? "Not about anything that I thought was really important. Why?" I ask.

"Well, I mean. I think of what your mom did, and how you'll have to find some way to forgive her. And that's not fair…for you to find out that I did too? That I left something out. Something important. That's kind of like a lie of omission?"

I open my mouth. My cheeks warm. She doesn't know the truth about the video. The truth I've been hiding from everyone. This isn't about me. I lead her back inside.

"I want you to know the truth about me," she says.

I take a deep breath. "Okay. Okay." Adam's standing in the middle of the living room. He stares at us as we walk to the couch. Amy sits first and her shoulders slouch over. I sit beside her and put an arm around her shoulder. She's so tiny.

"Do you want me to go?" Adam asks. "So you two can talk alone?"

Amy looks up and stares at him, long and hard. "Are we friends?" she asks him.

He nods.

"I mean real friends?"

"Of course." Adam nods solemnly.

"If you and Morgan fight or break up, I'm taking her side," she tells him, lifting her chin.

I duck my head to hide my smile.

"Deal," he says. "But we can still like each other in secret." He winks at her.

"You can stay," she says to Adam. She takes a deep breath and sits up taller on the couch. "I have an appointment tomorrow. With my oncologist."

The phone rings, but I don't even look at it.

"I've been in a holding pattern. It was a good run."

Adam and I glance at each other. My face flushes. The hair on my arms stands on end. I turn back to Amy, frowning. The phone rings again.

"I'm pretty sure my cancer is back," she says slowly.

Things happen for a reason, I hear my mom say. I close my eyes. "No," I say. "No."

She pats my hand. My breath is gone. I can't breathe. I open my eyes and stare at her face. "You're going to be fine," I tell her. "You're going to be fine."

There's a slight twist to her mouth and her eyes are sad. "I've had a feeling for a while. I just kind of know. My dreams." She pauses. "I know. And it's okay, Morgan. It's okay."

"Damn," Adam mutters, and he sits on her other side and pulls her in for a hug. She tolerates it for a moment and then wiggles away. The answering machine picks up the phone.

"The stats aren't on my side this time," she says.

"Screw statistics," Adam and I yell.

The words hang in the air and then Amy starts to giggle. She holds her stomach and giggles on and on. Adam and I watch her without joining in. Finally she calms down and turns to me. "I came to tell you. And I wanted to ask—if you don't mind, if you're not busy tomorrow—will you come with me? To the doctor?" she asks.

"Of course," I tell her, my heart swelling with love and worry. "Of course."

"Do you work?" She looks at Adam. "I think I'm going to have to book time off from work."

"You're in good with the boss," he says.

"I'm not working," I tell her. "I'll be there."

She smiles. "It's not for me," she tells me. "I want you to be there for my parents."

I reach for her hand. "I would be honored."

"I'm sorry I never told you before."

"I'm glad you did now," I tell her.

I'm terrified.

chapter twenty-two

15.   An apple a day keeps the doctor away.
#thingsithoughtweretrue

It's been raining for four days in a row. My hair is a frizzy mess. I'm 308 away from reaching five thousand followers, but it's Amy who's watching closely now. She's actually getting close to me in followers, but she wants me to get to it first.

I can't believe we go back to school in two weeks, but the good news is that Amy's dad is going to let her transfer to our high school. Once she's feeling better. Meanwhile, she's been seeing different doctors all week. Scans, blood work, and a ton of other tests I don't understand. Her dad and mom are there for all of it. They've done this before. They're way too familiar with the doctors and tests. I've joined them a few times, taking time off work to go with her. Today Adam picked me up, so we could both visit her. She's in the hospital. A different one from my mom, but the same smells, same uniforms, same clusters of people and patients wandering around dazed.

Amy is lying on a bed in her private room and has surgery scheduled for the next day. With her tiny frame and her hair cut short, she really does look about twelve years old now. We walk inside her room and a man is standing with his back to the door—Amy's dad. He turns and smiles. I notice again how his teeth are extra white. Bought and paid for. He can afford luxuries. Unfortunately, other than privacy, there's not a lot money can buy when it comes to cancer.

"Look, Amy. Morgan's here." The gratitude in his eyes humbles me.

"Of course. And Adam too," I say. Adam politely shakes Amy's dad's hand.

"The infamous road-trip crew," he says and smiles. "It's all this one has been talking about the past week, how much fun she had." He reaches down, and the way he touches Amy's forehead so gently swells up an urge to cry in my chest.

"I should take a moment while you have company to go get a coffee. You want anything, Amy?" he says.

"Maybe some water? I'm so thirsty I think I could drink the Pacific Ocean with a straw."

"Probably not a good idea, Amy bear." He touches my shoulder when he passes by me to leave the room. "I'll get you some ice chips," he says and I smile after him. We've had a couple of chances to talk.

"Where's your mom?" I ask Amy.

"She was here. She had to go to a meeting. She's coming back. How many followers you at, Morgan?"

I tell her the number and she squeals. "You are totally going to make five thousand this week!" she squeals. She's definitely obsessed. I don't want to talk about that though. I move closer to her bed where Adam's standing, looking down on her. "So they finally managed to get you here," Adam says.

"I'm a friggin' pin cushion. They're staging me," she tells him.

I don't know exactly what they mean but don't ask. They talk in medical speak, and I walk over to the window and open the navy curtains. At least she has a better view than my mom's room. I scrunch up my nose, not wanting to think about my mom's heart. I prefer to think she doesn't have one.

"I'm having the surgery tomorrow," she says. "Splenectomy."

I spin around slowly. Amy is looking at me. Her dad already told me, but I pretend to look surprised.

"Piece of cake," Adam says.

I walk to Adam's side and look down at her, trying not to let the fear inside me show on my face.

"Easy for you to say," she's saying to him. "No one's carving you open like a Thanksgiving turkey to remove your spleen. Anyhow." She waves a finger at both of us like she's a teacher and we're her bad little pupils. "You two? You're totally together now. Aren't you?"

"Totally," Adam says and winks at her. My cheeks turn bright red and I open my mouth wide.

"Good. I told you my bracelets were magical. I expected this." She leans back against her pillow. Her face is paler than usual, I notice, and she seems tired. "Does everyone at Tinkerpark know?"

"No!" I say. "We're keeping it secret." I don't want everyone knowing about it.

"Why?" she asks. "Are you ashamed of each other?"

"No," I say and notice Adam doesn't say anything.

"Morgan," Amy says, "are you worried about what people think? You do know you're kind of an asshole sometimes."

I laugh. "You're right. I am."

"Wait, are you embarrassed to be dating me?" Adam asks, grabbing at his heart and pretending to be shocked.

"No. Well, maybe at work, since you're a manager." I make air quotes on the word *manager*.

Amy clucks her tongue. "You're better than that, Morgan."

My cheeks heat up. "Never mind me," I say. "How about you? How are you feeling? Are you okay?" I resist putting my hand up to feel her forehead as if she's a little girl.

"Yeah. Great." She doesn't look up though, and she twirls her ID bracelet around and around her wrist. She doesn't have her usual string bracelets on. I wonder if the hospital made her take them off. "You know, for someone who has cancer." She tries to grin but isn't quite successful at making her lips turn up.

"You beat it once; you can beat it again," I say to her.

"Come on. Amy doesn't need that kind of stuff," Adam says and frowns at me. I wonder if he's mad I haven't wanted to "come out" at work as the girl he might sort of be dating—maybe.

"No Hallmark card-isms," he says, and the words sting and my cheeks warm. I'm worried I'm doing this all wrong, and he's kind of confirming it by critiquing me.

"And you know that because you're going to be a doctor?" I ask a little too snarkily and put my hand on my hip.

"It's a routine operation, but you don't have the right to minimize how she feels about it," he says, narrowing his eyes.

"Whoa." Amy waves both hands in the air without sitting up. "No fighting allowed, you two. It's bad for my health." She glares at Adam. "And I know what she meant. People don't always know what to say."

I grit my teeth. "I'm sorry if I sounded like a jerk."

"I forgive you," Adam says.

"I was talking to Amy," I snap, even though he's trying to joke. I think we're both angry at the wrong person. Or maybe the situation. It's not easy to see Amy in a hospital and not be able to do anything. I've been shoving down bad feelings for days, and they're piling on top of each other, trying not to spill out at the wrong person.

"I'm so glad you're my friends. Don't fight," Amy says, trying to bring us back together. "Our trip was so much fun…" She glances at me. "Other than your dad, I mean, and, uh, your mom." She stops. "Have you talked to them?"

I shake my head and pretend to search for something in my purse. Bob and his wife have been calling lately. Texting too, but I've ignored them. I don't know what to say yet, what I even want from them. And besides, I've been preoccupied with her.

Mom and I aren't talking. Well, I'm not talking to her. It's been surprisingly easy to give her the silent treatment, but it adds more layers to my mountain of repressed feelings.

"What time is your surgery?" I ask Amy. "I want to be here when you wake up—if it's okay with your parents." I tug on the sleeve of my Tinkerpark shirt.

She scowls. "I don't know."

Adam rests his butt on the bed so he's sitting beside her. "We totally should have picked up that hitchhiker. Don't you think, Amy?" he says to change the subject.

"You are such a dork!" she says but smiles. "We'd be in pieces on the side of the highway by now." She giggles. "I never would have guessed Morgan could change a tire. Right? Or that you were afraid of cows."

"I'm not afraid of cows," Adam interrupts. "I don't like them. There's a difference." He glares at her, but it's a mock glare. She makes a chicken clucking sound and they both laugh.

"I loved that hostel, even though I thought I was going to hate it. I loved those old ladies from England. If I ever visit, they're going to make me real tea."

The two of them chatter about our road trip, and I reach for my ChapStick in my purse. I swipe it on and cross my arms.

"And what about that whale and that cute little boy…" Amy is saying.

"How can you not know what time your surgery is?" I blurt out. They both stare at me.

"Do the doctors drop in whenever they have an urge to do an operation? They don't schedule things at this hospital?" I can't take more pretending. The antiseptic smell in the room is making me nauseous. The walls are too stark. It's all so loud, the hospital sounds.

"Morgan," Adam says and gets to his feet, "she's going to be okay."

"I know that." Her eyes blink at me, hurt. But I can't stop. "I don't want to talk about that stupid trip. I don't want to talk about it anymore."

Adam stands and frowns. He adjusts his glasses and then looks down at Amy. I follow his gaze. She's staring at me. Her lips are down and quivering. Her eyes fill with tears.

The trip where Adam and I first kissed. Where Amy became my best friend.

"I'm sorry," I cry to both of them. "I didn't mean that. I'm a self-centered jerk. I didn't mean it."

No one contradicts me. A buzzer rings down the hall and feet shuffle past the door outside. "It wasn't all great for you," Amy says.

I sit down on the side of her bed and shake my head back and forth. "No," I repeat. "There were good parts. Really good parts. You. Adam. Me." I glance back. Adam's leaning against the wall, his expression neutral. "I'm sorry, Amy. I didn't mean it."

Amy reaches for my hand. "I know. I understand what you meant. Don't worry." She turns to Adam. "And so does he."

Adam nods, and she looks out the window before turning back to me. "For me, it was the most amazing thing ever. Maybe that sounds awful. Maybe I'm the one being self-centered and selfish." I shake my head, but she smiles at me. "No. You're dealing with a huge family thing, and I feel bad for you, I do, but I have to admit, I had the time of my life."

"I know," I say softly. "And it's okay. I get it."

Amy reaches over and touches my hand. "For so long, my life has been all about cancer. Everything revolved around it. Even when I out-lived the survival rate, I was still getting tested and watched. Even when I got my black belt in karate, it seemed like I got special treatment. I wondered sometimes if I really deserved it. I was treated differently because they were afraid I might break. But then, when I got the job at Tinkerpark, no one knew and I met you guys. And the trip came up and…it was perfect. Not perfect for you, but perfectly real. You know?"

I wish I could take back my tantrum. "I'm sorry," I say again. Adam comes over and sits beside me.

"It's okay. It's just that I got to be normal. Perfectly normal. You know?" She smiles at both of us. "I'd already started to feel it. I knew it was coming back. But for that weekend, I had two best friends, and for a while, I got to forget."

Adam and I both nod. We don't know—of course we don't know. Not really. My throat stings. "We're still best friends," I say to Amy.

Adam puts an arm around me and then bends over so we're leaning toward Amy. "Group hug!"

Amy laughs and we gently squeeze all together.

"I love you guys," I whisper and vow in my head to make Adam chocolate chip cookies from scratch, to get Amy to five thousand followers on Twitter before I do, and to give myself a personality transplant for my dorky behavior.

"You're not going to try to make out with me too?" Amy jokes.

Adam makes kissing noises at her and we break apart. Then Adam makes another joke about picking up hitchhikers and I watch and smile, feeling like the Grinch as my heart grows to a bigger size. She doesn't want to talk about surgery or her health. She wants to be treated like a normal person.

Like me.

"So," I say, "I heard Jake came for a visit." I smile at her.

Adam stands and stretches his arms in the air. "Girl talk. Is this girl talk?" He walks over to the window, pretending to check out the fake plant, putting some space between us, but I know he's still listening in.

A tiny smile curls up her lips. "It was nice of him. My mom and dad like him. He's a nice boy. He's been by the house too."

"You know his motives aren't entirely pure, right? You know he has a crush on you," I tell her.

Jake is the only one at home who's talking to me. And he talks about Amy a lot.

She sticks out her tongue and wrinkles up her nose. "Boys don't have crushes on me."

"Uh. Apparently they do," I say. Finally there's color in her cheeks. She bats her eyelashes and picks at the comforter on her bed.

"Not when they know about the cancer," she says softly.

I snort. "Give yourself some credit. And Jake too. You're much more than a girl with cancer. He doesn't just want you for your giant boobs. He has discerning taste, unlike his twin."

She shakes her head and pick pick picks at the comforter without smiling. I glance over at Adam and he lifts his eyebrows. "Jake's a good guy, Amy," I say softly. "And I'm only teasing about your giant boobs."

We both look down at her flat chest and start laughing at the same time. "He wanted to ask you out." My words come back to my ears. "Wants to," I say. "He wants to ask you out."

"Hmm. Well, maybe he can take me to the hospital cafeteria after my surgery." She rolls her eyes.

"Now that's romantic," Adam says.

"Jake is good with stuff," I tell her. "Real stuff. You should have seen him with my mom when she had her surgery. Now, if it were Josh…" I shiver. "He almost passed out just being in the hospital."

"He's nice," she says and covers her mouth and giggles. "Jake, I mean. But I would never date him if it put our friendship in jeopardy. No offense to your brother, but if I had to pick between the two of you, I'd pick you. You're my best friend."

"That," I tell her, "is the nicest thing you've ever said to me." And then I smile. "But I won't tell Jake. And I would never force you to choose. He's a big boy. You're a big girl. Well, in theory. You're actually kind of a miniature person."

She rolls her eyes again. "You're not very nice to sick people, are you?" Her voice is lighter now. Happier.

"She's totally not," Adam agrees. "She's kind of nasty."

She glances at Adam. "Aren't you supposed to be at Tinkerpark, bossing people around?"

He pushes his glasses up on his nose. "I'm going in later to work. I rescheduled my time so I could soak up your sparkling personalities." He gestures at the two of us. "My aunt is being pretty awesome about my schedule."

Amy's smile fades quickly and she turns to Adam. "Do you mind if I have a moment alone with Morgan?" I have a flashback to my mom saying the same thing, and my heart swoops.

"Of course not." Adam walks back to the bed and leans down and kisses her on the cheek. "I'll see you out there," he says to me as he leaves. I watch him go, and when I turn back, she's still holding her cheek where he kissed her.

"He's good stuff," she says to me. "You should stop hiding your relationship with him at work. How would that make you feel if Adam was doing it to you?"

"You're right," I tell her and grab the chair in the room and pull it close to the bed and sit. "I am the jerk once again."

"You're not so bad." She stares at me. "I want you to do something for me," she says. "For both of us. And you're not going to like it. But I want you to do it anyway."

And then she tells me what it is.

chapter twenty-three

16. Potatoes are only good for baking.
     #thingsithoughtweretrue

I'm tempted to tell Theresa I don't need my usual break when she comes to relieve me in the gift shop. Amy was absolutely right—I don't want to do what she asked. But as much as I'm dreading it, I have to go through with it. I want to be able to tell her how it went as soon as she's out of her surgery.

As I walk toward the staff room, super slow, I type a new tweet.

Hermits have no peer pressure, I type. I put my phone away and sigh. I look forward to this as much as I do getting my annual pap smear. But Amy wants me to do it. I figure the bravery required from me is nothing compared to what she's going through with her cancer and upcoming surgery. I don't really get exactly what she hopes I'll accomplish, but whatever.

I stop outside the staffroom, breathe deeply, and then before I can run the other way, I strut inside with my head held high, ignoring the jumpiness in my stomach. From the corner of my eye, I see a red shirt at the table closest to the door. He's leaning back in his chair with his legs splayed out in front of him. But with my chin held up, I don't see his feet right in my path. In slow motion, I start the trip. A déjà vu swirls around my head, but before I fall all over the floor, I grab onto the arm of another red shirt boy walking toward the table.

I smile at him with relief. He's a very nice-looking red shirt boy, with firm and round muscles. He pretends to drag me into the seat with him, but I regain my footing and stand straight up. "Thank you," I manage and he grins.

"Sorry 'bout that," says the boy with the trippy feet.

"No. I totally meant to do that," I say and spontaneously wink. "I wanted to check out those biceps." I pat the arm of the guy who caught me and the rest of the guys at the table laugh. It's with me though, and not at me, and though my cheeks burn and the little girl inside me longs to run and cower in the corner, I think of Amy.

Use your Twitter voice, out loud, she told me. *Don't hide in the bathroom anymore. Let people see who you are.*

One of the girls at the end of the table tilts her head, watching me and narrowing her eyes. I would recognize that look anywhere. The mean girl gleam. Her lips turn up, but the expression is pure evil. I lift my chin and prepare myself.

"Aren't you Morgan McLean?" she asks sweetly.

I force myself to look her straight on. "That's the rumor."

She giggles. "And there's plenty of those about her," she whispers to her friend. She either thinks I'm deaf or she doesn't care if I hear. I know which one I'd pick.

"I've already heard most of them," I tell her. "And they're all lies. But thanks for caring."

She glares at me and then starts singing the song, under her breath.

All the eyes at the table are on me now. I lower my eyes and breathe deeply. I could walk away, tail between my legs—let her win. But I think of Amy, lying on a table, getting her spleen cut out of her body with a sharp scalpel, and I look at the mean girl and smile, showing all of my teeth. And then I turn around and whirl my hips in a circle. "Wiggle, wiggle, wiggle, YEAH," I sing.

The guys at the table whoop and clap. I keep dancing and turn to face them. They're smiling at me and laughing. With me. Even the other girls. But not the mean girl. She glares, and her eyes get even narrower. "Oh my God," she says. "That was so embarrassing. Dancing around in *boy's* underwear, having *everyone* see it."

I just don't care anymore if she doesn't like me. I care a little that she's basing her feelings on something that isn't really me, but I'll show her. Me. Twitter girl personality.

"I happen to have sensitive skin," I joke. "I'm allergic to girl's underwear."

She rolls her eyes but I smile at her. I don't have to take it, not from girls like her—not from anyone really. I am who I am. I don't need her approval. I'll own what I did. Who the hell is perfect? Sure, my mistake got broadcast all over the world, but I'm willing to put it behind me. "At least I wear underwear," I shoot at her, the same way I'd sass Josh or Jake, people who don't intimidate me. I'm tired of intimidation.

"Burn," the guy with the muscles says and grabs me by the waist and dips me back, and then he stands, lets me go, and makes a muscle man pose. "I'm sexy and I know it," he shout-sings.

Another girl from the table jumps up and starts singing along with him, and the two of them groove out while others start hooting and clapping.

"Man," calls the guy who almost tripped me, "how did you make your underwear swing around like the guys in that video?"

"I put a potato in the front," I tell him. "They're not just for baking anymore."

They all laugh and whoop. Refusing to hide and be embarrassed is working.

"You have a nice butt," someone else says, and there's a wolf whistle from the table. My cheeks burn but I keep smiling.

"You're, like, super famous. I heard they mentioned the video on Jimmy Fallon's show."

The kids at the table buzz with questions and comments about my so-called fame. I'm shocked to hear that these people actually admire me because of the video going viral. I've been hiding and they thought I was being a snob. I guess it proves something. The reality TV generation—we're kind of an odd one.

I glance over and see the mean girl pretending to be interested in her fake nails. I realize she's actually jealous of my attention. I almost feel sorry for her. Almost.

The guy who tripped me stands and walks to the next table, grabs a free chair, and brings it back, putting it down beside him and patting it. "Sit with us, dancing queen." I'm pulled down to the empty seat as the kids talk among each other about the number of people who saw the video. None of them seems to remember or comprehend the extent of my humiliation. This is completely not what I thought people were thinking.

I'm embarrassed that I'm kind of digging the kids swarming over me. It's not such a bad thing to have gorgeous guys telling me my butt is cute. Most of these kids go to my high school, and a few of them are in the super popular group. Lexi would freak *out* if she knew they were sucking up to me now. I imagine telling her. All I have to do is call her back. We could be hanging out with them our senior year. Things would go back the way they were. Better. We'd be the it girls we always wanted to be.

It would change everything for us.

And then I look around.

I remember why I'm really here, why I'm doing this. It's because of Amy. Because she asked me to take back my life, to stop hiding. Sure, it's awesome that I'm being embraced instead of ridiculed, but honestly, it could have gone either way.

It wouldn't have mattered. I'm not the same person I was. Because of her. And yes, because of me.

I glance across the room to the table where the managers hang out, ostracized by the rest of the staff. No one wants to hang with fun-suckers. Adam is at the table, chewing a sandwich, watching me and pretending not to be. He pushes his glasses up his nose and I smile, thinking of his lips—and how much I like him. And how incredibly true and brave Amy is and what a good friend she is to both of us. A real friend.

"Thanks," I say to the guy who got me the chair as I stand. "But I came here to sit with my friend."

I wave at Adam and he looks around to make sure I'm waving at him and then he lifts his hand. The uncertainty makes my heart fill with a fierce protection.

"You're friends with Goggles?" someone says.

His nickname.

"That Adam dude is a dickhead," someone adds.

I smile. It doesn't matter what these people say about us. It really doesn't. "They pay him to be a dickhead," I say. "And he's an awesome kisser." The table falls completely silent and then I walk toward Adam. The smile he's trying to hide behind his sandwich is the best thing I've seen all day.

Hunter, another younger manager, grins at me when I sit beside Adam. "Oh, look who's joining the cool kids table. It's Adam's girlfriend."

Adam pushes his glasses up on his nose. "Yeah. It is," he says and puts his arm around me.

I pull out my phone and take a picture of the two of us at the table so I can show it to Amy later. "You making new friends?" he asks, gesturing to the table of red shirts.

"Nah. I just tripped on the way in. Amy made me face them. And she made me use my Twitter voice out loud. It worked. I think they actually liked me."

"They've always wanted to like you. You're famous." He smiles. "Amy also ask you to Harlem Shake the masses?" He grins. "This girl can dance," he says to Hunter.

"I heard," Hunter says with a grin.

Adam smacks him, and it makes me like him even more.

There's a new text on my phone, so I open it.

> It's Lexi. You getting these texts?

A few seconds later, she wrote one again.

I'm sorry. :(

The happy bubbles in my brain begin popping.

"What's up?" Adam asks as he sips at his Coke. He's learning to accept my phone habit, which bodes well for our future.

I hold up the phone and show him the message. He lifts his eyebrows, takes another bite of his sandwich, but doesn't comment. He chews, watching me type.

"I forgive you," I type. But that's not the whole message. I type more.

I forgive you, but I can't hang out with you anymore.
Friends don't do that to each other.

She has to deal with what she did, as much as I do. I glance at Adam, dying to add something about my fabulous new boyfriend. And my new best friend. But I think of Amy. And how brave she is. And I want to be a little more like her. I press send and let her go. And then I tuck my phone in my pocket.

"It's not fair," I tell Adam.

"What Lexi did?"

"No. Amy. She's done nothing to deserve being sick. Nothing."

He nods and I lean closer to him, wishing we could make her better.

My phone beeps again to let me know I got another text. I glance at it, frowning when I see it's from Jake.

Come right home. Right now.

chapter twenty-four

17. In the end, people get what they deserve.
#thingsithoughtweretrue

Adam holds my hand. "It's going to be okay," he says for the
millionth time. I can hardly breathe. Jake's not picking up
his cell phone or answering my frantic texts back. I've tried the
home line, but no one's answering that either. I want to scream at
Jake for not picking up.

It's my mom. I know it. My mom and I haven't talked since
the fight. Not really. She's been falling all over Adam, practically
greeting him at the door with a shoe in her mouth when he comes
to get me. Now I'm horrified how badly I've been treating her.

When we finally get home, I run through the front door. Jake
meets us in the doorway, staring at us with wide eyes.

"Morgan." He looks like he's trying hard not to cry.

"What?" My mom is dead. I know it. Her heart has gone and
done what she predicted—failed. "Is it Mom?"

It's my fault. I did this. By refusing to forgive her. She died thinking I hated her, that I would never forgive her. Adam steps closer
to me and his body heat warms my side. I squeeze my eyes shut. I

don't hate her. Not really. I thought I had time to work things out in my head. I needed time. I planned on talking to her when I was twenty-one or something. A sob escapes from my chest. I figured I had lots of time.

Jake grabs me by the shoulder. "No. Listen to me. Mom is fine. She's with Josh." His face is so pale he looks like he's going to be sick.

"Where'd they go? Jake, what the hell is going on?"

"Amy's parents called. They had Mom's cell number because of your trip." Jake presses his lips tighter. "I saw her this morning. I was planning to ask her out. When she got better, you know. She's supposed to get better. She's so cute. Real. We had a, like, a…connection." He shakes his head.

"Oh my God—Amy?" I say.

The walls of the hallway tighten and the air becomes harder to breathe. I step away from Adam, trying to get space, to breathe.

"She's gone, Chaps." Jake's voice fades out, as if I'm listening to him from inside a tunnel. "Her surgery was moved up. She went into cardiac arrest on the table. She died almost instantly."

I'm the one shaking my head now. "No, she didn't."

I wrap my arms around myself. I'm freezing.

"Shit," I hear Adam say, but he's in a tunnel too. I can't feel his warmth even when he wraps both arms around me and pulls me into his chest.

"No, she didn't." I stare at Adam's shirt and see it's getting wet. But I'm not crying. I'm not making noise. My body makes no sense to me.

The doorbell rings. We all stare at it.

"She can't die. She's only eighteen," I say to both boys. It's not possible. Not fair. It's not fair. Jake walks to the front door and opens it.

Lexi is standing outside. I stare at her. Jake stares at her. Adam has no idea who she is.

"You can't forgive me?" she says. She glances at Adam with his arms wrapped around me. Her eyes flash with something. Hatred? Envy? "You knew. You pretend you had no idea, that you're the innocent one. But you knew I posted that video."

"What the hell?" Jake says.

I'm shaking. I know what she's talking about, but it's so incredibly stupid I can't even believe I thought it mattered. None of that matters. But here she is. Because it makes no sense at all.

"Lexi," I say, and my voice sounds calmer than it should. "This is *not* a good time."

"Why? You don't want *your boyfriend* to find out the truth. Adam Ranard? Really? I thought we had standards, Morgan."

"Morgan," Adam says, "who is this?"

"Lexi," Jake says, and she takes that as some sort of invitation and steps inside the house.

"We go to the same school, Adam," she tells him. I know her well enough to know it pisses her off that he doesn't know who she is. I stare at her like she's a stranger.

"I need to go," I say. "I need to go right this minute and see Amy."

"You can't go there now," Jake says. "It's too late."

"Who the hell is Amy?" Lexi demands.

"Lexi, you need to leave," Adam says kindly, despite her earlier insult.

Jake puts a hand on my back, trying to move me to the living room. I grip my toes to the uneven tiles in the hallway, a project that we never get around to fixing. "We *need* to go see Amy." I try to shove past Lexi, but Adam and Jake each grab me. Adam puts his arm around my shoulder again and Jake lets me go.

"Morgan. We can't." Jake runs his hands over his short hair.

Lexi frowns, clearly not happy she's not getting the attention she thinks she deserves. "She knew," she repeats to us all. "She pretends she didn't know, but she knew I posted that video. She could have stopped me before anyone saw it. This is just as much her fault as it is mine."

My cheeks burn but my hand clenches into a fist.

Jake's mouth drops open and he finally looks at Lexi, stares at her really. "Are you kidding me?" he shouts. "Get the hell out of this house. Someone we *care* about just died and you're here to try and blame your stupid decisions on my sister? Go." Jake grabs Lexi by the arm, opens the front door, and pushes her outside.

My ears are burning; my head is a mess. None of this makes sense.

My phone rings. I glance around and automatically grab it from my pocket and click it on. "Hello?"

Adam is frowning like there's something wrong with me. He's right. There is.

"Morgan. It's, um, Bob. Bob White."

I stare at the phone. Shocked. Now?

"What?" I ask bluntly.

"Um. I want to talk to you. I've tried calling a few times and you haven't called back."

He has no idea how colossally bad his timing is. But it's like I can't stop making things worse for myself. "That's because I don't want to talk to you." In some far-off part of my brain, I realize he doesn't deserve such fierce anger. Am I punishing him, or am I punishing myself?

He's shocked into silence so I make it easy for him and hang up. I hear the door to my dad slam shut. I close my eyes and see Amy's face. Her disappointment. I struggle to keep in the tears. I'm ruining things. But it's what I deserve. I deserve this. I deserve to have him hate me. I'm a horrible person and I do horrible things.

"Who was that?" Adam asks softly.

"Wrong number."

The three of us stand in the hallway, trying not to cry, not able to talk, trying to figure out what to say or do when we hear a car pull into the driveway. I follow Jake outside. Adam is beside me, his arm still around me. Lexi is gone.

Mom's in the passenger seat of Josh's car. She jumps out with the car still running and hurries toward us. She rushes at Jake—and then she runs past him and comes for me.

Adam lets me go and my hands fall to my side. "Mommy," I whisper. She wraps her arms around me and holds me in tight. I inhale the familiar scent. She smells better; the smoke scent is gone.

"It's okay, Morgan," she says in my ear. "Everything is going to be okay." I cling to her like a little girl. I'd forgotten these—her soothing hugs. The hug when I didn't get the badge I wanted in Girl Scouts. The hug when the other girls made fun of me for bringing my mom for the father-daughter picnic. The hug when

Greg Pierce, the boy I liked in sixth grade, asked Lexi to slow dance instead of me. The mom who had my back.

Some things have changed. Her body is bonier. Her long hair gets caught up in my teeth. But the hug is the same. And with a rush, I wish I could take back what I said to Bob. But he'll probably never forgive me.

"I had a dream about Amy last night," she says. And I listen to her tell me her dream the way I've listened to hundreds of dreams before. And she doesn't let me go but leads me back inside the house, explaining that Amy is going to be fine now. That's she's at peace.

As short as the time was that I knew Amy, I know nothing will be the same without her. And I know I let her down. I wonder if she knows. And if she'll ever forgive me from wherever she's gone to now. I hope it's a better place. She deserves a better place.

chapter twenty-five

I'm alone in my room. Adam's gone home, and the boys and Mom are chatting quietly in the living room. I feel like I'm holding my breath. I can't get full sips of air. I sit cross-legged on the bed, staring at the blank wall.

I need to call Amy's parents, offer my condolences. Say something. Do something. Show them people care. But my insides feel grated and chopped up. I swallow and swallow and finally reach for my phone lying at my feet. Taunting me. I turn it on and click to my Twitter page. My heartbeat spikes when I notice the follow status. I'm at 5,002 followers. I made it.

I close my eyes and imagine Amy squealing and jumping up and down. I imagine her so excited the words tumble out over top of each other. So much for that. This doesn't change one single thing. Reaching five thousand followers brought the opposite of good.

There's a knock at my door, and it pushes open before I can respond. Jake walks in. His face looks how I feel—wrecked.

"You okay?" he asks.

"Not really. I can't believe it. I can't believe she's gone. It doesn't seem real."

"I know. I keep expecting her to text me. I keep finding myself about to text her," he says.

"People my age shouldn't die."

"No."

We're both quiet, thinking how wrong it is. And how unreal. It's so hard to digest. How could this happen? Amy was good. She'd been through so much. She had so much ahead of her.

Jake shifts from foot to foot and stares at everything in the room except me. "I know it's not a good time to ask, but I really need to know. Is it true?" he finally asks. "What Lexi said?"

I blink. Frown.

"Did you know she posted that video of you online?"

I hear the disappointment in his voice, and it adds a layer to the shame I've tried to bury. Jake is struggling with this on top of everything. He doesn't want to believe the worst about me. My heart aches more. "Does it matter?" I ask softly.

He hangs his head and then slowly shakes it. "No, I guess not, not in the whole scheme of things," he says softly, but then he sighs. To him, it does; it matters a little. He doesn't want it to be true. "I believed in you, Chaps. And so did Amy."

I stare at him. And then I nod. For Amy, I'll tell him the truth. Exactly what I've told no one else. Amy would want me to tell the truth. I close my eyes and breathe, still not wanting to accept that she is gone.

"I knew," I tell him softly. I sigh. "I saw Lexi post it. I didn't stop her."

His eyebrows lift.

"I thought, you know, it'd be funny. Maybe people would think I was cool. I didn't know what it would turn into. I didn't know it would go viral and everyone would see it. I erased it after she left. But it was too late."

"You erased it?"

My cheeks burn and my body folds up even more. "I've been so ashamed. I mean, Lexi was right. I wanted people to like me." I take a deep breath and tell him the rest. "I found out later Lexi also e-mailed it to a boy at school—from my account. She thought he had a crush on me, so I think she was trying to get back at me, because she had a crush on him too. She was always so competitive about boys. Anyhow, he sent it to other people. And from there…"

He shakes his head. "You erased it though. She did this by e-mailing that boy. It got out because of them. There was nothing you could do about that once it was sent."

I raise my eyebrows. Shrug. I never thought of it that way before. "Maybe. I don't know. It doesn't really matter. I'm the one who did the dancing."

"Everybody does stuff like that, Morgan. But you didn't post it. To me, it matters," he says. "I knew it wasn't you."

"It shouldn't matter," I tell him.

"I know. But you're my little sister. I didn't want it to be you. And you didn't ask her to post it. Or send the e-mail. She did it behind your back. She set it in motion. Not you. There's no way you had control over what happened."

My relief makes me feel weak. "Do you think so?"

"I do. This wasn't your fault, Chaps. No matter how hard you've been trying to convince yourself it was. You didn't ask her to do it. She did it and she's the one who was wrong. Not you."

God knows where Jake picked up his values in our faulty family tree, but I'm grateful for them. And for his support.

"Thank you," I tell him, and maybe I don't quite believe it yet, but I'm starting to.

I remember how many times he's stood up for me over the years. My protector.

"It was my dad who called," I tell him. "When Lexi was here." I stare down at my feet, at my chipping toe nail polish, blushing. "I told him to never call me again."

Jake sighs and walks to the bed and sits down beside me. "Yeah. I kind of figured. It was bad timing, you know. You just found out about Amy. You can call him back. Explain it. He'll understand."

I shake my head. "But Mom wouldn't like it."

"Chaps. You don't always have to please everyone else. Sometimes you have to look out for yourself. "

I stare at him and blink. And finally the tears come. Because he's right. And he sounds exactly like Amy. I miss her so much. And I miss what she might have had with Jake. I still can't believe she's gone.

chapter twenty-six

It's my first funeral and for that, I suppose, I should consider myself lucky. But it's awful. Until now, I kept thinking it was all a mistake, that someone would clear up the misunderstanding. I kept expecting her to walk in and start babbling to me. But this. This makes it real. Horribly real. My friend is gone. My stomach has knots and my throat's sore from swallowing.

The church is a nondenominational one. Amy's parents are seated in the front pew. An old woman in a wheelchair sits in the aisle beside her mom. Her skin is thin and creviced, and her chin wobbles and shakes. I guess it's a grandmother, but Amy never mentioned her. It doesn't seem fair that she's there and Amy is the one in the casket.

I can't bear to look at her. Not yet. We're all seated in the aisle behind her parents and off to the right, but they haven't turned their heads. Adam is on one side of me and my mom on the other. Jake and Josh are beside her. Adam's parents sit behind us. His little brother is home with a sitter.

Before the sermon begins, I turn and look around, touched to see the church is crammed tight. Amy would be impressed. I recognize faces from Tinkerpark, some of the showgirls, the other girl who works in the snack shop. I'm embarrassed to realize I don't know her name and make a mental note to find out. Amy would have known.

There are a lot of other kids our age. Adam whispered that they're from the private school Amy went to her only non-homeschooled year. I think she would have liked going to school with Adam and me...less fancy, more friends.

I slip my hand inside my purse and sneak out my phone. Trying to be discrete, I hold it up and snap a picture of the crowd.

"Morgan," my mom whispers and smacks at my hand, but I ignore her. I think about posting the picture on Twitter later. To show our friends. Her account has more followers than mine does now. I think she'd like the tribute, but then I think about it and decide no. Amy didn't want me to live my life on Twitter, and she doesn't have to end her life on it. The people that are here are here. I'll print out a picture later and leave it with her family. I put the phone away and soak in the moment—as much as it sucks to do that.

When the minister has walked in and is seated, a choir at the front begins singing "Amazing Grace," the first song I learned on the recorder in sixth grade. My mom wraps her arm around me and presses her head to mine. I rest against hers for a moment before moving away. We have a lot to work through, but I know Amy would be happy to see that we're trying.

Tears are flowing in that church. So many, I imagine, if we collected them, there would be pails and pails of tangible sadness.

I blink as the minister begins to speak. His voice is low and soothing. He's young with dark, curly hair that I think might have the gray dyed out. He has cowboy boots on under his white robe. The biblical part of the sermon is brief and then he talks about Amy. He talks about her irreverence, her charm, and her bravery.

And when he is done, he turns to the crowd.

"Would anyone like to come forward to share their memories of Amy?"

I jump to my feet. I will not allow one second of an awkward pause for my friend. Not one. I ignore all the eyes on the back of my black dress as I walk up the aisle, trying to walk less like a duck and more like a lady in the high heels I borrowed from my mom.

I manage to navigate the stairs to the podium and move down the mike so it's close to my mouth. "Amy was my friend," I say to the crowd. In the back of the church, a baby cries. I know how it feels. But I swallow hard and keep going. "I didn't know her long, not long enough. But in the short time I did, she was the best friend I ever had."

I glance at Adam and he nods in approval.

"And, man, she could talk." I smile, remembering. "Her heart was big. She was forgiving and didn't judge and she was…true. She taught me to embrace the truth. Even the hard ones." I glance at the minister, and my cheeks redden and I stop for a minute to get myself back on track. "Amy was…amazing." I glance at her mom and dad and then quickly away so I don't lose it. My hand goes to the bracelet she made me, and I wind it around my wrist. I remember her telling me it was magical. I wish she would have kept it for herself.

"Shortly before Amy passed on," I pause and swallow, "we went on a road trip. Amy, me, and my…boyfriend." Adam hides his mouth behind his hand, but Jake lifts his thumb in the air. I smile. Amy would approve. "Along the way, we learned a lot about each other. A lot." I smile down at the mike. "Amy wasn't afraid to share." I stop and blink and swallow the growing lump in my throat. "She helped me realize what was important and she never made me feel silly about being wrong." I finally glance at her parents, hoping they don't think I'm being disrespectful or trite, but they're smiling through their tears.

"She was beautiful. She really was. And right before…the last time I spoke with her, she made me promise her I would show the world who I am. As if she knew she was leaving me." I take a deep breath and stare down at my borrowed shoes. "I will be forever grateful to Amy, for showing me the difference between things I thought were true and things that really are." I pause and the tears domino up in my eyes, ready to tumble out. "Like that only the good die young," I say and hiccup a little as I hold in a sob. "I miss her."

I step down from the podium then. It's blurry as I make my way back to my seat, but Jake walks past me, on his way to the podium, to say something else about the Amy he knew.

• • •

After the funeral service, Amy's parents host a gathering in their home. The house is cleaner. Emptier. I'm standing beside her dad, leafing through a portfolio book he wanted to show me, at some of the things Amy made and sold in her Etsy store. I see how talented she was and touch my bracelet again. I do that a lot now. Adam wears his and Jake is wearing both of the ones she gave him. I guess he decided to keep Josh's for himself.

Amy's dad is busy chatting with someone on his other side; it seems like he's a work colleague the way they talk. Her mom is sitting in a chair beside the old woman in the wheelchair and their heads are bent as they talk. I search around the room until I see Adam. He's standing with a group of kids from Tinkerpark. A couple of the managers are here too. He lifts his glass when our eyes meet.

My gaze sweeps around the room, and I spot my mom. She's talking to someone, out of my sight, and I watch her nervously wringing her hands and chewing frantically on her Nicorette gum. I'm proud of her for giving up smoking completely. She loved it, and it hasn't been easy for her. She has a glass of wine in her hand and as if she feels my eyes on her, she turns and looks right at me and smiles a smile I haven't seen before.

For a moment, with the light streaming in behind her, she looks young and very beautiful. Lovely and frightened. Vulnerable. The hardness around her edges is softened. And then she points at me, and Bob White and his wife step into my sight. My heart thuds in my chest and I put down Amy's binder.

Adam is suddenly at my side, his arm around my waist. When I told him earlier what I said to Bob, he assured me I would deal with him again when I was ready. "You okay?" Adam whispers in my ear. I sense eyes on me and glance at Amy's dad. His eyes follow mine back to Bob.

"Your dad?" he asks. I nod.

"Yeah. I see it. Amy said you look just like him." He smiles with his overly white teeth. "This would make Amy happy, you know. That he came to you here."

"You're right," I say. I look at Amy's dad. "She loved you so much," I tell him.

He nods and presses his lips tight. "I know," he says. "But thank you." We both turn and watch Bob and Camille approach. Bob has visible sweat on his upper lip.

"Excuse me," Amy's dad says, and he slips away, goes to his wife's side, and puts his hand on her shoulder. She presses into it, and I look at them for another moment, hoping they will be able to get through this. Wondering how they will.

Adam removes his hand from my waist but takes my hand.

"We're late," Bob says when they reach me. "My apologies. It was the ferry."

"It's good to see you, Morgan," Camille says and steps forward and hugs me close. She smells like expensive perfume. When she steps back, Bob holds out his hand. I stare down at it and then look at him and we both start to laugh.

I take his hand and formally shake it. I really am my father's daughter.

"I hope it's okay. That we came," he says.

"Of course," I say but frown, thinking of what I last said to him. "I'm sorry."

He nods. He knows exactly what I'm thinking. "I wanted to see you. And your mother invited us to come. She told us what happened, that you were upset about Amy the last time we spoke."

"I'm sorry for how rude I was."

"Don't even worry about it," he says.

"We wanted to pay our respects," Camille adds. "We're so sorry about Amy," she says. "She was a lovely young girl."

I nod and yet another lump forms in my throat. "She was."

"She seemed like a good friend," Bob adds.

"She was a great one."

There's a pause.

"She called me, you know," he says. "Before the surgery. She wanted me to know that you were a good person, to give you time. And she told me I better be good to you when you did. She assured me you would."

"She did?" I shake my head and half smile at Amy's audacity.

"I really am sorry," I say softly to Bob. "About what I said to you when you called. I was very upset." I don't tell him that maybe I was testing him too, without even knowing it. I want to be loved for who I am, warts and all. Because I am far from perfect. I look at him and see we're both realizing it at the same time. That it was a test.

"Don't apologize. You and I are going to mess up a lot along the way."

I nod, hiding a smile. He's implying that we have a future. And I want that very much. Jake and Josh appear at my side, their eyes burning with visible curiosity.

"This is Bob White and his wife, Camille," I tell them. "Jake and Josh."

"These are the twins?" Bob reaches to shake their hands. The boys are polite, but they don't remember Bob, not really. While they make small talk, I glance across the room. Mom is standing with Jake and Josh's dad. She smiles at me as she slips her hand into the crook of his arm. He leans down and whispers something in her ear. I raise my eyebrows and she rolls her eyes at me. I roll mine back. Maybe there are more reunions than one going on. Gross.

I turn to Adam, and he's laughing at something Bob said. I nudge him in the side. If he wants to be a good boyfriend, he really needs to stop getting along so well with my parents. Amy would have told him that. My heart sinks. I miss her way of telling it the way it was.

"Let me introduce you to Amy's parents," I tell Bob and Camille. As we make our way toward them, I hear one of the Tinkerpark kids saying something to one of the private school kids, asking if they saw me in the video.

I think of Amy. What she wanted me to do—show them who I really am.

I slip my hand into Adam's and hold my head high.

And then I wiggle my ass.

acknowledgments

There are so many people who have a hand in the book making process and it's an honor to be able to thank you. Like Brandon Norie and Heather Gurtler who let me pick their brains about doctor ambition and heart "stuff."

Thanks to Leah Hultenschmidt and Todd Stocke and the Sourcebooks editorial team for coming up with the title for *16 Things I Thought Were True* and to Leah for her always thoughtful and wise editorial massages. Also thanks to Gretchen Stelter for her keen copyediting eyes that caught so much, including my many Canadianisms. As always, the Sourcebooks team is a dream to work with from owner Dominique Raccah, to Jillian Bergsma and Cat Clyne (best name in publishing, hands down), to Derry Wilkens, publicity guru, to the super sales reps (who have the coolest jobs in the world)! Also the designers and artists and all the Sourcebooks family who get books made and into the hands of readers in one way or another, I bow to you and heartily fast-clap you!

I also love the great folks at Raincoast Books for doing such a smashing job distributing and promoting my books in my home land, Canada!!! Especially Jamie Broadhurst, Jocelyne Leszczynski, Crystal Allan, and the super sales team! Thanks, eh!

Special thanks to Linda Duddridge for her help with the later drafts of *16 Things* and for great listening ears and feedback from start to finish. Thanks again to Jennifer Jabaley and Lauren Bjorkman for their always amazing suggestions and catches and thanks to Denise Jaden who is my favorite first set of eyes that get me on track. Thank you also to Thalia Anderson, YA enthusiast, for reading and making wonderful editorial suggestions. And of course my agent, Jill Corcoran.

I'd also like to say thanks to teen librarians, who are so great at matching books with readers. Thanks for giving my books a chance and putting books into the hands of teenagers seeking realistic stories! It's a wonderful profession and I truly appreciate all that librarians do for authors!

Also to the many passionate YA book bloggers who support authors with such zeal. I've loved meeting so many of you and share your enthusiasm for young adult books! I hope to meet more of you in real life. In the meantime, here, have a gold star!!

Thanks to my Alberta writing pals for the support and friendship over the years as we travel the publishing process together, all of us at different stages but all of us devoted writers. To Leslie Carmichael, a funny and brilliant writer, the epitome of grace and quiet strength as she fights her battle with cancer, Angela Ackerman, Linda Duddridge, Deb Marshall, Gloria Singendonk, Stina Lindenblatt, Trish Loye Elliot, and Jan Markley. Also my new lunch writing friends and the good folks at Writer's Guild of Alberta!!

I also have to thank my husband Larry for making it all possible. LG+JM. And my favorite son, Max, for being you and for all of the future things I will be ripping off from your teen experience. You're a good kid. Keep up the good work.

I always love hearing from readers as well and thank you for reading this book and any of my others!! You can find me on Facebook or Twitter @janetgurtler or at my website www.janet-gurtler.com.

Lastly, for all people seeking truth. I hope you find it and that it's everything you want it to be.

Janet

about the author

Double Rita finalist Janet Gurtler recently moved to Okotoks, Alberta, with her favorite husband and son and a chubby Chihuahua named Bruce. *16 Things I Thought Were True* is her fifth Sourcebooks title. There are currently no videos of Janet dancing on YouTube or anywhere else online. This is probably a good thing. Visit Janet at www.janet-gurtler.com.

If you liked *16 Things I Thought Were True*, check out these other great titles from Sourcebooks Fire.

Racing Savannah

Miranda Kenneally

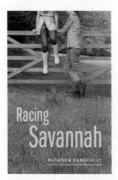

They're from two different worlds.

He lives in the estate house, and she spends most of her time in the stables helping her father train horses. In fact, Savannah has always been much more comfortable around horses than boys. Especially boys like Jack Goodwin. She knows the rules—no mixing between the staff and the Goodwin family. But Jack has no such boundaries. And with her dream of becoming a professional horse trainer herself, Savannah isn't exactly one to follow the rules either…

Praise for Miranda Kenneally:

"A must read! I couldn't put it down!" —Simone Elkeles, bestselling author of the Perfect Chemistry series

"An incredibly well-written, beautiful story that balances romance, drama, and comedy perfectly." —*Bookish*, on *Stealing Parker*